continued . . .

"The food-truck angle and the mouthwatering descriptions of the truck's offerings give this one a very appealing flavor."
—*Booklist*

"A lighthearted mystery with a fun premise, a hint of romance, and more tasty-sounding food than you can shake a food truck at."
—Smitten by Books

PRAISE FOR THE
PARTY-PLANNING MYSTERIES
BY PENNY PIKE
WRITING AS PENNY WARNER

"An appealing heroine whose event skills include utilizing party favors in self-defense in a fun, fast-paced new series guaranteed to please."
—Carolyn Hart, *New York Times* bestselling author of the Death on Demand Mysteries

"A party you don't want to miss."
—Denise Swanson, *New York Times* bestselling author of the Scumble River Mysteries

"Penny Warner dishes up a rare treat, sparkling with wicked and witty San Francisco characters, plus some real tips on hosting a killer party."
—Rhys Bowen, *New York Times* bestselling author of the Royal Spyness Mysteries

Death of a Bad Apple

A FOOD FESTIVAL MYSTERY

Penny Pike

AN OBSIDIAN MYSTERY

OBSIDIAN
Published by New American Library,
an imprint of Penguin Random House LLC
375 Hudson Street, New York, New York 10014

This book is an original publication of New American Library.

First Printing, January 2016

For more information about Penguin Random House, visit penguin.com.

ISBN 978-0-451-46783-6

Printed in the United States of America
10 9 8 7 6 5 4 3 2 1

Penguin
Random
House

To Tom

Acknowledgments

Many thanks to my writing group: Colleen Casey, Janet Finsilver, Staci McLaughlin, Ann Parker, and Carole Price; my wonderful fans; and a special thanks to Andrea Hurst, Sandy Harding, Isabel Farhi, and everyone at Obsidian / Penguin Random House.

"One taste of the poisoned apple and the victim's eyes will close forever in the Sleeping Death."

—The Wicked Queen

Chapter 1

"What smells so good?" I asked as I entered my aunt Abby's home through the back door of her San Francisco Victorian. The aroma of cinnamon, sugar, and baked apples perfumed the air and made my mouth water. I inhaled deeply, trying to fill my lungs with the intoxicating fragrance.

"Abby's Salted Caramel-Apple Tarts!" she exclaimed proudly as she lifted a tray of steaming-hot pastries out of the oven and onto the stove to cool. "It's my latest creation. I'm using caramel in the recipe and sprinkling it with salt. I'll let you taste one as soon as they cool down a bit. The flaky crust just melts in your mouth."

"Yum!" I stared at the lightly browned individual tartlets, willing them to cool off faster.

"Sit," Aunt Abby ordered. "You'll get drool all over my tarts."

I obeyed her command and took a stool at the island

counter that occupied much of the kitchen. Basil, my aunt's long-haired Doxie, nuzzled my red Toms.

"What prompted you to whip up something new?" I asked, petting the dog with one foot. "Your customers love the comfort foods you already serve. I hope you're not going to replace your caramel chocolate brownies with these. That could cause a riot."

Shortly after my aunt retired from serving cafeteria food at the local high school, she bought an old school bus, tricked it out, and turned it into a kitchen on wheels. For the past year, she'd been serving "old-school" comfort food in her Big Yellow School Bus at Fort Mason, where a dozen other food trucks gathered. Since I was between jobs, I'd been helping her out by making sandwiches, mixing up mac and cheese, and taking orders from hungry customers. Truth was, I'd recently been let go from my job as restaurant critic at the *San Francisco Chronicle* and hadn't yet finished writing my soon-to-be bestselling cookbook featuring food truck recipes. Unfortunately I wasn't much of a cook—I was more of an eater—but I was quickly learning how to make potpies in bulk.

"No, my *pretty*," my aunt said, assuming the voice of a wicked witch. "These are for something *special*." And then she actually cackled.

I laughed at this silly side of my sixtyish aunt. Yes, she could be eccentric, but there was something mischievous behind those twinkling Betty Boop eyes that even her Shirley Temple dimples couldn't hide. "What are you up to, Aunt Abby?"

She handed me a newspaper clipping and plopped down on the stool next to me.

I picked up the article and scanned the headline:
ANNUAL APPLE FEST OPENING OCTOBER 1ST.

I looked at my aunt, puzzled. "What's this about?"

"Read it!" she demanded, her smile as wide as her bright eyes.

While I skimmed the article, Aunt Abby hopped off her stool and busied herself making coffee, no doubt to wash down the caramel-apple tart I was hoping to taste soon. There was nothing special about the story—just a three-paragraph piece about a popular attraction in California's gold country.

Nestled in the rolling Sierra foothills of El Dorado County is a wonderland of apple orchards and apple farms, apple wineries and apple breweries, just waiting to bring you a variety of sweet, tart, and tempting apple treats. The area, known as Apple Valley, stretches from Placerville to Pollock Pines, providing the perfect place for a fruitful getaway. You'll find apple delights, from apple-cranberry cake to zucchini-apple bread, all prepared from the freshest farm ingredients.

While you're there, be sure to sample such homemade specialties as apple crisp, apple strudel, apple bread, apple donuts, apple butter, apple cider, caramel apples, baked apples, and everyone's favorite—all-American apple pie.

Take the scenic drive along Highway 50, or ride the shuttle, which begins at Apple Annie's Farm and ends at Adam's Apples, with stops along the way at the many apple orchards, food tents, and food trucks, and the A-MAZE-ing Hay Maze. Come pick your favorite apples and taste the apple treats, all fresh from

farm to fork. Remember: An apple a day keeps the doc-
tor away—as long as you buy your apples from an
Apple Valley–certified grower!

The piece, included in the "What to Do and Where to Go This Fall" section of the newspaper, was written by someone calling himself Nathan "Appleseed" Chapman, a descendant of the Johnny "Appleseed" Chapman family and the organizer of the Apple Valley Festival. Although I liked apples as much as the next all-American, I'd never been to the area, about a two-hour drive northeast from San Francisco. I got my apples from the local market, and only the green ones, which I cut and dipped in peanut butter. And sometimes chocolate.

"Is this where you got the idea for your apple tarts?" I asked.

Aunt Abby set a latte down in front of me. I encircled the hot cup with my hands to cut the fall chill and bring on the warmth. Was that cinnamon I smelled wafting from the coffee?

"Not just the idea for tarts, Darcy. I've signed up to serve them during opening weekend at the Apple Fest in four weeks."

"What are you talking about? Are you entering a contest or something?"

"Nope," Aunt Abby replied. "The festival committee invited selected food trucks to join in the festivities, and I applied. Guess what? I'm taking the school bus up for the weekend! Doesn't that sound fun?"

She turned her back before I could make a face.

While a weekend in the country sounded nice, I had made reservations at the Butler and the Chef in the South of Market District for Jake's upcoming birthday, and had my own festivities planned. Jake Miller was the Dream Puff who owned his own cream puff truck, and we'd been seeing each other for the past few months. I'd really been looking forward to spending some alone time with him. Now I assumed I'd be dragged along to help her in her school bus–turned–food truck. I sipped my coffee and watched my aunt drizzle melted caramel on the top of the tarts, then add a dash of salt. When she was finished, she scooped one of the tarts onto a small plate and brought the still-steaming treat to me.

"Seriously? You're really going up there in the food truck?" I leaned over the apple tart and inhaled deeply.

"Doing what?" came a sleepy voice from the door-way. Dillon, Aunt Abby's twenty-five-year-old son, stood in the entryway looking like a zombie, his dark hair sticking up porcupine style, and a two- or three-day stubble on his chin. He wore a holey Tom and Jerry T-shirt and baggy flannel pajama bottoms decorated in Minecraft images. Naturally he was barefoot, and he really needed to do something about his toenails.

"Dillon!" Aunt Abby said cheerily. "Perfect timing! You'll have to taste my salted caramel-apple tarts."

Dillon had a knack for showing up when his mother was baking. He had some kind of sixth sense when it came to food. He lumbered in and took the stool across from me, then eyed my tart. I pulled it back and wrapped my hands around it like a prisoner hoarding food from other convicts.

"So, what were you guys talking about? Are we going on a trip?"

Before Dillon had a chance to grab my fork out of my hand, I stabbed the tart, broke off a bite, and ate it. Since I'd moved into Aunt Abby's RV in her side yard, Dillon and I had had a bit of cousin rivalry going. He was only four years younger than I, but he acted more like a teenager at times. It didn't help that his mother spoiled him rotten. "Mmmmmmm," I murmured, closing my eyes. When I opened them again, Aunt Abby and Dillon were staring at me. "Wow" was all I could add.

Aunt Abby beamed. Dillon turned and looked at her hopefully.

"Here you go, dear," Aunt Abby said, setting a caramel-drizzled tart in front of him. "You want coffee?"

Dillon didn't answer, too busy stuffing his mouth with the warm fruity pastry. My aunt and I looked on in awe as he wolfed it down in three large bites. "Good," he said simply. "Can I have another?"

"No," Aunt Abby said. "I'm taking the rest to the busterant this morning to see how the customers like them before I serve them at the Apple Fest."

I shook my head at Aunt Abby's made-up word, "busterant." Since her food truck was actually a converted school bus and not a truck, she coined the term for her half bus, half restaurant.

"What fest?" Dillon said, getting up and heading for the refrigerator. He opened the door, took out the milk, and drank right from the carton.

I gagged a little.

Aunt Abby explained her plan to Dillon. Opening

day of the festival was in four weeks and she hoped Dillon and I would join her and help serve her apple tarts. She must have caught my hesitant look.

"Of course, there will be some perks," she added.

"Like what?" Dillon asked.

"I've booked three rooms at the Enchanted Apple Inn, a bed-and-breakfast farm, for the weekend. My old friend from cooking school owns the place, so you'll get to see a real working apple farm."

Dillon and I looked at each other skeptically.

"Plus," my aunt continued, "the fest is offering apple wines and beers, a bunch of craft booths, scooter rides, a hay maze, and even a scarecrow contest! Doesn't that sound fun?" Her dimples deepened with her widening grin.

"Dude, I don't know," Dillon said. "I've got a bunch of stuff to do on the computer, like update your Web site and maintain your Facebook and Twitter accounts. . . ."

"And I was planning to take Jake out for his birthday that weekend . . . ," I added weakly.

"No excuses. Dillon, you can bring your computer with you. I checked with my friend Honey and she has Internet service there. And, Darcy, apparently you haven't talked to Jake this morning?"

"No, why?"

"I got him to sign up too!"

"Jake's coming?" He hadn't mentioned it when I talked to him last night.

"And so is Wes," Aunt Abby said. "That is, if he can get the time off. Then we'll all be up there together!"

OMG. My nemesis, Detective Wellesley Shelton, had been dating my aunt for several weeks, and I still wasn't used to it. Most of my encounters with the very big, very intimidating detective had been interrogations about various homicides that had occurred recently. I couldn't imagine sitting around the breakfast table making small talk with the man.

"But—" I started to argue.

She cut me off. "Plus, I'll pay you overtime."

Dillon wiped off the milk mustache. "I'm in."

I sighed. I could truly use the extra money. "I guess we can celebrate Jake's birthday there with some apple birthday cake."

"Wonderful!" Aunt Abby said. "Now, let's get to work!" Basil, Aunt Abby's long-haired Doxie, barked in excitement. Maybe she thought she'd be getting some leftovers.

Ah well. So much for a romantic birthday weekend alone with Jake.

As soon as we got to Fort Mason, I ducked over to the Dream Puff truck to see Jake. We'd been spending a lot of time together, but he hadn't mentioned he'd be going to the Apple Fest. Aunt Abby must have talked him into it early that morning.

"Morning, Darcy," Jake called from the service window of his truck. Seconds later the door opened and I stepped up and into cream puff paradise. Jake wore his usual formfitting logo T-shirt and sexy jeans, covered by an orange-stained apron. I was tall at five feet ten, but he towered over me. The sparkle in his dark eyes when he looked at me made my heart skip a beat. He'd already prepared today's fall special—a cream puff shaped like a pumpkin, filled with pumpkin cream, and topped with caramel sauce and a green gumdrop to simulate the stem. Not only was it adorable; I was sure it was delicious. Jake was a master of cream puff creations, and I was his go-to taster.

"So," I said, my eyes lingering on one of the pumpkin puffs, "I hear you're joining my aunt for the opening weekend festival at Apple Valley."

He grinned. I melted a little. "What can I say? She has a way of wrapping me around her little manicured finger."

"Tell me about it." I rolled my eyes.

"She said you'll be there too, so I plan to make a reservation at the same B and B."

"Oh no," I said, then added, "you can just stay with me."

His grin widened. I melted some more.

"I'm hoping it will be a nice getaway and we'll have some time together," I continued. "I wouldn't mind taking a break from city life and all its recent drama, and spending a peaceful minivacation in the quiet country. Besides, the festival is offering apple wine. I'm a sucker for fruity wines."

"I prefer apple beer," Jake said as he filled more cream puffs for impending customers. "Bittersweet."

I scrunched up my nose. "I'll stick to wine."

"Seriously, it's good. You'll have to try it."

I glanced back at the cream puff I'd been eyeing seconds before.

Jake caught my unsubtle hint and pulled out another cream puff from the refrigerator. "Here. Try one of my Praline Apple Cream Puffs and tell me what you think."

I took a small bite and let the flavors of apple and caramel tickle my mouth, then dissolve away. "Killer," I said.

"Glad you like it. Hope the Apple Fest attendees do too." He offered me a napkin. "Actually the weekend sounds fun. I'll challenge you to a race through the hay maze."

"I was planning to celebrate your birthday at the Butler and the Chef," I said, "but Aunt Abby made me an offer I couldn't refuse. I guess we can celebrate up there."

"In our room at the bed-and-breakfast inn?" Jake raised an eyebrow.

"We'll see," I said coyly.

He laughed. "Tell you what. If I get through the hay maze first, you have to grant my every birthday wish. And if you finish first—"

"You have to do whatever I ask," I said, cutting him off.

Jake laughed again. "Deal," he said. "Sounds like I can't lose either way." He reached out a hand and we shook on it. My hand lingered in his. He pulled me forward and kissed the cream puff residue from my lips. It tasted even better than the puff itself.

There was no better way to start the day. Except maybe waking up in Jake's arms in a cozy bed-and-breakfast in the fall countryside.

I peered out the window. "I better get back to the school bus. Looks like a line is starting to form. Time for another hectic day in the truck trenches. I hope that weekend in the country isn't all work and no relaxation. I could really use some peace and quiet."

"I hope it *stays* quiet," Jake said as I headed for the exit.

I turned back. "What do you mean?"

He shrugged. "I went online before I signed up to see what the Apple Fest is all about."

"And?"

"Sounds like not everything in Apple Valley has been in apple pie order."

I frowned. "What do you mean?"

"Apparently something's been upsetting the apple cart lately."

"Will you quit with the apple metaphors and tell me what's going on?"

"Well, according to the American Apple Association, some GMO companies are trying to infiltrate the industry and it's causing quite an uproar among the farmers."

"GMO? As in genetically modified organism?" I'd read about GMOs while working at the newspaper and knew that GMO foods were controversial.

Jake nodded. "A couple of the articles claimed GMO apples are going to cut the organic farms to the core."

I rolled my eyes. One more apple metaphor and I was going to turn him into applesauce.

But, more important, what was my aunt Abby getting us into this time?

Chapter 2

"Aunt Abby?" I called as I mounted the steps of the school bus. "You've already got a line of hungry customers."

"I know," Aunt Abby said, handing me a fresh yellow apron emblazoned with the Big Yellow School Bus logo. "I can't wait to have them try my new apple treats. I just hope Dillon didn't eat them all." She shot a glance at Dillon, who was perched on a stool, checking his iPhone.

"I only had three," Dillon argued absentmindedly. As usual, he was tapping out a text message. "Or maybe it was four. Or five."

Dillon claimed he could multitask, but I thought he was just doubly distracted. He often spoke without thinking first, and his bluntness irritated me, but as Aunt Abby's only son, he was the apple of her eye and a genius when it came to computers. I only hoped his hacking skills didn't get him arrested one day. He'd already been in enough trouble at the university. I thought it was time he got his act together, in spite of his lack of social skills, but Aunt Abby coddled him too much. I also sensed he was unhappy I was living in his mother's Airstream. I was sure he wanted it for himself. Still, he'd helped me on several occasions, using his computer savvy, and I owed him for that.

"The tarts aren't that big, you know," he continued. "I could barely taste anything until I got to the last one."

While I shook my head, Aunt Abby smiled fondly at him. Her son could do no wrong in her eyes.

"Showtime!" Aunt Abby sang out, signaling the start of our business day. She pulled up the blinds and slid open the ordering window, ready with her pen and pad.

The next four hours went quickly with nonstop customers. We were always busier on the weekends, when more tourists were around. As usual, I was ready to collapse by the time Aunt Abby offered me a break around three o'clock.

I removed my food-streaked apron and dumped it into the hamper. "Wow, your new tarts were a hit, Aunt Abby!"

She gave her dimpled smile. "We sold out just after the lunch rush! I'll have to double the recipe for tomorrow."

"I'm glad they were a success. And they were perfect."

"Oh no." My aunt shook her head. "There's always a way to make something better. Maybe a bit more caramel and a little less salt. Or vice versa. I'll have to experiment tonight. But as soon as we clean up here, you two can go. I'll see you at home, after I stop off at the market and get a few things."

We finished doing the dishes, sanitizing the surfaces, and putting utensils away and had the bus ship-shape in record time. I checked Jake's truck as I headed for my VW Bug, but he'd already closed down for the day. Well, I'd see him soon enough. He'd invited me to dinner at his loft in SOMA, and I looked forward to whatever he was whipping up.

I left Fort Mason and drove home, thinking about the upcoming Apple Fest. As soon as I got to the Air-stream that was parked on the side of Aunt Abby's Russian Hill house—my temporary home—I cleaned up in the tiny shower and threw on black jeans, an orange V-neck sweater, and a pair of black Toms. Eager to do some research and check out the Apple Valley Web site so I could start planning the romantic part of the getaway weekend, I opened my laptop and logged on. The official Web site proved to be full of information on everything anybody would want to know about apples.

> *Apple Valley is a wonderland of orchards, farms, winer-ies, breweries, and bed-and-breakfast inns—the perfect place for an out-of-town getaway, a country picnic, or fun with the family. Come pick your own apples right from the trees or gather them from the convenient con-tainers, then sample the apple treats freshly prepared in our kitchens. You'll find dozens of varieties of apples to choose from, including golden delicious, Granny Smith,*

Pippin, pink lady, Rome Beauty, Fuji, Gala, and Mutsu, just to name a few. While you're here, learn about the joys of apple farming, which apples are best for cooking and which are best for eating, and savor the fruits of our labor while viewing acres and acres of apple trees, as far as the eye can see.

Whoever wrote this stuff made the place sound like Apple Eden. In a good way, of course, without the serpent and all that befell from *that* notorious apple incident. I clicked the link to read about local bed-and-breakfast inns in the Apple Valley area, then tapped on the Enchanted Apple Inn. The more I read, the more I wanted to leave today and not wait another four weeks.

Welcome to the Enchanted Apple Inn, a luxurious country estate nestled in the sprawling Apple Valley. Come rest your bones, replenish your spirits, and revive your romance at our beautifully restored Victorian home. The rooms are lovingly decorated in an apple theme, with baskets of your favorites at your fingertips. Stop by the tranquil duck pond, stroll through the ample gardens, and sample a complimentary glass of apple wine while you take in the scenic surrounding farms and orchards.

By the time I finished reading the flowery description, I was ready to move there, permanently. Was this place a slice of apple pie heaven or what? I could probably fill my Food Truck Cookbook with nothing but apple recipes.

I clicked back to the main site to see if there was anything I'd missed. Scanning down to the bottom of the Web site, I noticed a link that read "Note."

I tapped the link. *"We are proud to grow only natural, organic, and pesticide-free fruit in Apple Valley. Do not be fooled by artificially manufactured and genetically modified apples."*

That was an odd thing to add to the promotion information. I remembered Jake had said something about a controversy among the apple growers. My reporter instincts kicked in and I typed "GMO apples" into my search engine. A number of links to genetically modified apples appeared on the screen. I clicked the one at the top and read the headline.

Eden Apple Corporation— Are You Ready for Frankenfruit?

Wow. Jake was right. Apparently there was a worm in the apple industry. I couldn't wait to read more. Maybe there was a story in it that could get me back at the *Chron.* Then again, did I really want to go back, now that I was working on a cookbook featuring food truck fare?

Who wouldn't want a big perfect apple that doesn't turn brown when you slice it? Sounds too good to be true, right? But that's what's happening in the biotech world of genetic engineering known as GMOs—and these genetically modified organisms are coming to a restaurant, fruit stand, and school cafeteria near you. Basically untested, this brave new world of apple modification is unlabeled and drenched in toxic pesticides, posing health risks we've not even considered. But companies like Eden Apple, one of the major GMO producers, are growing, and they're pushing to have their Frankenfruit approved for sale to the general public. These mutants may soon take over the entire apple industry.

Well, I thought, here was scare-tactic journalism at its worst. But I had to admit, it had me at "Frankenfruit." I couldn't stop reading.

These newly created bad apples contain over forty pesticides that are especially toxic to children, yet some scientists say these tainted apples are "harmless." As the pro- and anti-GMO movements argue about safety, the Eden apple has not been tested by the FDA or USDA, and may only be labeled as a GMO product in code—a five-digit number beginning with the number eight—when it lands on the shelves. Without it, consumers won't be able to choose whether they want to buy and eat this freak of nature.

The controversy over these GMO fruits has raged for nearly a decade. But when the GMO apples appear on the shelves, the organic apples won't stand a chance. Why? Because the GMO apple will "look" perfect.

"They're not unsafe," argues Reuben Gottfried, the CEO of Eden Apple Corporation. "People have been eating GMO products for decades—soybeans, corn, papaya—all genetically engineered to resist disease and increase yields. Your so-called organic apples are subject to all kinds of pests and diseases, like winter

*moth, codling moth, aphids, sawfly, weevil, scab, can-
ker, brown rot—the list goes on. Thanks to science,
we've found a way to remedy those threats and prevent
acres of orchards from being destroyed."*

*"The truth is, these GMO apples haven't been stud-
ied properly," says Adam Bramley, president of the
American Apple Association. "If it's not organic, I don't
eat it," he states, "and neither should anyone else."*

My cell phone rang, startling me out of the engaging
article. I looked at the caller ID and answered, "Hi, Jake."

"Hey, Darcy. Sorry I didn't get a chance to say good-
bye when I left, but it looked like you and your aunt
were still swamped."

"We were! With cleanup, I didn't get out of there
until nearly four. Are we still on for tonight?"

"Looking forward to it," Jake answered. "I hope you
like sushi."

I gulped. I wasn't a fan of raw fish. I covered by asking, "You make your own sushi?"

"Yep. I'll teach you how to make your own rolls."
While I was impressed that he had mastered the art
of sushi, I could barely make a tuna sandwich. And I
wasn't sure I wanted to learn how.

"I'll probably turn them into cat food," I said, not
wanting to confess the truth if he'd already gone to
trouble.

"You just wait. I'll have you creating rolls almost
too beautiful to eat."

"Nothing's too beautiful to eat," I forced myself to
say—except sushi. "See you soon."

I hung up. I'd just have to grin and eat it, like those starving people on *Survivor* who had to swallow eels and bugs if they wanted to win a million dollars. If only it was for a million dollars.

Nuts! I'd forgotten to tell Jake what I'd found out online about the GMO controversy. Talking to him often distracted me from whatever I was doing or thinking. I knew he'd be interested, so I printed out a copy to take with me. If we ran out of conversation after making sushi art, at least we'd have something else to talk about. Of course, that wasn't usually what we did when we ran out of conversation. . . .

The first time I visited Jake at his loft in the South of Market area, I was struck by how much the area seemed to change every time I went there. SOMA, once mostly industrial warehouses, factories, residential hotels, and deserted buildings, kept transforming itself thanks to a continual stream of new start-up companies looking for low rents. The run-down sprawl between the Embarcadero and Eleventh Street, Market and Townsend, was now an eclectic collection of new businesses mixed in with hot nightspots, upscale art galleries, furniture showrooms, trendy restaurants, and the ubiquitous Internet and tech companies that kept popping up.

Many of the older buildings had been retrofitted and converted into lofts and living spaces for those who shunned the typical flats and apartments in the city. The core areas—South Park, the Giants Ballpark area, the MOMA, and Folsom—were no longer referred to as the "wrong side" of the Market Street trolley tracks. Popular restaurants and shops drew locals and tourists, bohemians and business folks, artists and entrepreneurs, hipsters and geeks, gays and straights, offering funky urban charm. Here you'd find such diverse cultural offerings as the Jewish Museum, the Museum of Modern Art, and the Cartoon Museum, all within walking distance of each other.

Jake had taken me to several of the more interesting restaurants in the area over the past couple of months. My favorites were the Butler and the Chef, a French bistro with a killer croquet monsieur, the Brickhouse Café, known for its eggs Benedict, and Beard Papa's Divine Dessert, offering hybrid pastry that is a cross between a croissant and a donut. If Jake ever decided to open up a Dream Puff outlet here, the locals would gobble it up.

I drove up to Jake's building and parked on the street, then entered the four-story former warehouse that featured large windows on every floor. I took the elevator to the top floor and stepped into the long hallway that led to Jake's loft. I recognized two young men who were holding hands as they passed by and we exchanged greetings before I knocked on Jake's door.

The door opened. "You made it!" Jake said, ushering me inside. He was wearing one of his Dream Puff aprons and held a long knife in his hand.

"Planning to kill someone?" I asked, grinning, as I stepped in and slipped off my jacket. "Like Moby Dick, maybe?"

The room smelled of soy sauce and cooked rice. I glanced around the wide-open area that housed the island kitchen and the sparsely appointed living space. Posters of colorful food trucks lined the walls, an obvious nod to his passion. I stole a look upstairs at the bedroom loft and spotted his cat perched on the railing. That would be Brimstone, the Cat from Hell. Jake had found it abandoned by the previous owner and the two now had a distant but respectful relationship.

"Ready?" he asked, calling my attention back to the kitchen. He retrieved a clean apron from a cupboard and placed it over my head, then reached around me and tied it in the back. I had no choice but to kiss him.

"Are you sure *you're* ready?" I asked, heading for the sink to wash my hands in preparation for handling raw fish.

"Hey, this is a piece of cake. You're going to love making sushi."

I took a deep breath and steeled myself for a lesson in the art of mastering fish rolls. "Bring it on. What are we going to make first? California roll? Hamachi? Spicy Tuna? Unagi? Fugu?" I'd been reading up in preparation for this.

Jake blinked. "Did you say fugu?"

I nodded. "I heard it was a rare delicacy."

"It's puffer fish."

"Yeah?" I said. "So? Maybe you create a new cream puff from it."

"I don't think so. It contains tetrodotoxin, and it's highly poisonous. You have to be trained and qualified to make fugu, and even then, I wouldn't risk eating it."

"Tetrodotoxin? Isn't that the stuff that's supposed to turn you into a zombie?"

"Only in old zombie movies," Jake said, handing me a sheet of nori. I knew what that was. Dried-up seaweed. Yum. Not. "Shall we begin?"

I forced a grin and nodded. My cell phone rang just as I was about to press sticky rice onto the dried seaweed as instructed by Jake. I looked at my phone screen lying on the counter nearby to see who was calling. Aunt Abby. With one somewhat clean baby finger I pressed the answer tab, then put the phone on speaker.

"Aunt Abby? What's up?" She rarely called me just to chitchat, so I figured it was something important.

"Sorry to bother you, Darcy, but I thought you'd want to know."

"Know what? What's wrong? Are you all right?"

"I'm fine, dear. Perfectly fine. But I just heard from Wes."

Detective Shelton? I was starting to get alarmed. "What did he want? Is it Dillon?"

Dillon had been kicked out of the University of California at Davis for hacking into the computers, ostensibly to show them how easy it was to break in. Unfortunately the dean called the FBI and Dillon left school in an attempt to avoid being arrested. He later explained his purpose to the feds, but he was now on the FBI's watch list, and he was sure they, the CIA, the NSA, the UC system, and the SFPD were going to apprehend him at any minute. It was not unusual to find Dillon in one of his several disguises, dressed as a custodian, a homeless guy, a disabled vet, or other "invisible" person to keep from being identified.

"No, Dillon's fine. He's in his room doing something on the computer. How's Jake?"

"Fine, Aunt Abby, but what's this all about?"

"Oh yes. Well, Wes called. He heard some news over the police scanner about a fire."

"Where? Near your house?"

"No, no, up in Apple Valley. In fact, it was some kind of storage building. Apparently there was a fire and a bunch of local growers lost a big supply of their apples."

"Wow. That's awful," I said, still wondering why she was calling with this news.

"But the interesting thing is," she continued, "the storage thingy belonged to the Enchanted Apple Bed-and-Breakfast Inn. That's where we're staying."

"Was the inn damaged?"

"No, I just called up there and the owner, Honey Smith, said her place is fine. But she sounded quite distraught. I asked if she wanted us to find another B and B, but she insisted we still come. Is that okay with you? I thought I'd check."

"Sure, I don't think it's an issue for us."

"I'm sure it is for her, what with losing her apple crop and shed and whatnot." She paused.

"Is there something else, Aunt Abby?" I asked.

"No, no, that's it. Except there was another fire a few days before that—at another farm. But Wes said not to worry. Sorry I bothered you. Enjoy your evening with Jake."

I thanked her for calling and told her I'd see her later, then hung up.

"Huh," I said to Jake, who'd been listening to the phone call. "You heard that, right? There have been a couple of fires up there." I thought for a moment, then asked, "So, how does an apple storage facility catch on fire? Is there anything flammable inside?"

"Not with the high levels of carbon dioxide usually used in cold storage," Jake said. Then he looked at me and frowned. "Why? You think it was suspicious because there were two?"

I shrugged. "I don't know. But it does seem like the Apple Valley area is having its problems. Maybe there's more going on there than meets the eye."

He pulled me close. "Well, you're the apple of my eye. Let's leave the investigation to the local police and get back to carving up raw fish."

Jake was right, I thought, as I took the knife he offered. I was probably making a mountain out of a valley. But that's what happens when your background is journalism and someone yells, "Fire!"

Chapter 3

After a few disastrous attempts at turning rice and fish into Wayne Thiebaud works of food art, I managed to end up with misshapen rolls that looked more like something Pablo Picasso would have made. I took a picture with my cell phone so I could send it to the "Nailed It" section of Pinterest.

Jake's efforts, on the other hand, were suitable for his own TV show. He presented me with an amazing masterpiece that was sculpted to look like a panda bear, made from crab, shrimp, avocado, and rice with black olive accents. To my surprise, nothing was made from raw fish. He'd known all along my dislike for most sushi and stuck with the cooked stuff.

The man was incredible.

After a delicious and delightful evening, fueled by wine and filled with laughs, we headed to the upstairs loft for a little more creative fun.

The next morning I drove home early to take a shower and get ready for another day in Aunt Abby's busterant. I asked my aunt if she'd heard anything more from Detective Shelton about the fire at the bed-and-breakfast inn—or any other fires. She relayed what the detective's counterpart at the Apple Valley Sheriff's Department had said: The sheriff there suspected arson.

Who, I wondered, would want to burn down a warehouse full of stored apples?

I didn't have time to think about it during the weeks that led up to our getaway. The days were filled with school bus food and Apple Fest preparations, broken up by too few dates and dinners with Jake. We were both so busy and tired from the business of food truck service, we hardly had time to enjoy each other's company in the hours we had leftover. My expectations for relaxation and recreation grew each day, and by the time of our departure on Thursday night, I had a bucket list of a dozen things I wanted to do with Jake while in apple country. Not all of them were about sex.

"All loaded?" Aunt Abby asked me after whipping up a simple but satisfying dinner of tomato-basil angel-hair pasta and salad. After clearing and rinsing the dishes, I'd gone back to the Airstream and retrieved my packed-to-capacity suitcase.

"Ready!" I said. "Suitcase is in my car, along with an audiobook, two bottles of water, and a box of See's chocolates to help keep my energy up on the two-hour drive. You?"

She gestured at the three matching Minnie Mouse

suitcases in the entryway. "Now if I can only get Dillon out of his cave and into the car, we'll be off."

"I'll help you out with the suitcases," I said. "Is Detective Shelton able to join us?"

Aunt Abby sighed. "Not tonight, I'm afraid. I'm hoping he can get away tomorrow, if nobody gets murdered in the city between now and then. We'll see."

I grabbed two of the suitcase handles while Aunt Abby pulled the third. She yelled down the hall, "Dillon! Come on! We're leaving."

"I'm coming! Jeez!" he yelled back. "What's the rush?"

Dillon appeared from his room wearing Ninja Turtle pajama bottoms and a hoodie zipped up to his neck, the hood hiding his hair. He carried a large paper bag in one hand and his laptop in the other.

"I want to get up there and settle in so we can get an early start tomorrow," Aunt Abby said.

I pointed at the paper bag Dillon held. "You're kidding. Your stuff is in there?"

"Yeah," he said. "I don't need much. And the bag's recyclable."

As if he really cared about that.

"Let's go," I said, before the paper bag ripped and dropped his "stuff" all over the entryway.

Aunt Abby led the way out the door, with her little Basil following at her heels. She'd made arrangements for him to stay at a posh doggy spa for the weekend, figuring he'd be bored cooped up at the B and B all day. One of the suitcases was devoted just to his toys and food.

After helping her into the bus, I hopped into my VW Bug and followed her to the dog spa. Twenty minutes later we were on our way to the peace and quiet of Apple Valley. Planning to caravan on the way up, I followed Dillon and Aunt Abby for a while until I couldn't stand the slow pace and drove on ahead. Jake had said he'd meet us there later tonight.

I couldn't wait.

Even though I didn't cook, I loved reading cookbooks and imagining the food, so I listened to an audio recording of *The Johnny Appleseed Cookbook* on the two-hour drive to get in the mood. According to the introductory bio, the book was by the same guy who had penned the article about Apple Valley—Nathan "Appleseed" Chapman. I wondered briefly if the author was really a distant relative of the wandering orchardist or was Chapman just using the alias to cash in on the famous Appleseed name?

By the time I arrived at the Enchanted Apple around eight o'clock at night, I was hungry again from listening to the apple recipes, and craving another one of Aunt Abby's salted caramel-apple tarts. As I pulled up to the circular driveway in front of the lattice-covered entryway, I figured I might have to do some recon in the inn's kitchen when everyone had gone to bed and see what I could find left over in the fridge.

The large house was something out of a fairy tale, with its ornate gingerbread, dormer windows, and ivy-covered roof. The driveway was dark, except for a few garden lights that lit the path to the front door. As I pulled my suitcase out of the trunk, I glanced around to see if I could spot the burned building Aunt Abby had told me about, but no lights shone on the rest of the property, making it impossible to get a glimpse of the ruined storage facility. I thought I smelled a trace of smoke still lingering in the air, but it could have been from the chimney. A lit fireplace would be a nice welcome, since the fall air had grown chilly.

I pulled my jacket tight, grabbed my suitcase, lumbered up the covered path, and rang the bell. The inn was painted Granny Smith green, with a red front door and an apple-shaped knocker. I was instantly greeted by a woman I guessed to be around forty, judging from a few gray hairs in her upswept hair and soft lines around her eyes. She wore comfortable jeans and a red sweatshirt embroidered with a basket of apples.

"Welcome!" she said cheerily, and reached out a hand. "You must be Darcy Burnett, Abby's niece. I'm Honey Smith."

I took her hand. "Nice to meet you."

"Come on in," Honey said. "Your room is all ready for you. Is Abby with you?" She peered at my car.

"No, she and her son, Dillon, are bringing the bus. She should be here soon."

I stepped inside, dragging my suitcase, and followed her to the front desk a few steps into the entryway. She stopped suddenly and touched her chin with her finger.

"Oh, um, I was going to have you sign the registry, but I think I'll show you to your room first and let you get settled in. I'm hosting a wine-tasting for my guests at eight thirty, so you can register then. This way." She flashed me a welcoming smile before leading the way.

I followed her past a dining area, then a parlor. I caught a glimpse of flames crackling in a redbrick fireplace and inhaled the smoky aroma. Three couches circled the fireplace, making a cozy gathering place for the guests. A table in the center held a dish of what looked like dried apple chips, next to a tray of ornate wineglasses. The whole scene was relaxing and inviting, and I let out a breath as I hoisted my suitcase and followed Honey up the stairs.

"We have a full house this weekend," she said as we reached the second-floor landing. "All five rooms are filled. In addition to your group, we have a writer who's doing a story on the Apple Fest for the newspaper—a man named Roman Gold—and his photographer, Paula Hayashi." She gestured down the hall. "Your room is here."

I wondered where Detective Shelton would be sleeping, then mentally groaned. Oh, that naughty Aunt Abby. I prayed I didn't have a room next to hers.

The nameplate read PINK LADY.

"I hope you like it."

I glanced back at the nameplates on the other doors: AMBROSIA, GOLD RUSH, PACIFIC ROSE, and WINESAP. Of course. All the rooms were named after apples.

Honey inserted the key into the lock, gave it a jiggle and a twist, then opened the door a crack. She stood back and handed me the key. "See you in the parlor in half an hour?"

I nodded, but before I could thank her, she spun

around and padded away. Holding the handle of my suitcase, I turned back to the door and pushed it open, then flipped on the light.

And gasped.

"Oh my God! You scared the crap out of me!"

I let go of the suitcase handle and took in the scene in front of me. Jake was sprawled on his side on the apple-decorated comforter, holding two wine flutes in one hand and a rose in the other. He wore his usual jeans, with a royal blue, button-down shirt. He looked amazing.

"What are you doing here? I thought you weren't going to be in until late."

"I wanted to surprise you," he said, grinning mischievously. "I let Honey in on my plan, came up early, and here I am. A glass of wine?"

"I may need a couple of glasses after that surprise." I sat down next to him and we both leaned in for a "hello" kiss. "Mmmmm," I murmured. "I'm so glad you're here."

"Me too," he whispered. He set the glasses and the rose on the nightstand and lay back on the bed, pulling me with him. Needless to say, we were a few minutes late for the wine-tasting.

Aunt Abby and Dillon had apparently arrived sometime in the last half hour, but being preoccupied, I wouldn't have noticed if the place had caught on fire and burned to the ground. When we finally entered the parlor, I found my aunt sitting on the couch facing the fireplace, already enjoying a glass of wine, her cheeks rosy either from the cold, the fire, the wine, or too much makeup.

"Darcy! Jake!" She raised her glass to the two of us in greeting.

An older man in an expensive-looking suit and a younger woman in a silky black blouse and colorful leggings sat a few inches apart on the couch to the left. While the man sat stiffly, the woman had her legs and bare feet curled up.

I went over and gave Aunt Abby a welcoming hug. "Glad you made it. Where's Dillon?"

"He's in his room, doing something on the computer. You know him."

Dillon wasn't especially sociable and preferred electronic gizmos to people. I had a feeling we wouldn't see him until morning when it was time to prep Aunt Abby's school bus for the festival.

"How was the drive?" I asked after Jake handed me a glass of wine. We sat down on the couch on the right and nodded to the two other guests on the opposite couch.

"Slow. The bus could really use a bigger motor or a jet pack or some wings or something. And Dillon drives like an old lady." She took another sip, then smiled at the nice-looking man in the suit. He wore black-rimmed glasses, had a trim beard, and short, neatly combed salt-and-pepper hair. He nodded at her, then shot a look at the attractive younger woman next to him. She gave a tight smile and ran her red-polished nails through her long black hair that fell over one shoulder. In spite of their ages—he looked forty-something, she had to be in her early thirties—I wondered if they were a couple. Their body language said no, but something in the look they exchanged left me curious.

Honey Smith swept in wearing a floor-length hostess gown that swirled around her as she moved. She'd added makeup to her pale face, and her hair was tucked into a French twist.

"Welcome, everyone!" she said. "I'm so happy to have you here for the opening weekend of our Apple Fest, especially my old friend Abigail Warner. Now, let me introduce the rest of you." She gestured toward Aunt Abby. "Abby owns a food truck in San Francisco. We grew up together in the city. Then I moved to the country and she stayed there. She's here to share her delicious goodies at the festival this weekend." She turned to Jake and me. "And this is her lovely niece, Darcy Burnett, who I understand is writing a food truck cookbook, and Darcy's special friend, Jake Miller, who's making cream puffs for the festival."

I blushed at the reference Honey used regarding Jake, but he put his hand on my knee, as if proud to be my "special friend."

Honey indicated the two strangers with her other hand. "Roman Gold is doing a story on the Apple Fest for an online publication. We're all so excited about that. I can't wait to read it. And this is Paula Hayashi, who's going to take pictures for the article. We're thrilled to have you both. Again, welcome, everyone. I hope you're enjoying the apple wine and apple chips."

Everyone nodded, mumbled "yes" or "thank you," then took sips.

"This wine you're drinking comes from the Wise Apple Winery," she continued, "run by Crystal Cortland, who will be selling her wares at the festival. It's made from some of the apples from my own orchard," she said proudly. Suddenly her face clouded over. "Unfortunately there won't be any new apple batches for some time—at least, not from my farm. You all heard about the fire I had a few weeks ago, when the storage building caught fire. It ruined the crop I'd stored up over the year."

Roman set down his glass and leaned forward. "I'm sorry about that. Any idea how it happened? I heard there were two fires, and that it may have been arson."

Ah, the reporter in him was already coming through.

"That's what Murphy O'Neil suspects. He's our county sheriff. But he doesn't know why or who or anything else. He and his officers are still investigating."

"Why would anyone do that?" Paula asked, frowning. "I mean, who would want to destroy a bunch of apples?"

Honey shrugged. "No idea. I'm friends with most everyone in the area. We all get along well, since we have so much in common. All I can think is that it's some outsider."

"What do you mean, an outsider?" I asked, the reporter in me also kicking in.

Honey pinched her mouth and shook her head. "Let's just say, it could have been someone who's in competition with our organic apples up here. If our crops are eventually sold off or destroyed, the competition could move in and replace them."

"But who's in competition with organic apples?" Aunt Abby asked, frowning.

The room went silent as we pondered the possibilities. Then Honey Smith said aloud the thought that had come to my mind.

"GMOs."

Chapter 4

Aunt Abby's frown deepened. "GMOs?"

"Genetically modified organisms," Honey said, shaking her head as she spoke. "But don't get me started."

I'd learned over time that when someone said, "Don't get me started," it meant I was in for a long tirade. Honey was no different. She continued, adding the occasional air quotes.

"These GMO companies think their stuff is the fruit of the future. They're growing what they consider 'perfect' apples, when in fact there's nothing more perfect than a naturally and lovingly grown apple. Even the name 'genetically modified organisms' sounds hideous. These people are playing God with their genetic experiments, and we all know what happens when scientists start fooling around with Mother Nature."

I could think of a few *good* things offhand—test-tube babies for childless couples, crossed crops that yielded new and plentiful foods, the arrest of certain diseases—but I decided not to argue with our hostess. She sounded as if her mind was made up, and I didn't want to do anything that might spoil this weekend. Instead, I took another sip of wine.

"And I'm not alone," Honey continued. "The whole valley is protesting these 'Frankenfruits' and we've all joined together to keep companies like Eden Apple Corporation from taking over our farms and businesses. First it was this drought we're in, now this."

Roman Gold set down his wine and looked up at Honey, who stood by the fireplace, her arms crossed.

"Do you really think the GMO companies are threatening your business?" he asked, his eyebrow raised in question.

Ah, the reporter was stoking the fire for his article. I'd learned quickly in the news business that there was nothing like a good controversy to get people to read your stories.

"Of course they are," Honey said. "Just ask anyone."

"I plan to," Roman said. "But I'd like to get your feelings about it first. Why are you so against modified apples?"

"Like I said, they're not natural," Honey insisted. "They haven't been well tested. They contain more pesticides. They cause disorders like ADD and who knows what else in children."

Uh-oh. She was beginning to lose her credibility with unfounded blanket statements like that. I watched Roman's reaction to see if he remained nonpartisan. He eyed her, as if digesting what she'd said, but I noticed he wasn't taking any notes or using a recorder. Maybe he had a really good memory.

"And you think these—what did you call them?— 'Frankenfruits' will put you out of business?" he asked.

"It's already happening. We recently lost the Jefferson Farm," Honey said, her anger visibly growing. "So tell me. If you see a big red apple on the shelf that promises not to turn brown after you cut it open and you compare it to a smaller one that *will* turn brown, which one are you going to buy? It's almost like comparing apples and oranges."

Not quite, I thought, but I got her point. I wondered what had happened to the serene and pleasant woman who had welcomed us to the inn. She seemed to be growing more and more hostile toward Roman Gold, as if she thought he was the enemy, not the GMO companies.

"And what about the environment?" Honey added, her voice rising. "All those pesticides can't be good for the land we use or the air we breathe."

Roman shook his head and sat back. "I don't know. It seems as if there will always be room for both. People like to have a choice. You have your die-hard organic food lovers and those who prefer perfection. Look at all the varieties of apples available. There are plenty of different kinds for everyone to enjoy."

Honey stared at Roman for a few seconds, as if sizing him up. I was afraid she might throw him out of her inn because of his pointed statements, but surely she realized he was just gathering information so he could present both sides for fair reporting. I guessed the situation was too close to home, so to speak, for her to understand the other side.

"That's easy for you to say, Mr. Gold, since you're not *in* this business," Honey said, gripping her wineglass tightly. "But my livelihood depends on my apple sales. What with my storage building destroyed, the threat of the 'New Apple' from Eden Corporation, and all the other pests and problems I have to deal with on a day-to-day basis, I'll be lucky to keep my bed-and-breakfast going, let alone my orchard. If I lose all this, I'm out on the street."

The growing tension between Honey and Roman was abruptly broken by the sound of someone knocking on the front door. After three quick raps, the door opened and the visitor let himself in. We all looked over at the grinning, ruddy-complexioned man with bright red hair. He wore a blue parka zipped to the neck, baggy denim pants, and work boots. He raised a gloved hand and gave a wave to the group, then removed the gloves and unzipped the jacket.

"Am I intruding?" he asked as he slid off his jacket, revealing a plaid flannel shirt and overalls. He swiped his curly red hair back in an attempt to tame it, but those curls would never be tamed. Besides, he needn't have bothered. He was pretty adorable just the way he was, with those freckles and that red hair, like someone out of a Norman Rockwell painting. I shot a glance at Aunt Abby and saw her eyelashes flashing double time, the incorrigible flirt.

"Red!" Honey exclaimed, moving from the fireplace to greet him. All of her building anger seemed to dissipate as she gave him a big hug. "I'm so glad you could stop by and meet my weekend guests."

"Well, you did invite me," Red said, suddenly looking a little self-conscious as he glanced at the group.

Honey wrapped an arm around the man and gave him a squeeze. "Everyone, I want you to meet my dearest friend and companion, Roscoe Cortland, the largest apple grower in the county. Everyone calls him Red. He owns the Red Apple Farm, just down the road from me. In fact, he's the one who first saw the smoke on my property and called the fire department. If it hadn't been for Red, I might have lost everything."

"Unfortunately not in time to save the storage building," Red added. Honey slid her hand into his.

"You did your best," she said. "I thank you for that."

He gave her a sweet smile. She blushed.

Well, how about that? These two were a couple! And why not? They looked about the same age— forty-something. Honey appeared to be single—she hadn't mentioned a husband, nor had I seen another man around the place. Besides, they had a lot in common. Like apples.

Roman stood up and reached out a hand. "I'm Roman Gold," he said, introducing himself.

Honey turned to Red. "Mr. Gold is writing an article about the Apple Fest and he's featuring my bed-and-breakfast inn. Isn't that nice?"

All of her hostility toward the reporter seemed to have disappeared.

"Nice to meet you," Red said. "If you want to see my farm, come by any time and I'll give you a tour."

Roman turned to Paula, who hadn't said a word and was still curled up on the couch looking sleepy. "This is my, uh, photographer, Paula Hayashi. She'll be taking photos for the article. Maybe she can stop by?"

Paula gave Red a half smile and said, "Hey." Her long black hair fell over half her face and she shook it back.

"Ma'am," Red said in greeting.

I thought I saw Paula wince a little. Still young, she didn't like the title "Ma'am," I sensed. Then again, what woman did, no matter what her age?

Jake rose and offered his hand. "Jake Miller."

Red shook his hand.

"This is his friend Darcy Burnett and Darcy's aunt, Abby Warner," Honey explained. "Abby owns a food truck and she's participating in the festival tomorrow, with her special salted caramel-apple tarts. And Jake makes yummy cream puffs filled with some kind of apple custard."

"Welcome, all of you, to our peaceful valley," Red said. I scooted over to give the man some room to join us on the couch while Honey reached for the bottle of wine.

"Got any of that apple beer, Honey Bear?" Red asked.

Honey smiled and set down the wine bottle. "I'll be right back."

Red grabbed a handful of apple chips that had remained untouched by the rest of us and settled back on the couch. After a brief go-round of banal questions from him such as "Where you all from?" and "How was the drive?" Abby, the shameless flirt, turned her green eyes on Red and batted her eyelashes. She just couldn't help herself, even if the man was attached to her friend.

"Tell us about *you*, Red," she said, taking a coquettish sip of her wine. "What's it like being an apple farmer?"

Red shrugged. "I don't know anything else. I grew up on the farm. My dad handed it over to me just before he died. My great-grandfather started out with pears until the blight wiped out the crop. That's when he turned to apples."

"Goodness," Abby said, "that must have been awful."

"A whole generation of growers was nearly ruined," Honey said, reappearing from the kitchen. She carried a large tray that held some kind of dessert—apple based, no doubt—along with a single "Wise Apple" beer. "That's why we're so concerned about our future crops." She set down the tray and handed the beer to Red. "I've been telling my guests about the GMO apple situation."

Honey sat down and began slicing up what looked like apple upside-down cake with some kind of glazed drizzle on top. It smelled heavenly.

Roman spoke up. "Honey seems to be quite worried about these modified apples, concerned they might have an impact on Apple Valley's industry. What's your take on it, Red, if I may call you that?"

"Red, it is." He took a slug of his beer before answering. "Well, we apple growers are concerned enough to band together and try to put a stop to this GMO nonsense. One of the farmers here, Adam Bramley—he's head of the American Apple Association—he organized a group called NoMoGMOs to fight them. None of us wants to lose our farms and our income, and we're not gonna just do nothing and let that happen, right, Honey Bear?"

Red Cortland was proving to be as passionate and outspoken as his Honey Bear. Was the threat of these GMO apples really that viable?

I remembered the recent fires and asked Red, "I heard Honey's fire was arson. Any idea who might have done that?"

Honey and Red shared a look. Red set down his beer and shifted his weight on the couch. "We're looking into it," he said mysteriously. "Meanwhile, I'm gonna make sure nothing like this happens again. Honey lives here by herself, you know, and I'm divorced, so we're talking about me moving in with her, now that some crazy fire-starter is running around the county."

"Oh, Red, there's only been two fires, and I'm fine. These people don't need to hear about all this."

Red shook his head. "You're a brave woman, Honey Bear, but until we catch whoever's done this, I won't rest." With that he took the proffered plate of apple cake from her hands, picked up his fork, and went to work on it as if he were plowing a field.

We made small talk for the next half hour—nice weather for fall, best places for various apple treats, what it takes to run a farm—avoiding the hot topic of GMO fruits. I was about to signal Jake that we retire when there came another knock on the door.

"Who could that be at this hour?" Honey asked, checking the clock that hung over the fireplace.

It was nine thirty, a little late for uninvited callers, and I hoped the night wouldn't drag on much longer with this new arrival. I was pooped and ready to hit the hay.

"I didn't invite anyone else," she added.

Honey went to the door and opened it. In stepped a tall, gangly man wearing khaki slacks and a long-sleeved brown V-neck sweater with a tan shirt underneath. He was good-looking, tall, with tan skin and a full head of mostly dark hair that matched his trendy goatee. By the look of the intruding silver along his hairline, I guessed him to be in his forties as well.

"Sorry to intrude," he said to Honey when he noticed us all the parlor, "but I saw the lights on and figured you were up. You have guests, I see."

"You're always welcome here, Nathan," Honey said. "We were just talking about the festival and my guests want to know all about it. I'm sure you can share a few inside stories and tips on where to find the best apple treats." She turned to us. "Everyone, this is Nathan Chapman, the festival organizer and the man to talk to if you want any information about Apple Fest."

"Chapman?" Roman said. "As in John Chapman, better known as Johnny Appleseed?"

Nathan grinned and nodded. "Yes, sir. I'm a descendant of his brother, Nathaniel. My great-great-granduncle helped turned this valley into apple orchards, a long, long time ago."

Nathan Chapman! I immediately recognized the name from the article I read and the audiobook I'd been listening to.

Nathan entered the parlor, nodded at everyone, gave me a leering smile with bloodshot eyes. I had a feeling he was drunk and undressing me with his eyes, and I looked away. Roman and Jake were about to rise when he said, "Don't get up. I'm just passing through." He returned to Honey still standing in the doorway and said quietly, "I wanted to talk to you about something, Honey, but I can see you're busy entertaining. It can wait."

"Are you sure?" she asked.

"No hurry at all," he answered, the grin seemingly frozen on his face.

"Well, why don't you join us for a glass of Wise Apple's new release?" she suggested.

Nathan's smile suddenly vanished. "You're serving Crystal's wine?" He shot a look at Red, who shrugged.

What was that all about? I wondered.

Honey linked her arm in his and dragged him back to the parlor. He stood between two couches, waving away offers to sit down, while Honey poured him a glass of wine. He took it and downed half the glass.

"Crystal harbors no ill will toward me, and I none to her," Honey said. "Just because her ex-husband and I are close doesn't mean she and I can't be friends. After all, this is a small community and we all need to get along."

Aha! So Honey Smith was seeing the winemaker's ex-husband. And everyone was fine with that?

"Well, thank you, then," Nathan said as he took the proffered wine. Honey brought him a chair from the chair room and insisted he sit down. He set the chair next to me and gave me another flirty smile. His alcoholic breath nearly knocked me over.

Paula leaned forward, distracting him from me, thank goodness. "So you're really a descendent of the legendary orchardist known as Johnny Appleseed?" Doubt laced her tone.

I studied Nathan Chapman and tried to remember what Appleseed looked like from my childhood books. Tall and lanky like the man in front of me?

"Yes, Mr. Chapman, is that really true?" Roman asked, eyeing him suspiciously. Just like a reporter to question everything.

"Indeed, it is," Nathan said. "My uncle never married and had no children, but his brother—half brother, really—had five children, including my great-great-grandfather. I was named after him."

"But didn't John Chapman do most of his planting in the Midwest?" Roman asked. "He didn't get as far as California, did he?"

I shifted, becoming more uncomfortable. While I wasn't terribly impressed with him, if he wanted to call himself a descendant of Johnny Appleseed, what difference did it make?

Nathan took a long gulp of wine before answering, then smiled, reminding me of a slick politician. "That's a common mistake. Like I said, my great-great-grandfather, Nathaniel, accompanied John on several of his many treks, before he married and settled down on his own farm. He's the one who actually brought the apples to Apple Valley, but Johnny is the more famous one because of his lifelong dedication to planting apple orchards. Thanks to me, he's a big part of our Apple Valley Festival. We even have a scarecrow contest named after him."

"Nathan's really put Apple Valley on the map with all he's done for the festival," Honey added.

"Interesting," Roman muttered, frowning at Nathan as if considering whether the man was telling the truth or not. I had a feeling he didn't believe a word of it.

"Nathan's also a vegetarian and an animal rights activist, just like his great-great-grand-uncle," Honey said. "Isn't that right, Nathan?"

The man nodded, trying to look humble, but he was clearly enjoying all the accolades.

"So, what's your take on the GMO apple controversy?" Roman the reporter asked.

Oh, great. We were going to be here all night. I poured myself another glass of wine and sat back, wishing I could just go to bed. With Jake.

"NoMoGMOs," he said, laughing as he quoted the name of the group Red had mentioned earlier. "Seriously, my ancestors never would have approved of this kind of scientific mumbo jumbo. Gene splicing, DNA, bacteria, insecticides. These superapples add up to superweeds, superbugs, and superchemicals from supercorporations who claim they're helping us farmers, when really they're cutting us out."

"You realize that GMO products have been on the market for years and are still facing the same stigma they did forty years ago," Roman noted. "Corn, soy, canola, zucchini are all GMO produce, just to name a few. My research indicates they're safe to eat and have the potential to feed millions of starving people, which the little farmer simply can't do. Isn't that important? Isn't this more about politics than science? In fact, isn't it antiscience?"

Wow.

I looked at Nathan for his reaction to Roman's baiting. He'd turned red in the face and the grin was gone.

"Who are you again?" Nathan asked.

"I'm sorry," Honey said. "I should have introduced all of you to Nathan. Where are my manners? Nathan, this is Roman Gold. He's doing a story about the Apple Fest. In fact, I thought you were the one who arranged for Roman to do the publicity."

Nathan suddenly flushed and cleared his throat. "Oh . . . uh . . . no . . . uh."

Hmmm. After all that grandstanding, now Nathan seemed to be uncomfortable talking to a reporter. Maybe he was worried going public with his opinion could damage his business? Before Nathan could continue, there was yet another knock on Honey's door. This was getting to be Grand Central Station.

"For God's sake! Now who?" she said, losing a little of her hostess polish.

As she opened the door, I caught a distinct whiff of smoke.

And it wasn't coming from the fireplace.

Chapter 5

"Oh my God!" Honey said as she stood at the front door. From the wide-eyed look on her face, I had a feeling she'd smelled the smoke too.

"Adam!" she said to the person standing on the porch. "What's happened?"

"Call nine-one-one!" a man's voice shouted. "There's a fire! My phone is dead!"

Red jumped up and rushed over to Honey. I stood, the hairs on my arms prickling, and joined them. The man at the door, dressed in jeans and a brown leather jacket, a cowboy hat, and boots, was gesturing wildly as he spoke.

Instead of pulling out her phone, Honey ran outside, followed by Red Cortland and Nathan Chapman. Meanwhile, Jake got out his cell phone and dialed 911, then called out to the group scanning the area, "Where should I tell them to go?"

"Oh dear Lord," Red said. "The smoke's coming from my farm!"

Red ran to his pickup truck and hopped in. Seconds later I heard the engine rev up; then the truck spun around and sped down the driveway and onto the road.

"Where's his farm?" Jake asked, still waiting for information to tell the operator.

"Next door!" Honey called out.

"What's the address?"

"Nineteen forty-seven Old Orchard Road." She ran back into the house, grabbed some keys hanging behind the front desk, and headed for her own pickup truck parked at the side of the house. As Jake gave the information to the operator, Nathan ran to his truck to follow them.

"Darcy?" Aunt Abby said, coming up behind me. "What's going on?"

Roman and Paula rose from their seats on the couch and joined us on the porch.

"Apparently there's a fire next door. It's Red Cortland's farm," I said. "Someone named Adam stopped by and told Honey to call nine-one-one."

"I smell smoke." Paula hugged herself against the chill as she walked to the driveway and glanced around. "How close is next door?"

I looked up at the moonlit sky and saw gray smoke drifting in from the east.

"Fire trucks are on their way," Jake announced, slipping on his jacket and pulling out his keys. "I'm going over there. They might need help until the trucks arrive."

"I'm coming too," I said, following him.

"Me too," Aunt Abby added, scurrying forward.

"Let's take my car," I said to Jake, so he wouldn't have to drive his cream puff truck.

He nodded and the three of us dashed to my VW Bug.

"We'll meet you over there," Roman called to us. He and Paula headed over to his late-model gold Lexus. Nice car for a writer, I thought briefly. Most of my writer friends had either inexpensive compacts like my Bug or money-saving Priuses.

I didn't have time to think about Roman Gold's financial situation—not with the sound of sirens approaching. They grew alarmingly louder as we drove to the end of the driveway. Before we could make the turn onto Old Orchard Road, two fire trucks whizzed by on their way to Red Cortland's farm.

I only hoped they made it in time to save whatever was on fire.

Red's farm "next door" was probably half a mile down the road. We arrived moments after the fire trucks and watched as firefighters quickly got the blaze under control. However, the burning barn looked to be a total loss. Under the streetlight, it looked to be nothing more than a black, skeletal two-story frame that no doubt went up like a match. The smoke was still thick and acrid, and set us all to coughing.

The three of us got out of my car. I grabbed a couple of bottles of water I'd brought along for the drive to Apple Valley and headed over to Honey, Red, Nathan, and the man Honey had called Adam. They stood on the periphery of the activity, watching the firefighters continue to hose down what was left of the smoking ruin. Lights from the fire trucks lit up the area, bringing the disaster into focus.

Red looked on helplessly, saying nothing, occasionally shaking his head. A few feet away stood Roman while Paula skirted the area taking pictures with a fancy camera she'd pulled from her bag. I eased up to Honey and noticed Red had his arm around her as if to comfort her. By her grim facial expression, she looked as if she was taking the fire harder than Red himself.

I raised the bottles and offered them to Honey and Red. Honey shook her head, but Red took a bottle, twisted opened the cap, and drank half, then wiped his mouth with the back of his hand.

"Looks like they've got it under control," I said, not knowing what else to say to a man who'd just lost his barn in a fire.

He nodded, but remained mute.

"Thank God none of the animals were harmed," Honey said.

I wondered what animals she was referring to. Did Red have horses or cows or other livestock on his farm?

"The dogs are okay," Red mumbled, motioning toward two golden retrievers tied up to a nearby tree with long lengths of rope, tails wagging, tongues hanging out. "They were sure scared when I got here," Red added. "Barking at the barn and running around like wild animals."

Concerned about the dogs, I looked around for a container, spotted a bucket a few feet away, brought it over to them, then poured in the water from the second bottle. The dogs lapped it up quickly.

"Who could have done such a thing?" Honey said when I returned to her side.

I frowned. "You think this was deliberate?"

"It had to be," Honey insisted. "This is the third fire in less than a month. That's no coincidence. Someone is trying to burn down our properties, I'm sure of it."

"That is troubling." Roman's voice came from behind us. I turned to see him studying the burned wreckage. "Do the firefighters have any idea how it started?"

"Not yet," Honey said, "but we'll find out—as well as who did it—if it's the last thing we do."

Roman's eyes narrowed, but he said nothing. For a reporter, I expected him to ask more questions, but he sauntered off toward Paula, who had stopped taking pictures and was now talking to the man—Adam— who'd alerted Honey about the fire. I guessed he was another apple farmer, although by the look of his Western apparel, he seemed more like a cattleman than an orchardist. At the moment he seemed enthralled by whatever Paula had to say, nodding and grinning, reminding me of a shy high school freshman talking to the head cheerleader. I wondered how he'd happened to be in Honey's neighborhood and spotted the fire. Did he live nearby too?

My random thoughts were interrupted by the appearance of a white SUV that pulled up close behind where we stood. It screeched to a halt and skidded a few inches on the gravelly driveway. Everyone turned to get a look at the new arrivals under the streetlight.

Two women got out of the car. The driver, a blonde I guessed to be around fifty, spotted Red and walked over to him. The woman's younger companion, around twenty-something, stood back, scanning the site. In the light from the streetlamp and the fire trucks, I could see the two resembled each other. They both had round faces, pert noses, and full lips. But the younger one's hair was brown and their figures were different. The older one might once have been slim, but she had filled out around the waist, probably from age. Meanwhile, the younger one was a head taller and still svelte. Mother and daughter? I guessed.

The older one grabbed Red's arm when she reached him. "Oh my God, Red, what happened?"

Red shrugged while Honey eyed her. "Don't know," he said simply. "Barn caught on fire. All the equipment inside burnt up. Don't know if I can salvage anything. Have to wait and see."

Honey addressed the woman. "It's all under control now, Crystal. The firefighters put out the fire. There's nothing more to do. It's over."

Crystal. The name rang a bell. Then I remembered, this was Red's ex-wife. I glanced back at the younger woman I guessed to be their daughter. She definitely resembled her mother more than her father, which was probably a good thing. While Red was adorable in his way, his round nose, bushy eyebrows, and small eyes would not have been attractive on his daughter.

"How did it happen?" Crystal asked, still gripping Red's arm. "You're always so careful."

Red shrugged. "No idea. Have to wait till the chief does his investigation."

Honey shook her head. "We don't need an investigation to confirm this fire was deliberately set. Three fires in such a short time? Somebody's trying to send a message."

"You think so?" Crystal said. "If that's true, someone could have been hurt, or even killed. I wouldn't put it past those GMO people who are trying to buy up everybody's property. How are Pippin and Mac?"

I realized she was referring to the dogs, named after apple varieties, but before Red or Honey answered, the younger woman joined the small group. "Sorry about this, Dad," she said to Red.

Red acknowledged her comment with a nod, then added, "It'll be all right, Tiffy. I'll rebuild. Don't you worry about it."

"Your dad's right, Tiffany," Crystal said. "He bounces back quickly, always has." She turned to her ex-husband. "Isn't that right, Red?"

I caught Honey rolling her eyes. What was going on between the two older women and Red? They could claim they were all on good terms, but at the moment, something festered underneath.

"By the way, Red, you missed Tiffany's maze run-through tonight," Crystal said. "I just picked her up from the festival site. Did you forget?"

Red glanced at his daughter. "Sorry, Tiffy. I got caught up. . . ." He shot a look at Honey, who looked away as soon as their eyes met. "Hope it went well."

"It was fine." Tiffany sighed. "Mom, I'm tired. I'm going back to the car. You coming?"

"I'll be right there," Crystal said. As soon as her daughter was out of earshot, Crystal turned to her ex-husband. "You know, Red, just because we're divorced doesn't mean you don't still have a daughter. You could come by the winery and see her once in a while, or show up at her events, or take her out for lunch sometime. She misses you, especially since you left so abruptly." Crystal shot a look at Honey.

Red didn't answer, his gaze fixed on the threads of smoke still wafting up from the water-soaked wood.

"This isn't the time, Crystal," Honey said sharply. "His barn just burned down, for God's sake. Leave him alone."

I thought there was going to be a catfight, but instead Crystal pasted a fake smile on her face, gave Red's arm another squeeze, and headed back to her SUV. She peeled off, her spinning wheels spitting gravel.

Red walked over to talk to one of the firefighters. Honey turned to us and said, "We should probably be getting on back to the inn. The fire's out. Not much more we can do here, and we've all got a big weekend ahead."

Roman, who'd appeared out of nowhere, added, "I agree. I'll go find Paula."

I noticed Paula was still deep in conversation with Adam, the man who'd alerted Honey to the fire. In spite of their differences in age and personality—she was obviously outgoing, while he seemed out of his league—the pair seemed to have hit it off quickly, judging by the way they stood so close to each other as they talked. At one point she put her hand on his arm and his grin widened. I wondered what Roman thought about that.

"Paula!" I heard him call to her.

Paula stopped her conversation and looked around, then spotted Roman and waved. "Be right there!" She pulled out what looked like a business card and handed it to Adam. He took it, smiled, tucked it into his pocket and patted it, then said something I couldn't make out. I didn't need to be an expert at body language to know she was flirting her ass off, though, and he was eating it up. Had she sensed a photojournalistic opportunity in talking with Adam, or was she actually attracted to the cowboy old enough to be her father?

None of my business.

Moments later she reached out and shook Adam's hand, holding it a second longer than necessary, and then laughed at something he said before joining Roman at his car.

I caught up with Jake and Aunt Abby, who'd been watching from the sidelines, and we headed for my car. After we climbed in, Jake behind the wheel, we followed Honey's truck back to the bed-and-breakfast.

"I'm going to turn in as soon as I straighten up a few things," Honey said once we were inside the house. The spark had gone out of her voice. "Let me know if there's anything you need. Otherwise, I'll see you at breakfast in the morning."

After locking the front door behind us, Honey

headed for the kitchen while Roman and Paula climbed the stairs, followed by Aunt Abby.

"Aren't you coming?" my aunt said, pausing halfway up.

"We'll be up in a few minutes," I answered, noticing Jake had wandered back into the parlor. I spotted him sitting on the couch by the now-dying fire, finishing his glass of wine. "See you in the morning," I called back to my aunt.

I followed him in and joined him on the couch. He poured me the last of the apple wine and handed me my glass.

"Not sleepy?" I asked him, enjoying this quiet moment by the fire. After he clinked his glass against mine and took a sip, he reached over and withdrew a long, flat box from a nearby shelf.

"You're kidding," I said as he set a box game on the coffee table. "You want to play Scrabble? Now?"

"Afraid I'll beat you?" he asked, opening it.

"I'm a wordsmith, remember?" I said. "You haven't got a prayer."

"Ah, but I'm a former attorney, and I know a lot of legal mumbo jumbo, like thereto and caveat and corpus."

I laughed. "So? I use words that sound real but aren't. Like preventative and conversate and irregardless."

"Bring it on, babe." Jake handed me a tile holder and set one in front of himself. "I'm onto your chicanery."

"You'll get no pretense from me, you . . . you . . ."

"What? Already at a loss for words?" Jake teased.

"Never!"

We selected our tiles. Mine sucked. Two *A*'s, two *O*'s, an *R*, an *S*, and an *N*.

Then we picked to see who went first.

Jake picked *B*. Lucky.

I took a deep breath, then turned over an *A*.

"Yes!" I said, pumping my fist. "You're going down!"

I spent the next few minutes trying to come up with a brilliant word to collect my double-word points. SON. RAN. ROO. NOR. Seriously? I needed at least a four-letter word to preserve my boasts, but all I could come up with were SOON, SOAR, and ROAN.

Too bad I didn't have a *C* or a *P*; then I could have spelled CRAP.

"Problem?" Jake said, looking smug as he sipped his wine.

"Just thinking," I said, stalling.

And then I saw it. I laid down my killer word.

"Boom!" I said.

Jake looked down at the double-five-point word.

ARSON.

Chapter 6

After a rousing game of Scrabble, Jake and I went to bed and enjoyed each other's company long after the competition ended. I fell asleep in his strong, protective arms, dreaming about him as a big bad biker and me as his leather-clad biker chick.

Unfortunately just as I was about to be swept off my feet and onto his Hog, my insomnia kicked in. Lying there in the dark, I became aware of muffled voices. I looked over at Jake, thinking he might be talking in his sleep, but he was snoring softly, out cold. I wished I could sleep so soundly.

I sat up, straining to hear the voices, and glanced at the time. It was after one a.m. The voices seemed to be coming from outside the window rather than outside my door. I slipped out of bed, pulled on my robe, moved to the window, then peered out. Looking down, I could just make out three—or was it four—dark figures standing in the shadows below. From their size and stance, it looked like at least two men and one woman and one I couldn't make out, but they were so obscured by the darkness that I couldn't see their faces. I had a hunch the woman was Honey Smith, since it was her house. While I couldn't be absolutely certain, who else could it be?

From my vantage point, the conversation looked heated, with gesturing, finger pointing, and arm waving. I opened the window and pressed my ear to the screen. I could hear the woman who I guessed was Honey and caught a few words between Jake's snores.

". . . right under our noses . . . ," I thought she said.

One of the men mumbled something, then pointed at Honey.

". . . ruin our festival . . ." and then ". . . run out of town . . ."

Another man—he was wearing a baseball cap—shook his head. Was that Red, Honey's farmer boyfriend? Then again, it could have been anyone under that hat. Maybe Nathan Chapman, the festival organizer? Adam Bramley, head of the Apple Association?

Or someone else?

I pressed my nose against the screen, trying to make out more details to identify the small group, but I was at the wrong angle and the dark was too penetrating. Curious, and knowing I wouldn't be able to get back to sleep anyway, I tiptoed across the room so as not to wake Jake, then opened the door. It creaked loudly.

I froze.

I looked back. He was still sound asleep. If that didn't wake him, I figured nothing would.

I stepped out and closed the door behind me. The hall was dark except for two small night-lights that barely lit the floor. I continued tiptoeing toward the stairs, praying I didn't step on a creaky board and alert the whole house. Each time I took a few steps, I stopped and listened for any kind of sound, but aside from the rhythmic ticking of the grandfather clock downstairs, all was quiet.

Slowly I made my way downstairs and tiptoed to the front door, which stood ajar. Sidling up behind the door, I peered out through the crack in the doorjamb, hoping to catch a glimpse of the people talking.

The door suddenly swung back and hit me in the head.

"Ow!" I cried, and reached for my forehead.

"Oh my goodness!" Honey said. "I didn't see you there! What are you doing?"

Uh-oh. Caught red-handed. I had to think fast, but with the oncoming headache, I wasn't at my best for lying.

"Uh," I said, rubbing my forehead. "I was. . . . just coming down to get a drink of . . . to see if you had any aspirin—I forgot to bring some and I've got this darn headache. Then I saw the front door was open . . . so I was going to close it. . . ."

Oh, what a tangled web we weave. At least the headache part was now true.

"I'm so sorry the door hit you!" Honey said. "I was just . . . uh, locking up and I thought I heard something outside. You know, these fires have got me a little jumpy. But it was nothing."

Ah, so we were both pretty good liars.

"Anyway, let me get you that aspirin. Or do you want Tylenol, Advil, Aleve?"

"Anything's fine." I massaged the small lump on my head. "I didn't mean to startle you like that."

"No worries," she said, heading for the kitchen. I followed her, wondering why she hadn't mentioned the men she'd been talking to outside.

"Is the bed comfortable? Are you sleeping all right?" She reached into a cabinet and pulled down three bottles of painkillers for me to choose from. I took the bottle of Advil and poured out a couple of pills.

"Oh yes, the bed's wonderful. I just have trouble sleeping anywhere. I'm a bit of an insomniac. The littlest thing wakes me and then I can't get back to sleep." At that point, I wondered if Honey might suddenly realize I'd overheard her talking.

Instead, she said, "I know how that is. Since the fire here, I've had trouble sleeping too, and now with this latest one at Red's . . ." She drifted off as she filled a glass with tap water and handed it to me.

I swallowed the pills and gave her back the glass.

"You know what might help?" she said, opening the freezer compartment of her refrigerator. "A warmed-up slice of my apple crisp, with a side of caramel-vanilla ice cream."

I started to demur, but when I got a glimpse of the dish she pulled out of the refrigerator, my tongue froze in my mouth. Who could say no to a serving of warm apple crisp with a side of caramel-vanilla ice cream? Not me.

"Have a seat." Honey gestured to the stool next to the kitchen island. I sat down, figuring resistance was futile. Not only was Honey insistent, but so were my taste buds. I had a feeling I would be wearing a larger clothing size after the weekend was over. But this little dessert break might also give me a chance to ask Honey about her clandestine nighttime conversation.

I watched as she cut two slices of the crisp, slid them onto a plate with a fancy spatula, and popped them in the microwave.

"So you didn't find anything?" I asked, after inhaling the sweet fragrance of cinnamon, baked apple, and cloves as she pulled the dessert out of the microwave.

She turned to me and frowned. "What?"

"Outside," I said. "You said you heard something outside and went to find out what it was. You didn't find anything?"

"Oh no. Must have been jackrabbits or foxes. We get a lot of wild creatures around here. The apples attract almost every kind of critter. Deer are the worst."

She continued to ramble on. Was I making her nervous?

"I'm glad it was nothing," I said as she slid one of the desserts onto another plate and set it in front of me. The ball of ice cream next to the warm crisp was already beginning to melt. I took a bite of both.

"Oh, wow," I said. And I meant it. "Best. Apple. Crisp. Ever."

Honey looked pleased. "Glad you like it. It's one of my favorites." She hadn't even touched hers.

"It's funny," I said after a few more bites. "I was lying in bed and I thought I heard voices. Maybe I dreamed it."

Honey pushed the crust away from her dessert, as if examining the texture of the apples beneath. "Voices?"

"Yeah, crazy, huh? They seemed to be coming from outside my window."

Honey set down her fork. "Oh, it was probably the TV. Sound travels in these old houses. I need to remember to keep it down."

TV? I hadn't noticed the sound of a TV on my way downstairs, or even when I reached the front door. No, it was voices I'd heard. Besides, a TV wouldn't explain the men I'd seen outside.

Honey was lying. The question was, why?

I finished my apple crisp, practically licking the plate, and patted my stomach. "That was incredible!"

"Would you like more?" she asked. "There's plenty."

"Oh no. If I eat anything else, I'll never get back to sleep. Thank you so much. That was delicious." So good, I'd almost forgotten my headache.

Honey smiled and carried the plates to the sink. Mine was clean. Hers was untouched, aside from the forking it had received. "I hope you can get some rest now. Those pills should kick in soon. In fact, take the bottle, just in case."

"My head feels better already," I said as I stood up and took the proffered bottle. I knew I wasn't going to get anything more from her tonight. And at this point it was too late to say I'd actually *seen* the others she'd been talking to. "Good night, Honey. Thanks again."

"It's my pleasure," she said warmly. "See you in the morning for breakfast. Hope you aren't tired of apples. We're having apple pancakes with a warm apple compôte, apple bacon, and apple bread toast."

I was so full I could barely muster any enthusiasm, but I knew I'd be hungry again in the morning. "Sounds lovely," I managed. "See you then."

"And sorry about the door!" she added.

"I'm fine," I said. With that I headed out of the kitchen, up the stairs, and back to bed, where Jake still slept, undisturbed. As I pulled up the covers and snuggled back into his arms, I couldn't help wondering why Honey hadn't told me about the men she'd been talking to outside. What was it I'd heard? *Right under our noses? Ruin our festival? Run out of town?* What had she meant? And who had she been talking to?

I closed my eyes. They popped open again as I had a last thought. While I was wondering what Honey Smith had really been up to outside, maybe she was wondering what I was really doing behind that front door.

There was no way I was going to sleep soundly the rest of the night.

"Ruin . . . run . . . right under our noses . . . ruin . . . run . . . right under our—"

"Darcy!" I heard a voice call from the shadows. I tried to find the source, but it was too dark.

"Darcy!" came the voice again.

I shot up in bed like a corpse coming back from the dead.

"What. . . .what?" I blinked and rubbed my bed hair. Disoriented, I looked around the strange room, softly lit by the morning sun peeking through the lacy curtains. I turned to see Jake lying next to me. He was frowning.

"Oh God, was I snoring?" I asked, blushing at the thought.

"No, you were talking in your sleep. I tried to wake you a couple of times, but you were in deep. Sorry if I startled you."

I closed my eyes and instantly recalled the nightmare I was having.

"What did I say?"

"Something like 'run, run.' Was someone chasing you in your dream?"

I sighed. "I guess. I can't really remember. Three or four people, holding lit torches . . ." I shivered at the thought and turned to Jake again. "What do you think it means?"

He shrugged.

"Don't you analyze your dreams when you wake up?" I asked, surprised. "I thought everyone looked for clues to their subconscious wishes and fears."

"Well, mine are mostly about food and sex. Pretty clear."

I elbowed him.

"But I think maybe the fire at Red's last night might explain yours."

"The lit torches?" I said. "You're probably right. As

for the three figures, I think I can explain that." I told him about hearing the mostly unintelligible voices from my window during the night, then going downstairs and trying to listen in on the conversation and getting hit in the head by the door when I got caught by Honey. I left out the part about the apple crisp, but I was sure it had contributed to my restless dream as well.

"So you don't know who the other guys were?" Jake asked, rolling out of bed. He slipped on his plaid boxers and stood up.

I looked at the ornate clock on the nightstand. It was a little after seven. I reached for my robe and pulled it on. "No. All I know is, it looked like they were having an argument. But the men were gone by the time I got downstairs."

"Well, I'm going to jump in the shower. We're supposed to be at the fairgrounds by nine to set up. The festival starts at ten."

"Don't use all the hot water," I called after him. With my robe tucked tightly around me to fend off the chill, I moved to the window and looked out, trying to recall more details of the scene I'd witnessed in the middle of the night. Maybe the whole thing *had* been a dream.

I glanced back at the nightstand. There sat the little bottle of pain pills Honey had given me for a headache. I peered into the antique mirror that hung on the wall nearby and lifted my hair from my forehead. There was a small bruised lump the size of a quarter from where the door had hit me.

That was no dream.

* * *

By eight a.m., all the guests at the Enchanted Apple were gathered at the large oak table in Honey's dining room for breakfast—all but Roman Gold. Even Dillon had managed to crawl out of bed and show up for Honey's apple pancakes. And he'd actually changed out of his usual morning attire—his cartoon pajamas—and was wearing baggy jeans and a *Star Wars* LEGOs T-shirt.

"Did everyone sleep well?" Honey asked. She stood at one end of the table, holding a pitcher of orange juice. I was a little relieved to see it wasn't apple juice. From all the apples I'd be eating over the weekend— and had already—I wouldn't have been surprised if I began to sprout apple blossoms.

The guests either nodded or mumbled, "Yes," to Honey's question. We offered to wait for Roman before digging in, but Paula said Roman wasn't much for breakfast, so we went ahead without him. Dillon broke the ice with the first bite and we all chowed down. Even after that midnight slice of apple crisp, I found I was hungry again. Must have been the country air. Besides, the apple pancakes with warm apple syrup melted in my mouth like apple butter.

After Honey made sure we were all served, she joined us at the table.

"I heard you had guests last night after we all went to bed," Jake said out of the blue.

I shot him a look and tried to kick him under the table but missed. I even thought about stabbing him with my fork. What was he thinking, sharing what I'd told him about last night?

Honey made a face and shook her head. "No. I went to bed right after all of you. You probably heard my TV. I sometimes turn it up too loud." She glanced at me.

Jake nodded, stuffed a bite of pancake into his mouth, and let it go. Thank God. But he'd made his point. For some reason, Honey was sticking to her lie about the midnight visitors. The question was, why?

"Well, I slept like a baby," Aunt Abby said. "Honey, that bed is so comfy. I hated getting up this morning." She turned to Dillon. "You didn't stay up all night on that computer, did you, dear?"

Dillon, his mouth full of apple pancake, just shrugged. His room had been on the other side of Jake's and mine, so even if he'd been up, he probably wouldn't have heard or seen the late-night talkers with his earbuds plugged in. And if Aunt Abby was out like a baby, neither would she.

"How about you, Paula?" I asked the young woman who was sipping her coffee, eschewing the high-calorie breakfast. Her room had also been across the hall, but maybe she'd done a little sleepwalking and had seen or heard something.

She looked up, as if coming out of a deep trance. "Huh?"

"I was just asking how you slept," I said, wondering what she'd been thinking about so intently.

"Oh, fine," she said, setting down her coffee. She patted her mouth with her cloth napkin, then rose. "If you'll excuse me, I've got a lot to do before the festival opens. Thanks for the breakfast," she said to Honey, nodding at her untouched plate. With that she left the table and headed upstairs.

The conversation turned to questions about the festival. We asked Honey what to expect, how big the crowd would be, what were the favorite attractions and foods at the festival. She was in the middle of telling us how many different types of caramel apples were available when Paula came back down the stairs.

"Honey?" Paula said, pausing on the bottom step. "Do you have an extra key for Roman's room?"

Honey frowned. "Why?"

"He's not answering my knock, and I know he has things to do this morning. I think I'd better wake him."

My first thought was, *So they weren't sleeping together.*

Honey backed her chair out and stood up. She went behind the counter in the front hall, opened a drawer, and pulled out a key. "I don't usually hand out extra keys without getting permission, so I'll go with you."

"Whatever," Paula said, shrugging. She turned and headed back up the stairs, with Honey right behind her.

We resumed our conversations. I was growing more intrigued about the festival with every detail Honey had shared. Other than the Chocolate Festival, I'd never done anything like this before and wondered how different it would be from our usual food truck business. I planned to gather a bunch of recipes for my work-in-progress cookbook, and I hoped the crowds liked Aunt Abby's offering. How could they not? She'd worked hard to perfect the recipe for her salted caramel-apple tarts and always took a lot of pride in her work.

"Well," Aunt Abby said, wiping her mouth, "I'd better get ready. Dillon, are you about finished with breakfast?"

Before Dillon could answer, the sound of loud pounding boomed from upstairs. Everyone turned toward the noise.

Then someone screamed.

I couldn't tell if it was Honey or Paula, but the hairs on the back of my neck tingled. Jake stood up and rushed to the stairs. I quickly followed, then Abby, then Dillon. We reached the top landing, one after another. Honey and Paula stood outside Roman's room, Honey with her hand to her mouth, Paula's mouth wide-open. The door was open, the key still in the lock.

Jake walked over to them and I followed him. We peered in.

Roman Gold lay naked, facedown, on the bed. A pool of blood had soaked the pillow and sheets around his head and chest. Some kind of knifelike instrument stuck out at the back of his neck.

Obviously Roman Gold was dead. Stabbed to death in bed.

While we'd all been in the house.

Chapter 7

"Call nine-one-one!" Aunt Abby cried, peering into the room between Jake and me, but Jake was already on it. He had his cell phone to his ear and was clearly waiting for an answer. Honey started to enter the room, but Jake extended his other arm to keep her and everyone else out while he talked to the dispatcher.

"What's the address here?" he said to Honey. She gave it to him and he relayed it to the dispatcher and disconnected the call.

"Oh my God, oh my God," Honey kept repeating, her hand still covering her mouth. "Should we do something for him? Like cover him up?"

"We wait for the police," Jake said, taking charge.

"What's that thing sticking out of his neck?" Paula said. I looked at her. She didn't seem overly upset that her coworker was dead.

Honey suddenly gasped.

"What is it?" Aunt Abby asked, putting an arm around the distraught innkeeper.

Honey shook her head. "Nothing . . . I thought . . . it was nothing."

"She's probably in shock," Aunt Abby whispered to me. "I saw on *Criminal Minds* that some people who witness a crime can go into shock."

Aunt Abby got most of her forensic information from television crime shows. I had a feeling she and Detective Shelton had some interesting discussions on the subject.

"Honey, why don't you make everyone a cup of coffee or tea while we wait for the police?" I suggested. Giving her something to do might get her mind off the dead man in her guest bed.

Honey began to ramble again. "Who would do this? Right here in my bed-and-breakfast?"

"I think the bigger question is, how did the killer get in?" Paula said, reflecting my thoughts. She turned to Honey. "Did you lock the front door last night?"

From inside the inn, Honey's keys were fairly accessible to anyone in the under-counter drawer that didn't appear to be locked. Anyone could have slipped into his room in the middle of the night, lifted the key, entered his room, and stabbed him. But it would have to be someone who knew about the location of the keys.

Honey looked bewildered. "I'm sure I locked it. At least, I think so. I . . ."

I remembered startling her as she came in the door. Could her embarrassment at bumping my head have caused her to forget to lock up?

Paula persisted, crossing her arms in front of her. "But you're not sure, are you? And *that's* probably how the killer got in."

"How do you know there was a killer?" Honey asked, facing her accuser. "Maybe he committed suicide."

Paula rolled her eyes. "Well, he sure didn't stab himself in the back of the neck, now, did he?" Paula's tone was growing increasingly hostile. Was she trying to blame Honey for Roman's death?

"Do you think he was killed while we were sleeping last night?" Aunt Abby added, stating the obvious.

"Won't know for sure until the coroner checks the body," Jake said, "but it had to have been sometime between ten, when he went to bed, and eight thirty this morning, when we checked on him."

"Hmmm," Aunt Abby mused. "This is like one of those Agatha Christie plots, where everyone is gathered at the summerhouse, there's a locked-room murder, and all the guests are suspects. Where's Poirot when you need him?"

I nudged my aunt with my elbow. This was not the time to compare a real murder to a fictional one. Even though she had a point. It *was* a locked room. We *were* all gathered at the inn. And we *could* all be suspects.

The sound of sirens jarred us all from our discussion. Honey ran down the stairs to let in the first responders while I leaned over the railing and watched from the second-floor landing. The door opened before Honey could reach it and a man wearing a sheriff's khaki uniform let himself in. It appeared Honey had a habit of not locking the front door, and the sheriff must have known this and felt comfortable enough to walk in. He was followed by a uniformed woman.

Honey pointed to the second floor, and the sheriff and deputy headed up. Right behind them, two paramedics rushed in, gloved and carrying large cases of medical equipment. Our small group shuffled back as the officers and EMTs shouldered past us and entered the room. One of the EMTs went directly to the side of the bed, knelt down, and felt for a pulse. The other stood by, talking on his radio. The female deputy hung back, waiting for orders, while the sheriff looked on.

After a few seconds, the first paramedic shook his head and stood up.

"Deceased," he announced.

"I'll call it in," the other one said. The EMTs lifted their bags and headed out, passing our little group by the door.

"Stand back, people," the sheriff said, taking command. I looked him over, wondering if I could judge his competence from his appearance. He was tall, pale skinned, freckled, with a white mustache and a paunch. His hat covered most of his hair, but short wisps of matching white hair were visible below the brim. I guessed he was in his mid-fifties, so he'd probably had some experience on the job. But had he had much experience with homicides out here in peaceful Apple Valley? I couldn't help wondering what Detective Shelton's take would be on all this. We'd know soon enough, once he arrived.

We shuffled back like cattle and resumed our spots at the threshold of the room.

"Anyone been in here?" the sheriff asked.

"No," Honey said. "Paula here and I discovered him when I opened the door. Then Jake called nine-one-one."

The sheriff looked over at the body, eyed the weapon sticking out of Roman's neck, and turned to us again. "Anyone know him?"

"I do . . . did," Paula said. "We worked together. I'm his photographer. He's a writer."

"What's his name?" the sheriff asked Paula.

"Uh . . . Roman Gold," she answered.

The wide-eyed young deputy took down the name in her small notepad. She was short and hefty, her latte-colored skin was makeup free, and she was hatless, her dark hair collected into a thick bun at the back of her head. I wondered if homicide was new to her. She looked fresh out of the academy. Her name tag read JAVIER.

"What was he doing here?"

"Uh, writing an article on the Apple Festival," Paula answered.

The sheriff turned to the rest of us. "I want you all to go downstairs and wait for me in Honey's dining room. I'm going to need statements from each of you. Honey, can you put on a pot of that good coffee you make? Bonita, will you escort these people to the dining room and wait for me there? I'll call the coroner and get Ravi over here."

"Copy that," the deputy said. She looked nervous in spite of the authority of the uniform and the heavy-duty, laden belt she wore. A rookie for sure, still trying to prove herself.

The sheriff looked as though he wanted to roll his eyes. Instead, he nodded a dismissal.

"If everyone will follow me, please," Deputy Bonita Javier said before she led us down the stairs. We found our places at the dining room table, where a plate of cookies awaited us. After a few minutes, Honey appeared holding a tray filled with cups of coffee. She passed them out, then took a seat.

I realized Dillon had disappeared somewhere between the breakfast table and the discovery of the body. No wonder. The cops had arrived. Dillon and cops didn't mix.

"How long are we going to have to wait here?" Paula said, checking her cell phone. "I have a lot of work to do."

Apparently she wasn't mourning the death of her friend so much.

"I don't want to sound callous," Aunt Abby said, "but the festival starts in less than an hour and I have a food truck to run."

"Sheriff O'Neil will be down soon," the deputy said, after taking a sip of her coffee.

Paula cleared her throat. "Uh . . . what about my coffee?" she said to Honey.

Honey looked at her. "Oh, did I forget you? Sorry. Would you like some?"

"If it's not too much trouble."

"I guess I could make another pot," Honey said, making no attempt to rise from the table.

"Never mind," Paula said, sounding irritated. She returned her attention to her cell phone.

We waited in silence, sipping our coffees. A few minutes later, there was a knock on the door. Honey glanced at the deputy for permission to answer it, then hustled over. The sheriff came bounding down the stairs as Honey opened the door. She welcomed in a woman wearing blue scrubs.

"Ravi," the sheriff said, greeting her from the bottom of the stairs.

"Murph," the woman answered in greeting. I guessed she was the coroner. "Where?"

Sheriff O'Neil pointed upstairs.

She nodded. "Lead the way," she said, and followed the sheriff up the stairs.

Honey returned to the table and sat down, wringing her hands. "Oh dear," she mumbled several times.

"It'll be all right," Aunt Abby said to her, patting her shoulder. "They'll find out what happened and who did this. Don't worry."

Honey nodded, but her absent gaze told me she wasn't really listening. We spent the next few minutes in our own worlds—Paula texting, Honey worrying, Aunt Abby comforting, Jake frowning, Deputy Bonita sipping her coffee and jotting some notes. As for me, I just wondered how the hell I'd ended up at another murder investigation.

Half an hour later, the sheriff and coroner came down the stairs. We all looked up, anxious to hear the answer to the big question: What happened to Roman Gold?

The sheriff shook hands with the coroner at the

front door and said good-bye. Then he ambled over to the table where we'd been waiting.

"Everyone, this is our sheriff, Sheriff Murphy O'Neil," Honey said, introducing him. She turned to him. "Any idea what happened, Murph?"

The sheriff frowned. "Ravi thinks the vic was stabbed between two and four in the morning, judging by the body temp. He was probably asleep—no signs of a struggle."

"What was that thing in his neck?" Paula repeated her earlier question.

Sheriff O'Neil dug in his pocket and pulled out a plastic baggie. He held it up. "Anyone recognize this?" He watched our reactions carefully.

Everyone shook their heads.

Except one.

The sheriff zeroed in on our innkeeper. "Honey?"

"It . . . it looks like one of my antique apple corers, but I don't have any idea how it got—" She stopped suddenly. The look of horror on her face could have meant several things. Horror at the thought of Roman being stabbed with it? Horror that someone used her antique corer?

Or horror that she could be implicated in a murder?

"You want to show me where it came from?" the sheriff asked her.

She bit her lip, nodded, rose, and walked into the adjoining parlor. We watched from our seats as she pointed to a framed display of antique tools on one of the walls. I hadn't noticed it before, among all the other antiques, knickknacks, artwork, and usual clutter found in many bed-and-breakfast inns.

Clearly, one of the six tools within the framed display was missing.

Honey's eyes were wide as she stared at the display. "I . . . I . . ."

"Bonita," the sheriff said. "Take Honey into the kitchen and make her some tea or something. I'm going to talk to the guests for a few minutes."

Deputy Bonita rose from the table and collected Honey, pulling her gently away from her fixated gaze. She led her to the kitchen and they disappeared from sight. The sheriff took a seat at the table.

"All right, do any of you know anything about this man's death?"

Interesting. If we'd been in the city, Detective Shelton would have questioned us one by one, individually and separately. Apparently out here in the country, the sheriff did things differently. We all shook our heads. When he asked where we'd been during the hours of two and four a.m., we gave our alibis. Aunt Abby said, "Asleep." Paula said, "Me too." Jake nodded and repeated, "Asleep." Then it was my turn.

I *hadn't* been asleep at two in the morning. And neither had Honey.

I confessed to the sheriff that I couldn't sleep and had heard voices outside.

"What kind of voices?" he asked, one eyebrow arching.

"Well, I thought there were three or four people—two

or three men and a woman—but I couldn't be absolutely sure. It was dark and they were in the shadows. I went downstairs to see what was going on, but by the time I got there, the men were gone."

"What about the woman?" he asked, taking notes in a small notebook he'd withdrawn from his pocket.

Uh-oh. I was just about to incriminate Honey. "I. . . .think it was Honey."

"How do you know?"

"She came in the door when I got downstairs."

Sheriff O'Neil looked up. "What were they talking about?"

"I couldn't make out the words. . . ."

In fact, I remembered hearing something like "run" and "ruin," but I couldn't be sure, so I didn't mention it.

The sheriff eyed me. "How did they sound?"

I shifted in my seat, uncomfortable with what I was about to say. But if I didn't answer the question truthfully, I'd be committing a crime by withholding possible evidence.

I glanced at Jake and Aunt Abby, hoping they'd save me somehow from having to say anything more. Jake shrugged. Aunt Abby just stared at me, her eyes wide.

I took a deep breath, then said, "It sounded like they were arguing."

Uh-oh. The murder took place in Honey's inn. The weapon belonged to her. And she and Roman had disagreed about GMO apples during last night's dinner conversation.

Had I just incriminated Honey Smith?

Chapter 8

Nobody else had anything to add, so the interrogation was short, if not sweet. Sheriff O'Neil let us get on with prepping for the festival, although we were already running late and knew we would barely make it on time. Oh well. I'd learned the hard way that a murder investigation always takes precedence over the food truck business—or anything else.

As soon as the sheriff was out the door, we headed upstairs to gather our things. Jake and I went to our room and brushed our teeth together over the single sink. I must say, it was comforting to share this ordinary task with him. He was adorable when he smiled with a mouth full of toothpaste. We got our jackets and my purse and locked the door after leaving the room. Although I realized locking up was no assurance that our stuff would be safe.

"Aunt Abby?" I said as I entered her room. Dillon

was sitting on her bed, texting. I'd nearly forgotten about him. "Where have you been?" I asked him.

He shrugged. "Had stuff to do."

"You mean someone to avoid, don't you?" I asked, baiting him.

"Hey, I don't know anything about who offed that guy," Dillon shot back. "That's the cops' job."

"You should have at least made an appearance," I countered. "When the sheriff finds out you were in the house and didn't come down for questioning, he's going to want to talk to you."

"Well, he's not going to find out unless you tell him," Dillon said.

I wondered if Honey would mention Dillon's absence to the sheriff, but I had a feeling it wasn't a top priority for her. She had other things on her mind, like who killed one of her guests practically under her nose. Not to mention the recent fires that complicated things.

"Stop it, you two," Aunt Abby said. "Or I'll smack the pair of you. And show some respect for the body in the next room."

I made a face at Dillon. He grunted.

"Need any help, Abby?" Jake said.

"No, thanks," she answered. "I need to put these two to work to keep them from bickering. You go on ahead."

Jake turned to me. "See you there?"

I nodded and he headed down the stairs to his cream puff truck.

Dillon and I took orders from my aunt and ten minutes later we were on our way to the Big Yellow

School Bus, our arms laden with chalkboard signs Aunt Abby had written up for the event to advertise her new apple delights. I looked for Honey to say good-bye for the day, but she was nowhere in sight. I wondered if she'd show up for a festival after all that had happened. As we walked to the bus, another car from the coroner's office pulled up and two men got out, dressed in protective cover-ups.

They were here to retrieve the body.

With a last glance back at the not-so-Enchanted Apple Bed-and-Breakfast Inn, I followed Aunt Abby and Dillon into the bus, wondering where Honey had disappeared to.

The twentieth annual Apple Fest was already in full bloom when we pulled up, with food, fun, and festivities galore. Honey had mentioned that ten thousand people were expected to attend and over thirty local farms and ranches were participating in the opening weekend. In addition to the dozen food trucks, there must have been three dozen large white canopies where vendors like Apple Annie's, the Big Apple, In Apple Pie Order, the Apple Polisher, Little Green Apples, and the Apple Cart were serving apple goodies. My mouth watered at some of the offerings— apple cinnamon rolls and strudels, apple cobblers and crisps, apple fritters and fries, caramel and toffee apples, apple butters, jams, and sauces, and apple wines and beers. They all claimed to be "Fresh from Farm to Fork." I hoped I got a chance to taste everything. Research for my cookbook, of course.

Across from the food vendors were maybe forty or fifty picnic tables, many already occupied by apple lovers. Beyond them I could see a corral offering pony rides, a bunch of trampolines, electric scooters to ride around the paved paths, a petting zoo for the kids, and the A-MAZE-ing Hay Maze. The only thing missing from this circus were the elephants.

Apparently this crowd hadn't heard or didn't care about the murder at the Enchanted Inn.

We parked the school bus next to Jake's truck, which already had a line. While Aunt Abby got out her apple treats to display inside the window, Dillon set up the signs and I put out napkins, plasticware, and packets of sugar, cinnamon, and allspice. We were ready for business in a matter of minutes and had a line by the time Aunt Abby slid open the service window.

The next few hours were mostly a blur of activity. Aunt Abby's salted caramel-apple tarts were a huge hit. People came back for seconds and thirds, in between visits to the other food trucks and apple vendors. I hadn't had time to think about the murder, but at some point it occurred to me that I'd seen no sign of Honey Smith at the festival. I figured, if she came, she'd at least stop by and say hello.

Maybe she'd learned what I'd told the sheriff about her arguing with those men. Would I find my suitcase on the porch when I got back to the inn? Worse, would I discover Honey Smith had been arrested for the murder of Roman Gold.

And would I be to blame?

Around four o'clock, after the crowd died down,

the vendors began closing up shop. I helped Aunt Abby clean the kitchen area and put away the utensils, then took a much-needed break and headed to Jake's Dream Puff truck to see if he was ready to close down. I wasn't hungry, having snacked on Aunt Abby's "failures" throughout the day, but it wasn't too early for a glass of apple wine. Hey, I was on vacation. Sort of.

"I've got a few puffs in the oven," he said through the service window. "I'll meet you at the wine tent. It looks like it's still open." He pushed some cash through the window. "Get us a couple of apple wines." He already had my heart. Now he could read my mind. I pushed the money back at him. "My treat."

I turned around and spotted the tent with a sign that read WISE APPLE WINERY. In my rush to head over, I tripped on a cord and nearly lost my balance.

"Whoa there, missy!" said the man who had grabbed me and saved me from an embarrassing fall.

I looked up to see Nathan "Appleseed" Chapman grinning at me. His breath smelled of alcohol.

"Thank you," I said, brushing myself off. "I need to watch where I'm going."

"Well, it looked like you were in quite the hurry," Nathan said. "Headed for the wine tent?"

I nodded. "Time for a break."

"Listen, maybe I could buy you a drink later? I've got to meet someone, but I'd like to get to know you better."

OMG. He was hitting on me! Did he not see me with Jake last night?

"Oh, that's really nice of you, but I'm meeting my boyfriend in a few minutes."

Nathan stepped back. "Well, if you change your mind . . ."

I nodded and quickly made for the Wise Apple Winery booth. When I got there, a middle-aged couple stood at the serving table with their glasses, chatting with a woman who was pouring wine. I immediately recognized the wine seller. It was Crystal Cortland, Red's ex-wife. I'd seen her last night at Red's place, after the fire. Standing silently behind her, wiping glasses, was their twenty-something daughter, Tiffany.

While Crystal talked with the couple enjoying her wine, I noticed Tiffany staring off to the side as if mesmerized by something—or someone. I glanced over to see what held her attention so intently and spotted none other than Nathan Chapman, gesturing to her and nodding to the left. I surreptitiously watched as Tiffany stole a look at her mother, then gave a tiny nod to the man. She set down the glass she'd been cleaning and disappeared out the back of the wine tent.

I turned to look at Nathan and caught him pulling a flask from an inside pocket. He took a quick hit and replaced the flask just as Tiffany appeared a few feet away. He glanced around, then followed her, keeping his distance. Moments later they were out of sight.

What, I wondered, was a man old enough to be Tiffany's father doing with Crystal Cortland's daughter?

Crystal, apparently oblivious of her daughter's disappearance, continued her conversation with the couple. I sidled up behind them and listened as they thanked Crystal for the wine and moved on. I took their place at the front of the serving table.

"May I help you?" Crystal said with a smile. She wore what looked like several layers of clothing—a long skirt, a peasant-style blouse, a long thin wrap, and lots of chunky jewelry. Her blond hair was done up with combs, with wispy tendrils cascading at the back. Her red roots were just beginning to show, indicating her natural color was beginning to grow out.

"I'd like to taste some of your apple wine," I said. Obviously she didn't recognize me from last night at the fire at Red's farm, but then it was hectic and dark, and I had only been an observer. I wondered if she'd heard about the murder at Honey's place.

Crystal set out a clean glass and poured a couple of tablespoons into it. "This is my Applewhite, one of my most popular wines. It's crisp and dry, with a light taste of oak."

I swirled the wine around the glass like the way I'd seen professional wine tasters do, then drank it down. "Mmm," I said. "Very good."

She got out a fresh glass, uncapped another bottle, and poured in a sample. "Now try this one. It's more of a dessert wine, with a fruity flavor. I call it Sweet Tiffany."

"Named after your daughter?" I asked, then downed the sip.

Crystal grinned. "Yes! How did you know?"

"I saw you at Red Cortland's farm last night, after the fire."

The smile faded as her eyes widened. "You were there? Are you friends with Red?"

"Oh no," I said quickly. "Several of us are staying

at the Enchanted Apple Inn and we heard about the fire, so we came over to see if there was anything we could do."

"Oh," she said, her eyes narrowing. "You're guests at Honey Smith's place. Then you must know about the murder."

I blinked. Apparently word *had* gotten out, at least among the locals.

"You heard about it too?" I asked, wondering how she'd learned the news. This being a small town, no doubt information spread faster than melting ice cream on a slice of hot apple pie.

"Of course," she said. "We don't get many murders here in Apple Valley. When something like this happens, everyone hears about it. Aren't many secrets in a place like this."

Yeah? I wondered.

"Did you know Roman Gold, the man who was killed?" I asked, curious about what she might know.

"Never heard of him. Supposed to be some kind of writer doing an article on the Apple Fest, but he never talked to me. Someone said he sounded kind of pro-GMO. That wouldn't have won him any popularity contests, at least not around here."

"It does seem like a lot of farmers are upset about the new GMO apples. But I hardly think his interest in them would get him killed. After all, he was just writing about the situation. As a journalist, he's supposed to remain unbiased." At least, that's what they told us in journalism school.

"Well, GMO apples don't bother me," Crystal said,

filling another clean glass with some of her wine. I thought she was about to offer it to me while we chatted, but instead she swallowed a couple of sips herself.

"You're not worried about them?" I asked.

"Oh, I sympathize with the growers, but my winery won't be affected, since bigger and prettier apples aren't really an issue for wine-making. Besides, it's going to happen anyway—that's progress—so we might as well accept it. Things happen that are out of our control. One day you have a farm. The next day it's burned to the ground. One day you're married. The next day he walks out on you. That's life."

She took another long swallow of wine and set down the glass a little harder than she should have. I was surprised it didn't crack or shatter into pieces.

"What do you think is going on with those fires?" I thought she might have some additional insight to offer after chugging that wine.

She frowned. "What are you, some kind of reporter too?"

I shook my head. "No, I'm working in one of the food trucks at the festival. The Big Yellow School Bus. And writing a cookbook featuring food truck recipes."

She brightened. "Why didn't you say so? I give vendors a discount on my wines."

"Great. Then I'd like two glasses of the Applewhite."

She poured the wine into the two glasses I'd used for tasting, apparently not concerned that they should be perfectly clean. Was the alcohol level affecting her wine-serving protocol?

"As for the fires," she said, "now, they're a real concern. My guess is someone is setting those fires to send a message, and who knows who'll be next? My winery? If I lose my business, I'll be left with nothing. My daughter and I would be in serious trouble. We can't live on her small income making crafts and setting up hay mazes and selling scarecrows. I hope they catch the bastard, and soon."

So, it sounded as though the fires worried her, but the dead man wasn't an issue. Interesting.

"That'll be ten dollars for the wine," she said. "With the discount. And ten for the two glasses. They're souvenirs, unless you want plastic cups."

Twenty bucks for wine and glasses? With a discount? Wow.

I gave her a twenty and picked up the glasses. "Thanks," I said. "Nice chatting with you."

"You too. Come by sometime over the weekend so you can meet my daughter, Tiffany."

"I think saw her last night. There's a family resemblance."

Crystal smiled proudly. "Yep. Got her mom's nose and eyes." She looked around. "Funny, she was here just a minute ago, helping me out. Now where'd she get to?"

I bit my tongue. No way was I getting involved in this potential drama. I already had more than enough drama to deal with on my own.

Chapter 9

I picked up my two glasses of wine and looked around for a nearby picnic table where Jake and I could sit down, take a break, and enjoy the drinks. I spotted a free one, sat down, and took a few minutes to relax, inhaling the smells of cut hay, hot cider, and horses around me. The trees in the nearby orchard dazzled with fall colors, and I wondered for a moment what it would be like to live in such beautiful country.

I glanced around and noticed almost all the food trucks were closed. Luckily I'd already collected a number of yummy recipes for my book, including apple donuts, apple sausage, and apple-cinnamon muffins. Most of the tents had lowered their front flaps, except for Crystal's wine tent and a few other merchants. But the amusements and attractions were still open, including the nearby A-MAZE-ing Maze, which had a line of kids, teenagers, and adults waiting to get lost among the hay bales and scarecrows.

I searched for Tiffany, wondering where she'd gone to meet Nathan and what they were up to. I had a feeling Crystal wouldn't be pleased. She seemed to keep a watchful eye over her grown daughter. But then, most mothers wouldn't want their twenty-something daughters fraternizing with forty-year-old men.

Jake arrived a few minutes later. By then I was half-way finished with my glass of apple wine and thinking about having a second.

"Hi," he said as he sat down on the picnic bench opposite me. He took up the glass of wine I'd brought him. "Thanks. I need this. It's been a long day."

"The wine's not bad," I said, taking another sip.

Jake glanced around, then turned to me. "Hey, are you ready to find your way through the labyrinth?"

It would be more like a rat trapped in a maze, I thought, wondering if I had a touch of claustrophobia. "Uh, sure . . . as soon as I'm done with my wine."

We chatted a few minutes about our day. Both of our trucks had lots of customers and we were kept busier than either one of us expected. Plus, we were both exhausted. It felt good just to sit and enjoy the wine as we made dinner plans. Jake mentioned a roadside café he'd passed on his way to the festival called the Peel and the Core and suggested we go there. I hadn't noticed the place, but it sounded interesting, and we decided we'd head over after a romp in the hay, so to speak.

Just as we finished our drinks, I saw Tiffany come out from the hay maze exit at the far end. She looked

as though she was in a daze, stumbling along, unfo-
cused. She shook her head, mumbled something to
herself, then glanced around several times, as if checking to see whether anyone was watching her. Luckily
she didn't spot me spying on her. Not with my glass of
wine in front of my face. Finally she headed for her
mother's winery tent.

What had happened in that maze to change Tiffany's behavior so dramatically?

"What are you doing?" Jake asked, apparently noticing my interest in Tiffany.

"Nothing," I said.

Jake followed my gaze.

"Don't look!" I said, not wanting Tiffany to notice
she had an audience.

Jake turned back, looking puzzled. "Don't look at
what? What exactly are you looking at?"

I sighed. "Tiffany, Crystal's daughter," I whispered
as if she might overhear me from several yards away.
"She just came out of the hay maze exit, looking as if
she'd seen a ghost or something. It was very weird.
Then she looked around to see if anyone was watching her."

"Someone is," Jake said, eyeing me. "You. Maybe
that's why she's acting a little strange."

I decided to tell him about my encounter with
Crystal. "I saw Tiffany earlier with her mom in the
tent, and then Nathan Chapman showed up, and then
Tiffany disappeared out the back of the tent, and then
when I stepped up to get our wine, Crystal started
looking for Tiffany because she wanted to introduce

me, and now Tiffany suddenly reappears from behind the hay maze." Nearly out of breath, I inhaled deeply.

Another movement from the hay maze caught my eye.

"Oh my God," I whispered. "Don't look now, but guess who just came out of the maze?"

"Who?" Jake asked.

"Nathan Chapman!"

The man glanced around, just as Tiffany had done a few minutes earlier, then pulled out his flask and took a long swallow.

I caught Jake staring at him. "I said don't look!"

Why is it when you say don't look, people look?

Jake sighed. "Darcy, what's the big deal? What do you think is going on?"

"I don't know, but something is. . . ." I nodded toward the Wise Apple tent.

"Can I look?" Jake asked sarcastically.

"If you're discreet," I said.

We watched Tiffany approach her mom, who stood behind the serving table. I had to strain to hear their conversation.

"Where've you been? I've been looking all over for you," Crystal said to her daughter.

Tiffany seemed to look through her mother. "Just . . . checking on the hay maze. Why?"

Crystal studied her daughter, her brow furrowed. "Checking on the maze? What on earth for? You hired college kids to do that."

Tiffany shrugged and glanced away. "Uh, J.J. said there was a loose bale, so I went to check on it. It's my

responsibility if the bales come falling down on someone, you know." Her voice was flat.

"Well, get J.J. to fix it. That's his job." Crystal looked
about to say something more; then she closed her
mouth. Her eyes narrowed. I glanced to see what had
caught her attention.

Nathan Chapman was approaching the Wise Apple
wine booth.

"Everything going well?" he asked cheerily, focus-
ing on Crystal. Tiffany suddenly turned away and
busied herself cleaning another wineglass.

"Fine," Crystal said, eyeing him. She turned to Tiffany. "Tiff, go get me a few more bottles of the Applewhite. I'm almost out."

Tiffany looked up at her mom, then stole a quick
glance at Nathan. She nodded and exited out the back
of the tent.

As soon as Tiffany was out of sight, Crystal turned
to Nathan. "We need to talk," she said, coming out
from behind the serving table. "Over here."

She walked a few feet away from the tent and out of
earshot. Nathan followed her. I could only see Crystal,
since Nathan's back was to me, but it was clear from
her expression she was angry. She said something I
couldn't make out; then Nathan shook his head, pulled
out his flask, and took a drink. All I could hear were
muted voices. It was obvious they were having an
argument. I wondered what they were fighting about.

I had a feeling it was about Tiffany.

After a few heated minutes, Nathan gave a last shake

of his head, then stomped off and out of sight. Crystal remained there for a moment watching him, then headed back to her own tent, just as Tiffany returned with the wine bottles. The young woman glanced around, frowned, and set the bottles down.

"Mother—"

Before she could say anything more, Crystal pulled down the front flap of the tent, closing the wine kiosk, and blocking my view of the two of them.

"Get in the back," I heard Crystal's muffled voice say behind the tent. "Now!"

Then nothing more.

"I guess that's the end of wine service for now," I said, turning back to Jake.

"What was that all about?" he asked.

"I told you something was up. I think it has to do with Tiffany and Nathan. I get the feeling Crystal doesn't like Nathan. She must suspect something too."

"You got all of that from just watching them for a few minutes?" Jake grinned. "Who are you, Sherlock Holmes?"

"Simple, deductive reasoning," I said, using a very bad British accent.

"And you came up with that scenario?"

"Look at the facts, Watson," I said. "Elementary, don't you think?"

"I think you should write romantic suspense novels instead of cookbooks. You really think there's something going on between Tiffany and a guy who's twice her age?"

I shrugged. "All I know is Tiffany seems naive and

kind of clueless, Nathan is some kind of alcoholic player, and Crystal acts like an overprotective mother."

"Or maybe she's jealous," Jake suggested.

"Jealous? Why do you say that?"

"Nathan and Crystal look about the same age. Maybe they were involved at one time, but something happened and now he's interested in the younger version of Crystal—her daughter."

"I doubt it. Crystal only recently got divorced."

"Maybe that's why her husband walked—because she cheated on him." His voice rose in excitement; his eyes were wide.

I slapped his leg gently. "You're making fun of me!"

Jake laughed. "Why the big interest in this, anyway? Shouldn't you be using that brain power to figure out who killed Roman Gold? For a reporter, that's more your style."

"I was a restaurant critic, not a reporter. And I have no idea who might have killed Roman Gold. Detective Shelton is supposed to arrive tonight. Maybe he can solve the murder."

"Well, how about we take a break from the Crystal-Tiffany-Nathan soap opera and do the maze? I plan to win that bet we have going."

I rose from the picnic table. Jake was right. What was I doing puzzling over this odd triangle? Maybe because, with my journalism background, it was my nature to be curious about people. But what went on inside hay mazes and closed tents was none of my business. There was a more pressing puzzle to be solved with the death of Roman Gold.

I had a growing concern that Honey's freedom was at stake—and I might have been the one who pointed that stake right at her heart. If I ended up being responsible, I'd never forgive myself—and neither would Aunt Abby.

Jake and I paid the entrance fee to a forlorn-looking college guy with long stringy hair and a vacant look in his eyes, then got in line behind a group of loud teenagers. While we waited for our turn, I read over the large sign posting the rules and tips:

THE A-MAZE-ING SCARECROW
HAY MAZE RULES:

NO SMOKING!
No alcohol or drugs.
No running. No horseplay. No bad language.
Stay on the path.
Use the bathroom before you enter. There are no
facilities inside the maze!
The field is 2 acres, covering 2 miles.
Average time to complete it is 1 hour.
No admittance an hour before closing.

I checked the hours—ten a.m. to six p.m. We'd just make it.

If you get lost, do NOT call 911. Call or text us
and we'll send in one of our maze runners. If
you call 911, you will be fined by the city for
wasting officers' time and resources. (Note: This

really happened to a family. The officers found them in 8 minutes. The family was uninjured but fined $500.)

Ha! I'd sleep overnight in the place before I'd resort to calling 911.

And finally the last rule, which was the same as the first:

NO SMOKING!

I pulled out my cell phone and tapped in "hay maze tips." I figured it wasn't cheating if I called it research. I found a site that read "How to survive a corn/hay maze without calling 911."

Perfect. I scanned the suggestions.

Bring a flashlight if it's dark.

I looked up. The sun was setting and it would be dark soon. Good thing I had my cell phone flashlight app.

Look for a watchtower and use it to see bigger sections of the maze.

The A-MAZE-ing Hay Maze didn't appear to have any towers.

Carry a stick with a handkerchief tied to the top to locate one another if you get separated.

Clever! Except I didn't have a stick or a handkerchief. The best I could do was take off my bra and wave it around if I got lost.

Use your cell phone GPS and Google Earth to find your way out.

Now, *that* was cheating. Seriously.

Orient yourself first. Listen for sounds of traffic, machinery, etc.
Notice where the exit is before you begin.
Keep an eye out for details along the route so you don't go around in circles.

Good tips. I listened for the sound of cars passing by and made a mental note that the entrance—and the exit at the other end—was not far from the highway. As for details along the way, I doubted I would notice variations in the hay, but maybe the scarecrows placed along the way would offer some clues.

If you get lost, follow little kids. They seem to know how to get out. But if you have no sense of direction, perhaps don't go in in the first place.

Very funny. I doubted the teenagers in front of us would be of any help. From the sound of their loud talk and frequent giggles, they'd either been drinking or smoking weed.

And finally:

Do not watch Stephen King's Children of the Corn*!*

Too late.

I laughed, but I began to wonder if I'd be the one who disappeared into the maze and was never seen again. I smiled at Jake. He smiled back. There was no way I'd let on that this didn't sound as fun as I originally thought it might be. Oh well. I wasn't going to chicken out now. What was the worst that could happen? And if I got desperate, I could always call 911.

Another bored-looking college kid guarded the entrance. He nodded for us to go ahead, after giving the teenagers plenty of time to get started, presumably so we wouldn't be able to follow them. That wouldn't have been hard. All we'd have to do is track them using the sound of their laughter and curses or smell of weed. I had a feeling the maze tips wouldn't help these tipsy teenagers.

After a few feet, Jake and I came to our first fork in the road. I looked at him, he looked at me, and we each headed in opposite directions.

It. Was. *On.*

I had my first panic attack after I'd been in the maze for nearly fifteen minutes and hadn't seen a sign of the exit, other people, or Jake. I stopped for a moment, tried to orient myself, then decided on a plan. I didn't have bread crumbs to drop, but I would "mark" some of the hay bales by tying pieces of hay into knots. That way I'd know if I'd been to a spot before and could try another path. Thank you, Hansel and Gretel.

Next, I remembered one of the tips about listening

for clues. I listened for a few seconds and thought I heard muffled sounds of cars but couldn't be sure where they were coming from. The hay bales must have created some kind of acoustic barrier.

Finally I decided I'd keep turning right, a trick I'd learned in Girl Scouts while doing outdoor orienteering. I'd forgotten the logic in that, but I didn't have a lot of other options, other than cheating and using my GPS, and I refused to do that. I wanted to beat Jake, fair and square—or I'd never hear the end of it.

After a few more minutes, I noticed I was straining to see the bits of hay I was tying into knots. It was getting dark. I switched on my cell phone flashlight and it flickered. I checked the battery. Only ten percent left. Great. Maybe it was time to whip off my bra and wave it around like a sailor lost at sea.

Two little kids ran past me. They'd come out of nowhere and disappeared just as fast. Punks.

"Hey, kids! Wait up!" I called, running after them. I turned a corner, thinking I heard them, but there was no one in sight.

I was alone.

It was getting dark.

And I didn't have a clue how to get out of this maze.

That was when I smelled smoke.

Chapter 10

Oh my God! Smoke!

The hay maze was on fire! And I was trapped like a rat with no clue how to find the exit. I did what anybody inside a flammable tinderbox would do—I screamed.

"Jake! Jake!"

I thought I heard my name being called, but I couldn't be sure. The hay bales seemed to muffle all sound. Trying not to panic, I pulled out my phone, saw I only had ten percent battery life left, and did exactly what the rules told me not to do—I called 911.

"Nine-one-one," the calm operator said.

I didn't have much time left on the phone.

"I'm trapped inside a hay maze!" I sputtered, not thinking straight.

"I'm sorry, but we don't handle those calls anymore," the operator said. "You'll have to call the maze operator and have someone locate you."

"Wait! No! The maze is on fire! And I can't find my way out."

"The maze is on fire?"

The female operator didn't sound at all convinced. I wondered how many crank calls she'd gotten that were similar.

"Yes! I'm at the A-MAZE-ing Scarecrow Maze at the Apple Festival. Please, can you send someone? There are other people in here too. A group of teenagers. Some little kids!"

And Jake.

The smell of smoke was growing stronger. I wondered how close it was to me. These hay bales could go up in flames in a matter of minutes if not seconds.

"Hello?" I said, when there was no response from the operator. "Are you there?"

"Please hold," the operator said.

She was putting me on hold!

And then my cell phone went dead. So much for using GPS now.

I stuffed my useless phone in my pocket and started rushing through the twisting and turning maze as fast as I could, hoping I'd stumble onto a way out.

"Jake!" I screamed after each corner I turned.

No response.

I kept running and screaming.

And then I thought I heard something. Sirens.

Thank God!

I was surrounded by walls of dry hay, ready to go up like a giant match. But would the firefighters be able to reach all of us in here in time?

The sirens grew louder.

"I'm in here!" I screamed, jumping up in hopes someone might see the top of my head bouncing up and down, but it was hopeless. These bales were stacked at least eight feet tall. There was only one thing left to do.

I unhooked my bra, slithered out of it, and began waving it over my head like a marooned castaway on a deserted island. I had no idea if anyone would see it, but I couldn't just wait inside the maze for the flames to lick my feet. I kept running around corners, waving my bra, praying I wasn't going in circles, praying I would find the exit soon—or that someone would find me.

Frantic, I turned a corner—and ran smack into Jake.

"Jake! Oh, thank God!" I said, embracing him briefly. "We've got to get out of here. The maze is on fire—"

"Calm down, Darcy. It's okay. We're safe," he said, holding me tight.

I broke loose. "No, we've got to get out. And make sure all those kids are out! Who knows how long it will take the firefighters to put out the fire?"

"The maze isn't on fire," he said calmly. "We're all right. Everybody's all right."

I frowned at him, not comprehending his words. "What do you mean? What about the smoke? The sirens? I don't understand."

"There was a fire. It's out now. But it wasn't the maze."

I stared at him. "How do you know?"

"I've been out of the maze for about fifteen minutes, waiting for you," he said, taking me by the hand and leading me down a narrow path. "When I smelled the smoke, my first thought was the maze too, but then I saw it was coming from another part of the festival area. I called nine-one-one and reported it, just in case no one else did. They got here in minutes and were able to put it out quickly."

"Anyone hurt?" I said, following his lead through the twisting maze.

"No, everyone's fine."

"Thank God." I stopped suddenly and looked at Jake. "Wait a minute. You've been out of the maze for *fifteen* minutes! While I was lost inside here this whole time, you found your way out and you've been *waiting* for me?"

He shrugged and led me on, turning and twisting confidently, as if he'd laid out the maze himself. "What can I say? I've got some kind of innate sense of direction. Most men do."

"Are you seriously saying men don't ask for directions because they don't *need* to? That's ridiculous!"

He shrugged.

He led me around another corner and stopped.

I looked up. There was the exit sign, right in front of my hot, sweaty face.

Jake knew better than to say anything, but he grinned and shrugged, as if he'd just gotten lucky.

"How did you *do* that?" I asked, amazed and irritated at the same time.

"Like I said, I was born with it."

I glared at him. "So you knew you had an advantage all along and made a bet with me anyway?"

"Yep," he said simply.

I shook my head. "Not fair."

"Sore loser?"

"Never! What are you going to make me do now that you've won?"

"I'll let you know," he said. "By the way, why are you carrying your bra?"

I felt my face fill with heat. Crap. I quickly wadded the undergarment into a ball and stuffed it into my jacket pocket. "Never mind," I said.

He tried to suppress a smile, but it didn't work. To make matters worse, he raised a naughty eyebrow.

"Oh, stop! Let's go find out about that fire. It's the fourth one so far—the third in two days. You said no one was hurt."

"Everyone's safe," he said.

I turned to him. "How do you know?"

"When I saw where it was coming from, I ran over to see if I could help, but the firefighters arrived and got it under control."

"Where was it?" I asked.

We exited. Jake took my hand and led me to over to the area that housed the food and craft tents. It looked as though one of the tents had caught fire, burning the canvas off the steel frame and leaving the vendor's table blackened and scorched and the area around it water-soaked.

"Oh no!" I said when I realized it was the Wise Apple Winery tent. "Where are Crystal and Tiffany?"

Jake pointed in the direction of some people who

had gathered around to gawk at the spectacle. I spotted Crystal talking to one of the firefighters, her daughter standing silently beside her.

I looked at Jake. "Does Crystal know what happened?"

Jake shrugged.

"The firefighters?"

He shook his head.

I couldn't help wondering if this fire was deliberately set.

I glanced around. Some distance away, standing in the shadows and watching the scene, was Nathan Chapman.

Somebody called my name. I turned around to see what looked like two big kids on electric scooters coming right toward me. One was short and petite and had a big smile on her face. The other one was a guy, tall and hunched over the handlebars. They both wore black helmets.

"Oh no," I said under my breath. Jake grinned at the spectacle that was Aunt Abby and Dillon. They looked absolutely ridiculous.

"What are you *doing*?" I asked my aunt as she came to a halt a foot away from me. Dillon did a figure eight around me before coming to a stop. They were smiling like oversize school children playing hooky.

"Riding electric scooters," Aunt Abby said proudly as she stepped off and tapped the kickstand with her foot. "It's fun! And great exercise."

Exercise?

"Where did you get them?" I glanced around for a vendor who was crazy enough to rent these two people any kind of vehicle.

She pointed behind her, but tents blocked my view of anything but more tents.

"It's a place called Scoot! You can rent these Razor electric scooters by the hour and they have these paved and dirt tracks you can ride on."

"Wanna try, Darcy?" Dillon asked me. He had a smirk on his face.

"Uh, no, thanks. I've had enough excitement for one day."

"You talking about the fire?" Dillon asked. "Yeah, we saw the smoke. That's why we rode over. What's up?"

"Aren't you supposed to stay on the designated path?" I asked.

"If you rent them, yes," Aunt Abby said, "but we were having so much fun, we bought these."

I blinked. "You *bought* those? You can't be serious!"

"Why not?" Dillon said. "They're awesome. They go up to fifteen miles an hour. And we can use them to tool around Fort Mason, Golden Gate Park, a bunch of places."

My relatives were both nuts.

"So, what's up with the fire?" Dillon asked again, gazing in the direction of the scorched tent.

I looked at Jake, praying he wouldn't tell him my side of the story—being lost in the maze, certain I was about to be incinerated, braless.

"Uh, apparently the Wise Apple Winery tent caught on fire somehow," I answered before Jake could rat me out. "We were just about to see if we could find out anything."

"Seems kinda hinky," Dillon said. "Isn't this, like, the tenth fire in Apple Hill? This place is jinxed."

"The fourth," I corrected him. "But that's not all," I continued. "The tent that burned—the Wise Apple Winery? It's owned by Crystal Cortland."

"Who's that?" Aunt Abby asked, scrunching up her nose.

"Remember the fire yesterday at Red Cortland's, Honey's friend?"

She nodded.

"Remember the two women who arrived a few minutes later?"

"The older blonde and the younger brunette? I remember," Aunt Abby said, and then it dawned on her. "Oh! She's Honey's boyfriend's ex-wife."

I nodded. "And it's her tent that caught on fire."

Aunt Abby frowned as she processed the information. "That's odd. Honey's storage building catches on fire. Her boyfriend's barn burns down. Now the ex-wife has a fire. Plus, wasn't there another fire before all this? It seems coincidental even for a small town like this."

"My thoughts exactly," I said. "Luckily no one's been hurt—or killed. It looks like Crystal and her daughter, Tiffany, managed to escape. They're standing over there—" I turned around to indicate where we'd seen them talking to the firefighter, but Crystal was now talking to the guy who'd alerted her to the fire at Red's.

"Oh yeah," Aunt Abby said. "What's his name again?"

"Adam something," Jake answered. "He owns the Adam's Apples Farm and heads up the American Apple Association."

How did Jake remember these things? I guess, being a former attorney, he had a knack for storing details and pulling them out as needed. No doubt a handy tool when in court. Being a journalist, I had to write things down so my information would be accurate—and I wouldn't forget it all.

"Nice-looking man, for his age," Aunt Abby said. "And isn't that the woman who's staying at the inn?"

I turned again to see Paula Hayashi standing a few feet away from the trio. She was holding up her camera and taking pictures. I wondered what her photos would have to do with the story Roman Gold was working on. And why she was still in Apple Hill when the journalist she'd been working with was dead. Was someone else coming to finish the assignment? The story couldn't have been that important. Could it?

Or had it turned into a different kind of story?

"Well, we've got to load these scooters into the bus and get back to the inn," Aunt Abby said. "I've got a bunch more tarts to make for tomorrow."

"I'm starving!" Dillon whined. "Can't we eat first?"

Aunt Abby looked at me. Uh-oh. I knew what she was about to ask.

"So," she said, "where are you two going for dinner? Maybe we'll join you, if you don't mind."

I forced a smile. It wasn't that I didn't want to dine with my aunt. I was just hoping to have a romantic dinner with Jake to celebrate his birthday, but she seemed oblivious of that. Oh well, that could wait until tomorrow for his official birthday.

"Uh, great," I managed to say. I looked at Jake. "Where's that place you mentioned?"

"It's called the Peel and the Core," Jake said. "It's back a few miles on the highway. We passed it on the drive up."

"How about we meet you there in about fifteen minutes?" I said. There was one more thing I wanted to do before we left the festival area. As Aunt Abby and Dillon hopped back onto their Razor Scooters and rode them the few yards to the school bus, I headed for Crystal and Tiffany, who were still talking to Adam. Paula stood on the sidelines—listening? I wondered.

"Where are you going?" Jake called to me.

"I'll be right back," I answered. "I just want to ask Crystal a question."

"Okay," he said. "I'll meet you at my truck. Try not to get lost."

"Very funny," I called back. Not.

I sidled up to Crystal, waiting for a break in her conversation with Adam.

"Are you all right?" I asked when there was a pause.

Startled, Crystal whirled around. "I beg your pardon?"

"I was just wondering if there was anything I could do," I offered.

Crystal's eyes narrowed. "You're that food truck girl, right? Staying at Honey's place?"

"Yes. I bought a couple of glasses of wine from you a little while ago. I just thought I'd check and see—"

"We're fine," Crystal said, cutting me off. "We're not liable for the tent, and my insurance will cover any wine loss. And Adam here has graciously found us another tent for my business. But thank you."

I turned to Adam. "That was nice of you, Mr. Bramley, right? I guess it pays to be head of the Apple Association."

He actually blushed, perhaps thinking it was a compliment.

"Any idea how the fire started?" I asked him. Three fires—or more—in such a short period of time certainly had me curious.

He started to answer, but Tiffany cut him off.

"The chief thinks someone set it on purpose. He said some kind of aerosol was used. He smelled it."

"But they don't know who did it," Crystal added, "and until this firebug is caught, we're all going to have to stay on high alert." She started to turn back to Adam, but he had stepped away during our brief chat and was talking to Paula.

Flirting was more like it. Paula kept pawing him and Adam was grinning like an embarrassed teenager.

Crystal frowned.

I glanced at Tiffany, but she wasn't paying attention to any of us. Her eyes were elsewhere. Once again I followed her gaze. She was looking at the man in the shadows.

Chapter 11

I was beginning to get creeped out by this guy who called himself Nathan "Appleseed" Chapman. I'd have to ask Dillon to do a little fact-checking on Nathan's so-called credentials and quasi claim to fame. I couldn't help wondering what was going on between him and Tiffany.

There I went again, but then, curiosity came with the territory. It's just that mine often got me into more trouble than I expected.

I headed back to the Dream Puff truck and found Jake packed up and ready to go. The Big Yellow School Bus had already left, and I guessed Aunt Abby and Dillon were waiting for us at the café. As we drove to the restaurant, I told Jake what I'd learned from Crystal—that the fire chief thought the fire was deliberately set. That caused the question: Who was the firebug? And why was he—or she—doing this?

The letters GMO popped up in my mind, and I wondered if that was the underlying cause. Would GMO companies do something this extreme to drive out the apple farmers and take over the business?

"Maybe Wes can make some sense of all this when he gets here," Jake said, referring to Detective Shelton, as we pulled up to the large parking lot of the Peel and the Core. The school bus was already parked at the far end of the large lot, along with a number of RVs and other oversize vehicles. Jake drove into an empty double-wide slot alongside the other rigs and shut off the engine.

"Darcy?"

Lost in thought, I looked at him. "Yes?"

He smiled. "I said, I hope you're hungry."

"Sorry, I didn't hear you. My mind's so scattered with all that's happened today."

He placed a hand on my knee. "Are you all right? I know you were scared in that maze. But I'm sure the employees keep track of everyone who goes in and comes out. There are probably some secret shortcuts they can use if someone panics or gets injured and needs to get out quickly."

I thought about Tiffany and Nathan's secret meeting inside the maze. Maybe there *were* some secret areas that only a few people knew about. But truthfully, being trapped in the maze while thinking it was on fire wasn't foremost on my mind at the moment. I couldn't get over that last image of Tiffany gazing at Nathan, who stood in the shadows. There was something going on between them and I was dying to know what it was.

He squeezed my leg. "Anything else on your mind?"

"What? Oh no, nothing." Since I didn't have anything concrete about the connection between Tiffany and Nathan, it wasn't worth sharing with Jake again at this point. But I was determined to find out more about them, especially Nathan. His public persona as head of the festival seemed a little too smooth, and I suspected it hid a secret that perhaps Crystal sensed.

"Okay, shall we?" He stood up from the driver's seat and led the way to the side door of his Dream Puff truck. He helped me down the steps, and I waited while he locked the place up. With his hand on my back, he guided me to the café, then held open the door so I could enter.

From the outside, the restaurant looked like an ordinary wood-framed ranch house, only this particular house sported a carved wooden sign that read WELCOME TO THE PEEL AND THE CORE. It hung over the front door and featured an apple peel on one side of the lettering and an apple core on the other. I had no idea what to expect when I went inside, but I certainly didn't expect what I got.

The interior looked like an old-fashioned country store, loaded with knickknacks that were set out on every available surface—windowsills, countertops, shelves, benches, and even the tables. Naturally all of the items featured an apple theme. There were blown glass apples, apple dolls, apple-shaped candles, apple tea towels—you name it, they had it in apple. The walls were painted to look like apple trees with faux branches and papier-mâché apples that appeared to grow out from the tree trunk murals. The place was packed. I could barely hear the country music playing in the background.

Not seeing Aunt Abby and Dillon in the waiting area, I glanced around and spotted them in a booth at the back of the restaurant. They were waving their arms in the air like construction workers at a road-block. I nodded, pointed them out to Jake, and we headed over.

After navigating around several tables on my way, I sat down next to Aunt Abby and set the apple-red napkin on my lap. "Popular place," I shouted, hoping they heard me over the noise, loud conversations, and music. "You're lucky you got a table."

"You can thank Dillon for that," Aunt Abby said. "He knows one of the waiters. Went to school with him."

"Nice going, Dillon," I said.

Dillon's long-haired ponytailed friend came over to take our order. Dillon introduced him simply as J.J. and I thought I recognized him. He turned out to be one of the kids working at the maze. I ordered an apple wine—the only kind of wine they served— while Jake and Dillon ordered apple beers, and Aunt Abby asked for tea. J.J. promised to return with our drinks and then take our food orders.

I looked over the menu, a stained eight-page booklet, touting all their specialties. Naturally everything had an apple touch. The pork chops came with applesauce, the ham and Swiss sandwich was on apple bread, and the chicken salad combined apples with walnuts. Much like Aunt Abby's school bus menu, the restaurant promised down-home cooking with a twist—apples.

When J.J. returned, I ordered the chicken salad, Jake had the pork chops, and Aunt Abby opted for butternut-apple harvest soup, which sounded delicious. Dillon asked for the burger with a side of apple fries dipped in caramel sauce.

As soon as J.J. walked away from the table, a couple sat down in a booth across from us. I immediately recognized Paula Hayashi and Adam Bramley.

Hmmm.

I held up my menu so they couldn't see me and whispered to the others, "Guess who just sat down behind you guys!" They all began looking around.

"Don't look!" I hissed.

Jake turned back, but Dillon continued to scan the restaurant until he spotted the couple. He shrugged. "So? It's that chick who's staying at the inn with us—the one who found the dead guy's body—and the guy who came and told us about the fire."

"Shhh!" I hushed him. "They'll hear you!"

Dillon rolled his eyes and took a gulp of his beer.

I peeked at them from behind my menu to see if they had spotted us yet, but they looked deep in conversation. Actually Paula was doing most of the talking while Adam more or less nodded from time to time. It was hard to hear them with all the noise in the café, so I couldn't make out anything they said. From Paula's animated expression and gestures, I wondered what she was so excited about.

After our food arrived, I tried to watch them surreptitiously as I picked at my food, hoping maybe I could make out snippets of their conversation. I even tried to lip-read Paula, but she moved her head too much for me to catch anything. Were they on a date? I wondered. Was Paula actually attracted to this balding, overweight farmer who had to have twenty years on her?

And what was it about older men and younger women in this town?

I was about to give up trying to listen in when I had an idea. Making sure to avoid Paula's view, I signaled Dillon's waiter friend over to our table.

"Is everything okay?" J.J. asked. He looked concerned that we might not be satisfied with our meals. In fact, I had hardly touched mine.

"Oh yes, fine," I said, keeping my voice low. "I was just wondering if you grew up in Apple Valley."

"Yeah. Been here my whole life, 'cept when I was at UC Davis. Now here I am with a college degree in business and I'm still waiting tables and working at festivals. Why?"

"I was wondering what your take is on the GMO apple competition."

He shook his head. "Funny you should ask. One of those GMO companies made my dad an offer he apparently couldn't refuse and he sold the place to them. Shocked the heck out of me. I'd gone to college to learn the business so I could take over the farm, then boom. I come home and there's no more farm."

"Your dad sold your farm to a GMO company?" I asked, making sure I heard him correctly.

"Yep. Company called Eden Corporation. Most of the other farmers won't sell to them, but my dad said he needed the money so he took it. I think he figured those GMO companies are inevitable, so why not get the best money he could?"

"Do you know what Eden is planning to do with your farm?"

He nodded. "They've already started. They tore down a bunch of the buildings and got rid of the old processing machinery, then replaced everything with all new state-of-the-art stuff."

"Have you been back to the farm and seen all the changes?"

"Nope. Only driven by. They're being very CIA about it. Everything's like this big secret. It's all fenced now, and I heard they won't let anyone inside that doesn't work for them."

Interesting, I thought. "Why all the secrecy, do you think?"

J.J. shrugged. "They probably don't want any of the other farmers to know how they grow the apples. Someone might burn the place down if they knew." He laughed.

Burn the place down?

"Thanks, J.J.," I said.

"Sure. Just don't mention I told you any of this. Like I said, a lot of folks around here aren't happy with my dad for selling his farm."

"I won't," I said.

"More water or anything?" J.J. asked before leaving us.

We shook our heads. I sneaked a peek at Paula to see if we'd attracted any attention by talking to J.J., but she seemed oblivious of us and enthralled with her dining companion.

"Are you going to eat your dinner?" Dillon asked.

While I'd been talking to J.J., I hadn't noticed that Dillon had wolfed down his dinner, pulled out his laptop, and was typing away on the keyboard.

"Seriously?" I said to him, nodding to the computer. "Can't you just text like everyone else?"

"Yeah, well, while you were pumping J.J., I was doing a little research. I think you're gonna want to hear this."

"What?" I leaned in to hear him better over the noise.

"Dude, I was just checking out Eden Corporation. The CEO there is some dude named Reuben Gottfried."

"So?"

"So, here's a picture of him." Dillon turned the laptop around so I could see the photograph he was referring to. "Look familiar?"

Aside from the absence of a beard and glasses, he looked a lot like the murder victim, Roman Gold.

Reuben Gottfried. Roman Gold.

Whoa. I started to say something, but Dillon held up a finger. "So then I did a search for Roman Gold. Wanna know what I found?"

Dillon continued to amaze me the way he could find out things few people knew. I had to admit, it was nice having a computer savant in the family, even if he was annoying most of the time.

"Of course! What?"

Dillon gave an "I know something you don't know" smile. So immature.

"Dillon!" I insisted.

"Can I have the rest of your dinner?"

"No!" I snapped, and pulled the plate toward me.

"Then buy me the apple hot fudge sundae and I'll tell you."

"Deal! Now spill it!"

Dillon hunkered down into his conspiratorial mode and glanced from side to side for spies or whatever. Aunt Abby and Jake leaned forward to hear when he finally began, "Dude, first of all, I couldn't find anyone named Roman Gold in any of the Internet searches I did. I found Roman gold coins, but that's it. Maybe that's where he got the name."

"So you think Roman Gold is a fake name?"

"Looks that way. But that's not all. I checked the news outlet he said he was writing for—the *Sacramento Bee*. No one there by that name."

"Why would he lie about his name and about his job?"

"I did a little more digging," Dillon continued, but stopped when J.J. appeared to clear our plates. I waited impatiently until he was done. Before he left the table, Dillon put in his order for the hot fudge and apple sundae, and so did Aunt Abby. When J.J. finally left, I leaned in again.

"What else?"

"So, I checked out that chick we were talking about. . . ." He nodded toward Paula.

"Is that a fake name too?" I asked.

"No, it's real," Dillon said, covering the side of his mouth. "But she's not a photographer for the *Bee*. She's not even a freelance photographer."

This was getting good.

"Who is she, then? Reuben's wife? Girlfriend? What?"

"She's a VP at Eden Corporation." Dillon more or less mouthed the words.

"Are you sure?"

"Check it out." He turned the laptop to reveal her corporate photo. Bingo.

"Wow!" I said, taking it all in. Aunt Abby's eyes were wide with interest. Even Jake looked impressed.

"And guess what?" Dillon added.

"There's more?" I asked, growing irritated at Dillon. Getting information from him was like peeling an apple with a fingernail.

"She works under, Reuben Gottfried. Dude, she's second in command."

Chapter 12

"Oh my God!" I said, staring at Paula as she continued to flirt with Adam. "Roman and Paula weren't covering the Apple Fest at all. They're actually spies for their GMO company."

Aunt Abby huffed. "And at the moment, she looks like she's doing some kind of Mata Hari thing on Adam."

"Who's Mada Harry?" Dillon asked.

"She was a spy during World War One," Aunt Abby explained patiently. "She used her feminine wiles to seduce information out of foolish men." -

Dillon frowned, no doubt processing the information, but he didn't pursue the subject. I'm not sure he knew what feminine wiles were, but he had the good sense not to ask. Given any encouragement, Aunt Abby would go into much more detail than was necessary.

"So you think Roman and Paula were trying to get

some kind of information from the local farmers?" Jake asked. "To what purpose?"

"I don't know," I said, "but maybe Honey knows something. Let's get back to the bed-and-breakfast inn and see if she can make sense of this."

Jake paid the bill for everyone, in spite of my efforts to share the tab. Sometimes I thought he was too good to be true. We all thanked him and then Aunt Abby, Dillon, and Jake headed for the restrooms. I lingered at the table a moment, as if making sure I had all my belongings, then crossed over to the table where Paula and Adam sat. They were intimately sharing a single apple strudel topped with a scoop of vanilla ice cream that looked divine.

I stopped abruptly, acting as if I was surprised to see them.

"Paula!" I said, feigning surprise. "What are you doing here?"

Paula pulled back her fork and sat upright. "Uh, hi . . . uh."

"It's Darcy. From the Enchanted Apple Inn. We're guests there, remember?"

"Yes, I know." She indicated Adam with her fork. "Do you know Adam Bramley? He's one of the biggest apple farmers here in Apple Valley. I'm learning so many interesting things from him about the apple business—for the article."

Adam blushed. Color seemed to come easily to those apple cheeks of his.

"The article?" I repeated. "Are you still working on that? I thought, with Roman Gold's death, the story might have been killed." Shoot. Killing a story was a common term for not publishing work that had been written, but what with Roman Gold being murdered, I could have chosen a better word.

"Oh, they're sending someone else to do the story," Paula explained. "So I'm still taking pictures and interviewing the farmers."

"I'm sorry about Roman," I said, trying to look sympathetic.

Paula lowered her eyes and mashed her fork into the remaining dessert. "Yeah. I hope they find out who did it."

I glanced at Adam. He'd practically turned into a stone, sitting there with no expression. What was it with him?

"Were you close to Roman?" I asked Paula.

"No, no. We weren't friends or anything like that. I just worked . . . I mean, I was just working with him on his assignment."

Yeah, right, I thought, remembering what I'd just learned from Dillon. "Do you have any idea who might have wanted him dead?"

"Me? I have no clue who might have killed him. Why would I?"

"Do you know if he had any enemies?" I asked.

"Why all the questions?" Paula asked, meeting my eyes. "What's it matter to you?"

I shrugged. "I just thought, since it happened at the inn where we're all staying—"

Adam, who had kept quiet until this point, cut me

off. "Maybe it had something to do with those fires we've been having around here."

Paula shot him a look I couldn't read.

"So you heard about the fire at the festival?" I confirmed.

He nodded. "I was there. Sounded like another case of arson to me. Just like at Honey's and at Red's and that other fire. I'll bet it's one of them Frankenfruit people, trying to threaten our farms."

I looked at Paula. Her face was flushed and her mouth tight.

Knowing what I now knew about her, I decided to put her on the spot. "What do you think, Paula? Have you heard anything about the GMO companies trying to move into the area? Companies like Eden Corporation?"

Paula set down the fork she'd been holding and sat back, crossing her arms. "No. Like I said, I'm just here to take pictures. But I doubt a big company like Eden Corp would resort to intimidation like that."

"Still seems suspicious," Adam added, "if you ask me."

Out of the corner of my eye, I saw Jake waiting for me near the exit. It was time to go.

"Well, it was nice to see you both," I said. "I better get back to the inn. Another big day for the food truck business tomorrow."

Adam nodded; Paula forced a smile.

"Have a nice night," I said. "See you at the festival tomorrow?"

"You bet," Adam said. "I'll be there for the Scare-crow Contest."

"Paula?"

"Absolutely," Paula answered. "Don't want to miss those photo ops."

I left the table, wondering if I should have called Paula on her lie about being a photographer. But I had a feeling I'd learn more if I kept my mouth shut—at least for the time being. Once her cover was blown, she might take off and the sheriff might never get to the bottom of those fires. Or the death of Roman Gold.

On the ride back to the Enchanted Apple, I told Jake what I'd learned—not much in terms of spoken words, but Paula's body language had chattered quite a bit. She'd reacted to the comments about the GMO company and even tried to defend them. However, I still wondered why she was spending so much time with Adam Bramley. What did she hope to gain from him? Access to information about his farm? Leverage for Eden Corporation? He might have seemed like a meek old guy, but those were often the ones with the most secrets.

We arrived at the inn to find Aunt Abby, Dillon, and Honey seated in the parlor, sipping apple wine next to a cozy fire. Honey looked tired. She still wore the khaki slacks, now wrinkled, and a beige blouse, topped by a knitted vest that featured apple pies and black birds. I wondered where she got all her apple-themed clothes. Not that I was in the market.

"Darcy!" Aunt Abby said. "You made it. You took

so long, I was getting worried, what with all that's going on around here."

I waved a greeting to everyone, then took off my jacket and joined the small group in the parlor. Jake hung our jackets on a coatrack by the door that was made from deer antlers and sat down next to me. Honey leaned over and poured two more glasses of wine—one for me and one for Jake.

"Sorry if I worried you," I said, after taking a sip. "I stopped to talk to Paula and Adam at the restaurant."

Aunt Abby's eyebrows shot up. Honey looked at me wide-eyed.

"Did you confront her about working for Eden Corporation?" Aunt Abby asked.

I looked at Honey for a reaction to Aunt Abby's announcement, but from her lack of expression, I sensed my aunt had already blabbed it to her.

"I can't believe she lied about her job," Honey said, "all the while sleeping under my roof!" She took a long swallow of wine, then added, "She's probably the one who murdered that . . . that traitor, Roman Gold."

"I don't think so," Jake said, setting down his wineglass.

"Why not?" Honey asked. "She sure doesn't seem very upset about his death."

"What's her motive?" Jake asked.

"Uh . . ." Honey shrugged. "I don't know. Maybe they were having an affair and he got jealous that she was flirting with Adam, and he tried to kill her, and she killed him in self-defense."

Wow, I thought. If she could come up with a motive like that, she should be writing murder mysteries, not running a bed-and-breakfast.

"Nah," Dillon said, leaning forward and resting his elbows on his bony knees. "Too obvious. First of all, we didn't hear any fighting or anything like that. And she wouldn't have done it with all of us around. At least, I wouldn't. Plus, I'm sure she's had plenty of other opportunities to kill him, since she worked with him. Did the cops get any prints on that stabby thingy?"

Honey shook her head. "Murph said the apple corer was wiped clean."

"Do you think he suspects that you did it?" Dillon asked Honey.

The room went deadly silent, except for Aunt Abby's gasp.

"Dillon!" she said.

Honey smiled. "It's okay. I realize things look bad in terms of the murder weapon and all. But I didn't have any reason to kill him."

"Except," Dillon continued, in spite of a glare from Aunt Abby, "you might have already found out he was the CEO of Eden Corporation and figured he came here to worm his way into the apple business." The kid really had no filter.

"Dillon, you're not helping," I said.

"Darcy's right, Dillon," Aunt Abby agreed. "Honey had nothing to do with it. I've known her a long time, and even though we haven't see each other much over the past few years, I'm always right about things like this, aren't I, Darcy? I've always been intuitive."

The last two times my aunt had been involved in a murder case, she was actually a suspect in one of them, so I could hardly call that unbiased intuition.

"Listen," Jake said, "until we know more, let's just take a minute and look at what we do know."

"He's right," I said, remembering the rules they'd taught us in journalism schools. "Until we know what, when, where, how, and why, we're not going to know who. So far we know what—Roman Gold was murdered. We know approximately when—last night between two and four. Where? In his room, which was supposedly locked. And how? With an antique apple corer. But the big question is why? If we can figure that out, we might be able to figure out who."

"I'll tell you why," Honey said, straightening her slouch. "He came here to spy on us farmers—me in particular—to find our weak spots, buy up our property, and then convince the rest of the farmers to convert to his growing methods. If you'll remember, he had a lot to say on the subject the night before he was killed."

A knock on the door startled us.

What now? Another fire alert? The sheriff come to cart Honey off to jail—thanks to me? Or just another drop-in visit from Nathan or Red or Adam?

Honey stood up, tried to smooth out the wrinkles in her pants, and walked to the door.

She peered through the peephole—something she hadn't done before the murder—and gasped. She stepped back, looking about to faint. Aunt Abby and I rushed over to support her, followed by Jake and Dillon. While Abby wrapped an arm around her, I yanked open the door to see who had caused her to be so alarmed.

Speak of the devil. It was Sheriff Murphy O'Neil. He wasn't smiling.

"Are you here to arrest me?" Honey blurted. She looked pale and drawn. Abby clasped her hand.

Someone in the shadows stepped out from behind the sheriff.

"Wes!" Aunt Abby said, letting go of Honey. Her face lit up when she saw Detective Shelton and she went over to give him a warm hug. "I'm so glad you're here."

Detective Shelton seemed a little taken aback by the welcoming committee.

"The gang's all here, I see," he said, eyeing each of us and nodding. Honey looked visibly relieved. Just the way I felt.

"Come in, come in!" Aunt Abby said, taking him by the arm. "How was the drive?"

Sheriff O'Neil followed him in after wiping his shoes on the WELCOME TO THE ENCHANTED APPLE doormat.

"You two know each other?" I asked, glancing back and forth between the sheriff and the detective as they stood side by side in the entryway. They were as different as night and day, and not just because they were black and white. Detective Shelton had at least five inches on Sheriff Murphy, towering over him at six feet plus. He'd also stayed in better shape than his country equal, I thought, noting Sheriff O'Neil's expanding paunch, compared to Detective Shelton's muscular physique. The sheriff's pale, freckled complexion and fine lines reflected his Irish background, while the detective's smooth coffee-colored skin made him look years younger than the Irishman. Both still had their hair, but Detective Shelton had only begun to gray, while Sheriff O'Neil's once blond hair had given way to mostly white. It was hard to believe they were the same age.

"Went to the academy together," Detective Shelton said, acknowledging his peer. "Long time ago, right, Murph?"

Sheriff O'Neil gave Detective Shelton's shoulder a buddy slap. "We were just kids. Can't believe we're both still trying to catch criminals."

Looking more relaxed now that she wasn't being arrested, Honey took the men's coats, then herded everyone into the parlor. Detective Shelton sat down beside Aunt Abby while Sheriff O'Neil stood by the fireplace, warming his hands.

Honey disappeared into the kitchen while the two lawmen reminisced; then Honey returned with two more wineglasses and handed one to Sheriff O'Neil and one to Detective Shelton. "You must be Abby's friend from the city," she said to the detective.

Aunt Abby blinked. "Oh, I'm so sorry. I forgot to introduce you. Honey, this is my boyfriend, Wes. He's a homicide detective for the San Francisco Police Department. Wes, this is my old friend Honey. She owns this adorable bed-and-breakfast."

Did my aunt really just call Detective Shelton her boyfriend? OMG.

The detective stood up, grinning sheepishly, and shook Honey's hand. "Nice to meet you. Abby's told me a lot about you. I understand you had some trouble here last night."

There's a cop for you, I thought. Getting right to the elephant in the room.

Honey nodded and glanced at Sheriff O'Neil.

"Wes stopped by my office when he got to town," Sheriff O'Neil said. "I was telling him about the murder on the ride over. We don't get many homicides in Apple Valley and we can always use another expert set of eyes on a case like this."

Wes sat down. "Well, it's out of my jurisdiction, but if you need any help, Murph, I'm happy to do what I can while I'm here."

"You stopped off there?" Aunt Abby asked the detective.

"Common courtesy," Detective Shelton explained. "I don't want to step on any toes. I'm just here for a weekend vacation."

"Hey, you're always welcome here," Sheriff O'Neil said. "And this murder case is a real puzzler. So far we don't have many leads other than the weapon and opportunity."

Honey bowed her head, as if sensing the sheriff might be referring to her. After all, it was her so-called weapon and she certainly had plenty of opportunity. She lifted the bottle of wine from the coffee table and poured herself another glass.

"So, fill me in," the detective said after taking a small sip.

Aunt Abby and Honey took turns sharing the details

with Detective Shelton, although I had a feeling he'd already learned most of the information from Sheriff O'Neil.

When they were done, Aunt Abby asked, "So, what do you think, Wes? Any hunches?"

He raised an eyebrow. "So, Dillon, you said Roman Gold was hiding something?"

Dillon took in a breath and was about to answer when the sheriff sucked the wind out of his sails with two words: "Reuben Gottfried. Yeah, we know."

Dillon frowned.

Detective Shelton steepled his fingertips. "So, the CEO of this mutant apple company is murdered—with an apple corer, no less. The killer knew where to find the weapon *and* the key to Gold-slash-Gottfried's room. Then the killer went upstairs and stabbed him without any of you hearing anything, leaving you to find the body the next morning. Have I got that right?"

We all nodded silently. Somehow the detective had managed to make us all sound like accomplices for being sound asleep at the time of the murder.

"And these fires," he continued. "You think they might be related?"

"I'm sure of it," Honey said. "Those GMO people are targeting us apple growers, so they must think setting fires to our places will intimidate us."

"Then why would someone murder the CEO of the company?" Detective Shelton asked.

"Because one of the farmers found out he set the fires and killed him," Honey said.

"Wasn't the latest fire at the festival tent set after Gottfried was killed?" Detective Shelton asked. "Wouldn't that indicate the CEO wasn't the fire-starter?"

There was silence among us.

"Just spitballing here," Jake said, "but what if Roman or Reuben or whoever he is and Eden Corporation was in competition with another GMO company for the land up here? Maybe someone from that company knew what Roman was up to and decided to eliminate the head of Eden."

Detective Shelton turned to the sheriff. "Got any leads on other companies in this area competing with this Eden Corp?"

"Not that I know of," he said, "but I'll check."

More silence as we sipped our wines.

"Maybe," Honey said quietly, "someone who doesn't like me is trying to make it look like I murdered my own guest in my own house with my own weapon."

Detective Shelton's eyebrows rose. "Do you have any enemies, Ms. Smith?"

She looked at Sheriff O'Neil, as if he might know of some, then shrugged. "I don't think so. I've never done anything bad enough to cause someone to do this."

Sheriff O'Neil cleared his throat and then said, "Maybe the fires aren't related to the murder at all. Maybe we're dealing with two separate crimes here— murder and arson. Someone murdered the CEO of a GMO company. Someone else set the fires in the area."

"Seems awfully coincidental," I said. "If we can find a connection between the two, I think we can find both the murderer and the firebug."

The front door of the bed-and-breakfast suddenly swung open. Everyone turned to see who had entered.

In stepped Paula Hayashi, followed by Adam Bramley. One from each camp, I thought. Paula represented the GMO company, while Adam was head of the American Apple Association. How had they become so chummy?

The smiles faded from Paula's and Adam's faces when they turned and found us all staring at them.

"Wow," Paula said, removing her coat. "This is just like an Agatha Christie mystery with all of you gathered in the proverbial parlor." She looked at the sheriff. "I'll bet you're playing the part of Hercule Poirot in this potboiler?" Then she turned to Detective Shelton. "But who are you supposed to be? Miss Marple's alter ego?"

Uh-oh. She didn't know who she was dealing with.

The detective set down his glass and stood up, rising above us like a mountain. His dark, piercing eyes narrowed as he focused on her.

"I'm San Francisco Homicide Detective Wellesley Shelton. And if you're a guest here, I'd like to ask you a few questions."

Boom, lady! You've been served!

Chapter 13

That stopped Paula Hayashi in her high-heeled tracks. Adam Bramley looked as if he wanted to disappear into the wall behind him. The rest of us just enjoyed watching Detective Shelton do his thing.

Sheriff O'Neil gestured toward the parlor. Detective Shelton entered, sat down on the couch that was flanked by the other two couches, then turned around and said, "Have a seat" to Paula and Adam. Adam bowed his head as he made his way inside while Paula hesitated a moment before entering. She glanced at Sheriff O'Neil, then took a seat on the couch on the detective's left while Adam slumped into the couch on the detective's right. Neither Paula nor Adam looked at each other, as if both wanted to distance themselves from the other.

Detective Shelton looked back at the rest of us standing nearby. "Would you all excuse us, please?"

Sheriff O'Neil turned to Honey. "Why don't you wait in the dining room until we're done here? Honey, would you be kind enough to get everyone some coffee?" He pulled the sliding wooden doors to the parlor closed.

Disappointed at not being able to witness his interrogation, I veered to the dining room to wait for news from the interrogation.

"No coffee for me," Aunt Abby said. "I'm going to bed." She yawned as she detoured toward the stairs.

I stopped and turned to her. "You're not going to wait up and see what they find out?"

"Wes will tell me . . . later." She smiled. I knew what that smile meant, and it had nothing to do with what the detective might or might not tell her later.

Dillon started to follow her up.

"Dillon? You too?" I called to him.

He shrugged. "I got a few things I want to check. I'll catch you later."

I turned to Jake and Honey, who stood in the doorway to the dining room.

Honey sighed. "I'm going to go clean up the kitchen. It's a mess from all my baking. Would you two like some coffee?"

I shook my head, not wanting the caffeine to keep me up. Jake said no and thanked her.

As soon as Honey left, I looked at Jake, still standing at the edge of the room. "Well, I guess it's just you and me."

"Yeah, about that," Jake said, then pressed his lips

together for a moment. "I'm bushed. What do you say we call it a night? It's been quite a day, and we have to get up early again tomorrow."

"Seriously? You're abandoning me too? I have to wait down here all by myself?"

Jake took my hands. "First of all, you don't have to wait. I'm sure Detective Shelton will fill us in tomorrow at breakfast. Unless, of course, he can't. And second, aren't you tired? You worked all day in the school bus, then got lost in a hay maze that you thought was on fire. Besides, didn't you grill Paula on the way out of the restaurant and essentially find out nothing? I doubt Paula or Adam will share much with the detective either. There's really nothing more we can do tonight. At least, in terms of solving a murder." He gave me a sexy grin.

In spite of being disappointed that he wasn't going to hang around for the results of Detective Shelton's inquiry, I melted a little. Maybe he was right. I hadn't slept well the night before, and hoped that night I'd get at least a few hours of uninterrupted z's, although I doubted it. While my body ached for rest, my mind was boiling like a pot of hot apple cider.

Jake nodded toward the stairs and I followed his lead.

"All right, you win. I'm tired too. I just wish I could do something for Honey. She seems depressed about all this, and probably worried about her implication in the murder."

"Let the cops handle it," Jake advised. "Sheriff O'Neil seems fairly competent, in spite of being a small-town officer, and you know Detective Shelton is sharp. If Paula or Adam knows something about the murder, the officers will find out—eventually."

I knew they were capable, but it wouldn't hurt to do a little investigating of my own. "What if there's another murder?" I shivered.

Jake stopped on the second-floor landing. "Darcy, there's no reason to think that. I'm sure Roman Gold was murdered for a reason. Don't go imagining we have a serial killer in our midst. You're perfectly safe here and so are the others. Roman had something to hide and it got him killed."

I nodded as he unlocked our door and opened it for me.

"I need a shower," he said once we were inside. "Join me?"

I laughed. "Are you saying I need one too?"

"Nope. Just thought you might like a soapy body massage. I'll even wash your hair."

I blushed and giggled as we entered the room. "You get the soap; I'll get the shampoo."

Twenty minutes later we were clean and cuddling in bed. Jake put his arm around me, and I nestled onto his chest. In a manner of seconds I heard regular sounds of his soft breathing. I envied how easily he could fall asleep.

I lay awake for the next half hour, going over the events of the day, the murder and the fires, and the detective's interest in talking with Paula and Adam. What was up with Tiffany and Nathan? Who killed Roman Gold? Who was setting those fires?

I sighed and began counting my breaths, something

I did to help me get to sleep. The answers—if there were any—would have to wait until morning. I just hoped we all woke up and found ourselves alive.

I must have slept like the dead, because I didn't wake up until Jake nudged me. He was already showered, shaved, and dressed. "Breakfast time," he whispered, and kissed me.

I bolted upright and glanced at the clock. "Why didn't you wake me!" I fluffed my flat hair, rubbed my eyes, and swung my legs out of bed.

"You looked so peaceful, I didn't want to disturb you. I figured you needed the sleep."

"Yeah, but I need breakfast too! And I need to get ready for work. Where are my clothes? My shoes? My hairbrush?" I ran around the room collecting various items necessary to put myself together. "You go on down. Save me a seat and some food. And coffee."

Jake smiled at my wild-eyed dance of panic. "You sure? I'm happy to wait for you."

"No! Go! I'll be down in five minutes."

He arched an eyebrow. Apparently he didn't believe I could work a miracle in such a short time. I'd show him.

As soon as the door clicked closed, I pulled on yesterday's jeans and a fresh top and slipped on my dusty Toms. I ran a brush through my hair and then scrunched it to trade that "just got out of bed" look for an "I meant to wear it this way" style. As promised, I was down the stairs in five minutes flat. Maybe six.

Aunt Abby, Detective Shelton, Dillon, and Jake

were all seated when I arrived at the dining table. Paula was conspicuously missing, plus our hostess. And the dead guy, of course. Honey appeared seconds later from the kitchen with the first breakfast plates. The smell of apple sausage and apple waffles with caramel syrup perfumed the air.

"Good morning, Darcy," Aunt Abby said as I sat down next to Jake. The others smiled or nodded.

I immediately took a sip of the coffee from one of Honey's dainty porcelain cups. After a good jolt of caffeine, I managed to say, "Good morning, everyone." I nodded at the empty chair. "Where's Paula? Did you ask her—" Before I could finished my sentence, everyone looked up at the staircase.

Out of the corner of my eye, I saw Honey tremble as she set down a plate in front of Detective Shelton. "Oh my goodness," she whispered. "I hope she's all right. Maybe I should check on her—"

We heard a door slam upstairs.

Paula appeared at the landing, dressed in tight black capri pants, a plunging red sweater two sizes too tight for even her, and a long colorful knitted scarf that hung around her neck like a stole. She stopped when she realized we were all staring at her.

"Ask me what?" she said, making a face as she continued down the steps. "You all look like you've seen a ghost. Did I forget to zip my pants or something?" She laughed, apparently thinking she was funny, then stopped again at the bottom of the stairs. "Oh. . . .wait a minute. You all thought . . . because I was late . . . that I might be dead or something." She laughed again and seated herself on the other side of Detective Shelton. "Sorry. Not this time." She smiled at the detective, who ignored her. Aunt Abby, however, caught Paula's flirtatious grin and glared at her.

I decided to provide a distraction before a food fight broke out.

"So, Detective Shelton. How do you like it here in Apple Valley? A nice change from the city?"

Honey reappeared with two more plates, then spotted Paula and frowned. She set the plates down in front of Jake and me and quickly returned to the kitchen.

Detective Shelton shrugged. "Fine if you like peace and quiet. Me, I'm a city guy. I can't sleep unless I hear sirens wailing, horns honking, trucks backing up, and neighbors playing loud music."

Paula laughed. "Me too," she said. "Country life bores the hell out of me. I can't wait to get back home and away from all this healthy fresh air."

Honey brought in plates for Dillon and Paula. After serving them, she sat down, plateless, and sipped her coffee. "Please begin," she said, noticing her guests had waited until everyone was served.

"Aren't you having anything, Honey?" Aunt Abby asked. She looked worried for her friend and rested a hand on her shoulder for a moment. "This breakfast is delicious."

"I don't eat much in the morning," Honey said. "But I'm glad you're enjoying it. The apples are from my orchard, of course, and the caramel syrup is my own secret recipe. Be sure to pour it on your waffle while it's still hot."

Dillon and Detective Shelton didn't hold back and dug in as soon as permission was granted. The rest of us savored each bite. All except for Paula, who ignored her plate of food and focused on her coffee.

I wondered what Detective Shelton had learned the previous night, and whether the sheriff had confronted Paula about her real job, but it wasn't the time or place to ask, so I decided to see if I could subtly find out more about her. She'd mentioned "home," so I thought it would be a good place to start. "So, where is home?"

"Here and there," she said, adding more sugar to her coffee. "In my work, I travel a lot. You know how it is."

"In your photojournalism work, you mean?" I asked pointedly.

"Uh, yeah. Always on the go."

"That's funny," I said, setting down my fork. Enough of this charade. "Actually I heard you're in the apple business too."

"What?" she said, looking at me as if I were crazy.

Honey glanced me, then at Paula.

"No, of course not," Paula said. "I told you before, I'm here to take pictures for an article. My publisher should be sending another writer down today. What's with the questions?"

Before I could ask another question, there was a rap at the front door. We turned to see Sheriff O'Neil let himself in. Was this a social call? Or business? I wondered.

"Morning, everyone," he said as he headed toward the dining table. "Sorry to disturb you, but I need to have another word with Ms. Hayashi."

Paula sighed. "Look, Sheriff, I told you and the cop here everything I know about the murder, which is nothing. This is starting to become harassment. I'm just trying to do my job and you're not making it easy."

"And what job would that be, Ms. Hayashi?" Sheriff O'Neil asked. "Because you're no photographer, like you told me last night. It's time to cut the crap, lady. You're a vice president at Eden Corporation, something you neglected to mention."

"You neglected to ask me," Paula shot back.

I glanced at the sheriff. I wondered if he'd held on to the information last night to see if Paula might reveal something important—or incriminating.

The sheriff bit his lip, as if to keep himself from speaking in anger, then calmly said, "You realize, Ms. Hayashi, withholding information borders on interference with a police investigation. You could be prosecuted for obstruction of justice."

Paula threw her coffee spoon down on the table. "We have lawyers for that kind of thing," she said. "Coming here was my assignment and I was supposed to keep it to myself. Who told you, anyway?"

"I don't name my sources."

I glanced at Dillon, but he was hunkered down, busy shoveling waffle sections into his mouth. I was certain he was the one who'd somehow tipped the sheriff. Then again, maybe Aunt Abby had told Detective Shelton and he'd shared the information with the sheriff. Or the sheriff figured it out on his own. Either way, the bad apple was out of the bag. I was just surprised it had taken so long.

"Well, you'd better be careful relying on anonymous sources for your information," Paula snapped. She rose from the table. "That's pretty sketchy police work. I've committed no crime, so if I'm not under arrest, you'll have to excuse me. One of the farmers is showing me the ins and outs of the apple business."

"I wonder if he'll still be interested in providing all that information once he learns who you really are and who you really work for," Sheriff O'Neil said.

I thought it was interesting how tenacious the sheriff was being. I figured he would have held back that information until he had more on Paula, but maybe he was baiting her, thinking she might say or do something incriminating. He was certainly sharper than he looked.

Paula's face reddened even more under her heavy makeup. She licked her lips, as if trying to come up with a response, then threw her napkin down over her coffee mug and stomped out of the room and up the stairs.

I looked at the sheriff. "So, where *did* you get your information?"

The sheriff glanced at Detective Shelton, who cleared his throat but said nothing.

Aunt Abby raised her hand as if she were in grade school. "Um, that would be me."

"Mo-om!" Dillon said. "I told you not to tell him! He'll know it came from me."

"But he had to know, Dillon. Otherwise, that's obstruction of justice, right, Wes?"

"It's okay, Dillon," Detective Shelton said. "The sheriff and I already knew."

Dillon frowned at him. I sensed he was disappointed not being the only one who could dig up information.

"So, what does that mean?" Honey asked. "Is Paula a spy? Is that GMO company really planning to take over our farms? It's already happened at the Jefferson Farm. You know we can't compete with apples that grow faster, require less water, are pest-resistant, and look perfect. That's why Roman was here, right? To spy on us." Tears welled in her eyes.

I saw her statement as proof that she had nothing to do with Roman's death. But the sheriff and detective might have felt she'd just provided a motive. Get rid of Roman and eliminate the threat.

"There's something else," Sheriff O'Neil said, taking Paula's vacated seat. He pushed her untouched plate aside and folded his hands on the table. "I talked with a few of the farmers—Adam, Nathan, Red. When I asked them where they were the night Gold was murdered, they admitted they were here at the inn."

Honey's face flushed. "Oh, I'm sure they left before . . . before anything happened. It couldn't have been very late." She glanced at Aunt Abby, Dillon, Jake, and me. "You all saw them. Remember, Red stopped by and had some wine. Then Nathan dropped in and then Adam told us about the fire?"

"But they came back later that night, didn't they?" Sheriff O'Neil said to Honey.

Honey frowned.

"You were heard arguing with them," the sheriff added.

Honey flushed and shot me a look.

Uh-oh. She knew I was the one who'd told the sheriff that I'd overheard her with the men. I hadn't know how many, but apparently it had been all three.

"Yes, well . . ." Honey looked down at her feet, obviously flustered. "Like I said, we were just having a discussion. It was nothing. I don't even remember—"

"Tell me about your conversation with them, Honey," the sheriff insisted.

She looked up at him, frowning. "All right, yes, they came back here that night. We talked about the drought, then about the festival. They were upset. Something about one of the vendors getting more space than the others. Honestly, that was all we talked about, Sheriff. It had nothing to do with the GMO apples or Eden Corporation or Roman or anything else. In fact, none of us had any idea Roman worked for Eden Corp."

I was no detective, but it was obvious from her lack of eye contact and nervous hands that she wasn't telling the whole truth. And from the frown on the sheriff's face, I had a feeling he'd sensed this too. Had the three men said something different to the sheriff about why they'd been by so late at night? Something other than their discussion about the festival?

When he'd announced that both Roman and Paula worked for Eden, Honey seemed genuinely surprised. So, was she holding something back? And why?

Chapter 14

When the sheriff was done with his questions, we returned to our rooms and gathered our things for the second day of the festival. Friday had been well attended, but even bigger crowds were expected today. Aunt Abby still had plenty of prepping and baking to do, as did Jake. We headed over to the festival site in our food trucks and Jake parked next to us along the side of the road designated for the mobile vendors.

Dillon and I helped Aunt Abby with her tarts, and soon the Big Yellow School Bus smelled like caramel-apple heaven. I caught Dillon sneaking a few "damaged" tarts, but I saved my appetite for one of Jake's fresh apple-infused cream puffs, right out of the oven. With only a few minutes before the festival was set to open, I offered to get coffees for Aunt Abby and Dillon, then swung by Jake's truck and suggested a trade—a coffee for a cream puff. We made a deal, and

I went in search of a coffee vendor among the other food trucks.

To my surprise, I spotted a familiar truck at the end of the line, and my heart leaped. The outside of the truck sported a cartoon drawing of a sexy witch stirring a large caldron of what was supposed to be witch's brew—in this case, coffee. The Coffee Witch was in town!

I waved to Willow, the young woman behind the service window. Willow was part of the Fort Mason food trucks crowd, and her bewitching coffees always garnered a long line of caffeine-addicted patrons. She'd been a big help with solving a murder a few months before and was always handy to have around for intel. Even while whipping up coffee drinks, she seemed to hear all the gossip. I wondered if she'd already learned anything interesting with the apple crowd.

As usual, her mostly black hair was dyed blond at the tips, cut at an angle, and moussed into spikes. Fast, perky, and full of energy—no doubt fueled by caffeine—Willow was busy serving her magical elixirs that ranged from Simple Spells (vanilla lattes) to Potent Potions (double-shot mochas) to Enchanted Espressos (triple-shot espressos). I had a feeling the Coffee Witch would make a whole bunch of new fans here in Apple Valley, once they fell under her addictive spell.

I waited my turn, then stepped up to the window. "Willow! What are you doing here?"

"S'up, Darce?" Willow said, leaning over on her elbows. "You didn't think you guys were gonna do this gig without me, didja? Thought I'd run up here today and check it out."

"I'm so glad you did! I could use a good jolt. Don't tell me you have some kind of apple-infused coffee drink."

"They wouldn't let me in if I didn't," Willow said. "Wanna try my cinnamon-apple latte? It's really spicy and goes really good with all those apple desserts they're selling around here. I'm calling it the Wicked Queen's Cuppa Poison."

"Sounds awesome," I said. "I'll take four."

"Comin' up," she said, turning to her espresso machine. "Hey, I heard someone got murdered up here," she shouted over the noise of the coffeemaker. "Déjà vu, eh?"

"Yeah," I said. "Someone at the B and B where we're staying was killed. What have you heard?" Back at Fort Mason, the Coffee Witch was the place to go for the latest dirt.

She shrugged as she worked and spoke over her shoulder. "Guy in the Apple Fun Funnel Cakes truck said it was some writer. Probably stuck his nose in where it didn't belong."

"Yep, that's what we writers do," I said.

Willow laughed. "I didn't mean you. Besides, you're not a regular writer."

I smiled patiently. In her early twenties, Willow was still young and didn't always think before she spoke. Then again, maybe she was right. Maybe I wasn't a "regular" writer, now that I was working in a food truck while writing a cookbook.

"So, you gonna solve the crime again like last time?"

Willow set the four paper cups of coffee into a carry tray and pushed it toward the open window.

I handed her some bills. "Oh, sure. In my spare time, when I'm not slaving away in the school bus for Aunt Abby. Or maybe I'll just let the cops handle it this time." I grinned.

"Well, if you need any help, let me know. Remember how I helped you solve that last murder?"

I smiled as I took the cardboard tray filled with coffees. "Will do."

"Oh, hey," Willow said. "See that tall old guy over there?" She pointed out the window. I turned to see Nathan Chapman talking with Paula Hayashi. He stood close to her, grinning, and had his hand on her arm. She, in turn, leaned in and touched his chest with her fingertip. Hmmm. Nathan without Tiffany? Paula without Adam? I wondered what these two were talking about.

"Yeah," I said, "that's the guy running the festival. Nathan Chapman. What about him?"

"Well, a few minutes ago, I thought there was going to be another murder."

I blinked. "What?"

"Seriously. He was ordering one of my cinnamon lattes and all of a sudden he started coming on to me. Can you believe it? He's, like, old enough to be my father. Jeez."

I thought about Nathan and Tiffany and their age difference, not to mention Paula and Adam. What was it with these May-December romances around here?

"Anyway, he was asking me my name and where I was from and what time I got off and stuff, and then this chick comes out of nowhere and starts saying something and shaking her head and then he tries to calm her down and takes her over by that hay maze and she looks like she's crying and he looks like he's trying to comfort her and she finally stomps off. Then he looks around to see if anyone was watching and takes off."

"Can you describe her?"

"The girl seemed about my age, not bad-looking but not that hot, if you know what I mean. Long brown hair. Oh, she was wearing an apron that had a glass of wine and some grapes on it."

Tiffany.

"Did you hear anything they were saying?" I asked.

Willow shook her head. "They were too far away and it was too noisy. But it's weird 'cause now he's, like, all over that chick with the long black hair. What a player."

Well, this was another side of Tiffany I hadn't seen. She wasn't exactly the quiet little mouse I'd guessed her to be. In fact, it sounded as though she had quite the temper.

I stepped aside to let another customer order coffee and surreptitiously watched Nathan and Paula for a few moments. Willow was right. From Nathan Chapman's body language, it was obvious he was flirting with Paula. That guy was something else.

"Thanks again, Willow," I called over to her as she handed the next customer his coffee order.

"No prob," she said, then added, "Hey, Darce. Remember. Let me know if you need any help solving the you-know-what." She glanced at the customer.

I nodded, then headed for Jake's truck.

I knocked on his window and it slid it open. "Here's your Poison Apple latte," I said, handing it over, "direct from our own Coffee Witch."

"She's here?" Jake asked.

"Yep," I answered, and held out my hand. "That'll be one apple cream puff."

He passed me the delicate puff pastry, nestled in a paper holder. "You headed back to the bus?"

I nodded.

"Meet you for a glass of wine after we're finished?"

"Can't wait," I said.

"And maybe another trip through the hay maze?" he added, grinning.

"Not funny. I'm never going in that hay maze again, ever."

He laughed. "Well, I heard there's a scarecrow contest later today, where people actually dress up as scarecrows. The most creative one wins some money. Shall we check it out?"

"As long as the scarecrows aren't too scary," I said. "Personally I think scarecrows are kind of creepy, like clowns. But then, maybe I've seen too many horror movies with scarecrows."

"Don't worry. I'll protect you."

I smiled. "Don't forget. I owe you a birthday dinner. I'll ask around for some restaurant suggestions. I'd like to find someplace nice. And this time, it'll be just the two of us."

"Sounds good."

I headed back to the school bus with the remaining coffees, planning to gear up for the onslaught of festival customers with a good dose of Willow's coffee concoction. But my mind was elsewhere. I couldn't help wondering if Nathan Chapman was really trying to hook up with Paula Hayashi.

Or was it the other way around?

With the increase in the number of weekend festivalgoers, the day sped by. Aunt Abby sold out her large supply of tarts a little before she closed up shop at four. She insisted on staying inside the bus to prepare more tarts for the final day of the festival, freeing Dillon and me to take a much-needed break. I tried to get her to join me, but her idea of relaxing was to do more baking.

"Are you coming to the scarecrow contest?" I asked her before I left the bus. Dillon had already fled on his new scooter, no doubt headed for one of the paths that went around the nearby orchards. I thought about absconding with Aunt Abby's scooter and joining him, then decided I'd probably run it into a tree, break an ankle, and spend Jake's birthday in the ER.

"I'll try," she said, already elbows deep in a bowl of floury mixture. "Go have some fun with Jake. You've earned it. I appreciate all your help."

I hated to leave her to work alone, but she'd insisted. Like Henny Penny, she'd always been the type of cook who preferred to do it herself. She only let Dillon and me help with the simple tasks while she took care of the heavy cooking. She could use a few tips on delegating, but there was no arguing with her.

I found Jake waiting for me at our usual picnic table with two glasses of wine. Disappointed he'd already gotten our drinks, I frowned and sat down.

"What's wrong?" he asked. "Don't you want any wine?"

"It's not that," I said, taking a sip. "I was hoping to use it as an excuse to talk with Crystal again. I thought she might know more about the fire at her tent."

"Sorry about that," Jake said, stifling a smile. "I forgot you were on the case. So, where's Detective Shelton when you need him, eh?"

"Seriously. Aunt Abby said he's out on a ride-along with Sheriff O'Neil to see how country law enforcement works." I took another sip and let the appley flavor linger in my mouth a second. "I don't suppose you learned anything more from Crystal?"

"As a matter of fact, I did. I can charm information out of people too, you know."

I raised an eyebrow. "Oh, really?"

"Besides, I think the old girl is sweet on me," Jake teased. "You know, some women like me for more than just my cream puffs."

I gently slapped his arm. "So what did she say?"

Jake set down his wineglass. "The fire was definitely set, at least according to Crystal. I didn't confirm that with the fire chief, but I don't think she has any reason to lie."

I nodded. "I figured as much, what with the other

fires also being deliberately set. Does she have any idea who might have done it? Does she know anyone who has a grudge against her, as well as Honey and Red?"

"She said she figured it had to be someone from the GMO company when it came to Honey and Red, but she couldn't come up with a reason for the fire at her tent. Maybe someone at Eden Corporation wants her winery too, for whatever reason."

"But she didn't think they'd be interested in the winery."

"She also mentioned the Jefferson Farm."

"Jefferson?"

"Yeah, remember J.J., that kid who waited on us last night at the restaurant? He said his dad recently sold their family farm to Eden Corporation. She thinks that's just the beginning. And she believes Eden will try to intimidate anyone who refuses to sell, even her."

"Wow," I said, and took another swallow of wine as a digestif for this information. Then I wondered— was this information real, or more just Crystal's opinion? "Do you think her suspicions are valid?"

Jake shrugged and glanced at the people milling around the tents, tables, and activity areas. The numbers were diminishing, but there was still a good crowd, mostly teenagers and young adults. I guessed they were here for the scarecrow contest, hay maze, scooter rides, trampolines, and other non-food-related fun.

"I do think the fires are connected, since they involve apple growers," Jake answered. "But the fires don't fit the murder of Roman Gold—aka Reuben Gottfried. That's the orange in the apple barrel. Crystal believes the person who killed Roman also set the fires and that everything is connected to Eden. If so, there's still a missing link."

I nodded. "I'll ask Dillon to find out more about Reuben Gottfried, see if there's any connection between him and one of the fire victims. Maybe he can dig up something we haven't learned yet."

"And maybe Detective Shelton and Sheriff O'Neil will turn up something," Jake added. "I have a feeling those two aren't just doing a ride-along. Detective Shelton's a lot like you, Darcy. If there's a puzzle, he's determined to solve it, even if it's not in his jurisdiction."

An announcement came over the loudspeaker, breaking into our conversation: *"Attention: The scarecrow contest will take place in fifteen minutes over by the hay maze. Come and vote for your favorite scarecrow. Remember, the winner receives a hundred-dollar prize!"*

I thought I recognized the voice as the man in charge of the festival—Nathan Chapman. He was certainly a busy man.

Chapter 15

I was surprised Nathan Chapman could tear himself away from the ladies long enough to do the job. The man apparently had all kinds of talents.

Jake and I moseyed over to the maze area where a nice crowd had already gathered. The side of the maze was roped off with bright red caution tape, creating a single-file aisle that I guessed would corral the line of wannabe contest winners. I saw a few contestants wander by, covered in makeup, stuffed with straw, and clad in patchwork outfits. Apparently folks around here enjoyed dressing up like scarecrows in hopes of winning the prize.

Tiffany appeared from a large tent marked with a sign that read SCARECROW MAKEOVERS, where contestants could change into their costumes in private before the contest. She seemed to be giving orders to her young staff, sending them in different directions, having them test the microphones, gesturing for them to keep the judging area clear from the slowly invading crowd. I recognized one of the guys helping her— J.J.—Dillon's friend from college.

I looked around for Nathan, thinking he must be nearby too, but I didn't see him. Maybe Crystal had given him another talking-to, discouraging him from hanging around her daughter. Or maybe he'd found someone else to hang with, like Paula or any number of young attractive women at the festival. I wondered where Crystal was. Still pouring wine at her new tent location and making sure the crowd got enough of her apple "juice"?

"This is one of the highlights of the Apple Festival," came a voice behind me. I turned around to see Sheriff O'Neil talking to Detective Shelton.

"You made it," I said to them.

"Darcy," Detective Shelton said by way of hello. "Jake. Have a profitable day today?"

We nodded. "Aunt Abby's tarts sold out completely," I said. "She's working on more for tomorrow. Have you seen her yet?"

Detective Shelton nodded. "I stopped by the bus. She said she'd meet me here as soon as she's done. That woman never rests. I admire her energy."

"No kidding," I said. "So, how was your tour of Apple Valley? Did you learn anything more about the murder?"

A few bystanders glanced at me when I said the word "murder."

Sheriff O'Neil frowned and said in a low voice, "Still looking into it."

Either that meant no or it meant the sheriff didn't feel like sharing anything with me or the people around us. No worries. I'd get it out of Aunt Abby later, after she got it out of Detective Shelton.

I turned back in time to see Tiffany duck into the scarecrow-prep tent again. A few seconds later Crystal popped out of the tent and retrieved a microphone from one of the teenagers, then disappeared inside once more. I spotted Paula, tough to miss in her colorful leopard leggings and too-tight zebra-printed top. Her long black hair rippled like a cascading waterfall down her back each time she spoke to Adam, who stood next to her like a puppy dog, looking as if he hung on her every word.

Aunt Abby scooted up on her new electric scooter. She'd freshened her makeup, but had missed the imprint of her hand on her neck made from what I suspected was flour.

"Just in time!" I said, and leaned over to wipe off the evidence with my fingertips.

She hopped off the scooter, hit the kickstand, and looked up at Detective Shelton, who towered over my petite aunt. "Did I miss anything?"

"Nope," the detective said, smiling down at her. Never had there been a more mismatched pair.

"Good!" she exclaimed, more excited about the scarecrow contest than I expected. I looked at her suspiciously.

"You're really into this, aren't you?" I said.

There was a twinkle in her eye. Yep, she was up to something.

Tiffany appeared again from the tent, holding a microphone, followed by Crystal and J.J. I spotted Willow, who had apparently sneaked away from her coffee truck. She was waving to J.J., who blushed and gave a quick wave back. Huh. Had Willow already made a friend? She was an attractive girl, but country-boy J.J. didn't seem to be in city-girl Willow's league. Still, there definitely seemed to be an attraction between them, the way they were grinning at each other.

Tiffany shouldered her way to the front of the crowd and stood at the center of the designated area, holding the mic and ready to speak. To my surprise, in the moments she'd been gone, she managed to transform herself into a scarecrow and now wore a long patchwork dress with puffy sleeves, wild mismatched socks, and leather boots. Her hair was streaked in a rainbow of spray-on multicolored dyes and braided into two pigtails. She'd drawn on oversize eyelashes, perky eyebrows, and large freckles with a brown eyebrow pencil, and rouged her cheeks and lips with apple red lipstick. I couldn't decide if she looked like some kind of monstrous rag doll or mad clown, but it was a noticeable change from the fresh-faced young country girl she usually appeared to be.

She cleared her throat, then began. "Ladies and gentlemen, apple lovers from everywhere, welcome to Apple Valley's Annual Scarecrow Contest!" The shy woman I'd met seemed to have come alive under that disguise.

Tiffany waved her hands to hush the eager applause. When the noise died down, she continued. "In a minute our ten human scarecrow contestants will be lining up along the side of the hay maze. I'll introduce each one by name and hold up the Clap-O-Meter, so you can clap for your favorite living scarecrow. The contestant who receives the loudest applause will win a one-hundred-dollar gift certificate to spend on anything here at the festival!"

Another roar of applause burst forth. Everyone, it seemed, was excited about the scarecrow contest.

"Oh, I'm so glad I didn't miss anything!" came another familiar voice behind me. I turned around to see Honey, her cheeks flushed, no doubt from rushing to the event.

"Honey!" Aunt Abby said, giving her friend a hug. "I was worried you weren't going to make it."

"Wouldn't miss it!" Honey said. "I was over in the scarecrow tent, helping Red. Every year he enters the contest. You should see him." She broke into smile. "He looks like he stepped right out of *The Wizard of Oz*."

"Red is dressed up like a scarecrow?" Aunt Abby asked, her sparkling eyes wide.

"Never misses this. Each year he comes up with something different, then sets the latest one up on the farm. He loves making scarecrows for his trees—it's kind of his hobby. He calls it his Orchard Army."

"I didn't know scarecrows were used in tree orchards. I thought they were only in cornfields," Aunt Abby said. "You can tell I'm not a country girl."

Honey laughed. "Oh, scarecrows are a staple around here. I'm surprised you haven't noticed. And they really work, not just on crows, but all kinds of birds and wild animals that dig up the seeds, trample the seedlings, and eat the fruit off the trees. A lot of folks have switched to using aluminum ribbons that shimmer in the sun and scare the critters away, but Red is old school—and a little superstitious. Scarecrows are supposed to be supernatural. You'll find stories about them in every-thing from Nathanial Hawthorne's work, to comic books, to horror movies. There are scarecrow festivals and contests all over the country."

"Wow," I said. "I didn't realize how popular scare-crows are." Thank goodness they weren't common in the city, I thought, or I'd be totally creeped out.

"Wait till you see the contestants competing today," Honey said. "I got a preview inside the tent."

Before she could tell us more details, Tiffany called for the crowd's attention again.

"All right, everyone! Are you ready for the scare-crow parade? Here they come!" Tiffany announced the contestants by their scarecrow names as they appeared from the tent and lined up along the side of the hay maze behind her. The standouts were a fisherman scarecrow named "Hodmedod," a hatchet-wielding scarecrow named "Lusty Bordon," a pirate scarecrow named "Jack Scare-oh," a bonneted, little old lady scarecrow named "Tattie Bogal," and a really hideous zombie scarecrow named "Jeepers Creeper."

"Which one is Red?" Aunt Abby asked Honey.

She blinked and strained her neck to see the contestants through the crowd in front of us. "I . . . I don't see him. . . . I wonder what happened. . . ."

"And now it's time to vote!" Tiffany announced through her mic.

I watched as she had J.J. hold the retro Clap-O-Meter next to each contestant. Every time the crowd clapped, the needle on the gizmo moved, measuring the amount of noise produced. Excitement seemed to be running high as each contestant was applauded.

One of the scarecrows I hadn't noticed before caught my eye. He—She? It?—was dressed in a green shirt and green tights, with a rope belt around its waist, and a red cape at its back. A hemp hood covered the scarecrow's head, with two eyeholes cut out. Straw stuck out from the ends of the sleeves, leggings, and hood. It was an odd interpretation of a scarecrow, and I wondered where the idea had come from.

Just as Tiffany announced the name of the mysterious scarecrow—"Jonathan Crane, aka Scarecrow from DC Comics"—I knew who it hid beneath that mask. But it wasn't the identity that gave it away—it was the familiar ratty tennis shoes.

"That's Dillon!" I shrieked to everyone around me.

"Where?" Aunt Abby asked.

I pointed. "Right in the middle of the scarecrows. Look at the shoes!"

"Oh my," Aunt Abby said. "I didn't recognize my own son!"

Jake and Detective Shelton just shook their heads.

"I hope he wins!" Aunt Abby said, suddenly beaming with pride. "Everyone clap for him!"

Tiffany continued to hold the Clap-O-Meter next to Dillon, garnering him a nice loud applause. But as she moved on, I knew he had some stiff competition from Jack Scare-oh and Lusty Bordon.

After the last contestant received his Clap-O-Meter results, the crowd hushed. Tiffany held up the mic to announce the winner. "First, I want to thank all of our scarecrow contestants today. They did an outstanding job, didn't they?" More applause. "Now, for our winner. The one-hundred-dollar gift certificate goes to. . . ." She paused and looked around at the crowd. "Scarecrow number six—Jonathan Crane, aka Scarecrow!"

We cheered like rabid sports fans as Dillon was awarded his prize. Without removing his mask, he thanked Tiffany and accepted the gift certificate. I gave Aunt Abby a high five, then looked around to see everyone's reactions. That was when I noticed Honey had disappeared.

Figuring she'd gone to the scarecrow dressing room tent to find out what had happened to Red, I didn't give it another thought. I glanced back at Dillon, still holding the gift certificate, and noticed J.J. running up to Tiffany. When he reached her, he whispered something in her ear. Willow watched him from a few feet away, frowning.

Tiffany's face went white when she heard what J.J. had to say, and she dropped the microphone. It landed on the hay-covered ground with a ping.

"Sheriff!" J.J. suddenly called out in our direction, his eyes wide.

Sheriff O'Neil shouldered through the crowd, followed by Detective Shelton. People nearby murmured as they began to realize something was up.

When the sheriff reached J.J. and Tiffany, the young man said something to him, then pointed toward the hay maze. J.J. started for the entrance, with the sheriff and detective right behind him.

"What's happening?" Aunt Abby said.

"I don't know," I answered, puzzled. I glanced around for a clue, but everyone looked as confused as I did. I caught a glimpse of Tiffany disappearing into the scarecrow tent. There was no sign of Crystal, nor did I see Paula, Adam, Red, or Nathan.

While another young attendant kept the curious onlookers from entering the maze, we milled about, waiting for someone to tell us what was happening. Ten minutes later, J.J. and Detective Shelton came out of the hay maze entrance. J.J. looked wide-eyed while the detective, his face a mask, was talking on his cell phone.

Aunt Abby hurried over to him. Jake and I followed.

"What's wrong? What happened?" Aunt Abby said after Detective Shelton hung up.

The detective spoke in a low, hushed voice to Jake. "Can you help that kid keep these people from going inside the maze?"

Jake nodded and began herding the crowd back from the entrance.

"Wes?" Aunt Abby persisted. "What's going on?"

The detective shook his head. "There's a body in the maze."

Aunt Abby gasped. "Oh my. What happened?" she whispered.

The detective frowned. "I don't know. The sheriff called his crime scene guys and the coroner and told me to keep everyone away."

"Any idea who it is?" I asked.

Detective Shelton shook his head.

"Man or woman?" I asked, trying to narrow it down.

"No idea," the detective said.

I frowned at him. How could he not know if it was a man or a woman?

And then I got my answer.

"Whoever it is was dressed like a scarecrow."

Chapter 16

Detective Shelton ordered the festival closed, per Sheriff O'Neil's wishes, and asked the college students working the hay maze to help steer people home. Only those of us who knew either Detective Shelton or Sheriff O'Neil were allowed to remain. Jake, Abby, Dillon, and I wandered over to a nearby picnic table and sat down to wait for further developments. Dillon was still dressed as a scarecrow but had removed the mask and the hay that had been sticking out of his sleeves and pant legs. He looked ridiculous in those tights.

"Has anyone seen Red?" Honey asked, reappearing from the scarecrow tent. She looked a little frantic and was obviously worried about her friend.

We shook our heads. "I'm sure he'll turn up," Aunt Abby said.

"You might ask the sheriff," I suggested.

Honey scanned the area and spotted Sheriff O'Neil

talking with Detective Shelton. She headed over and I followed her, curious about the man's whereabouts myself.

"Sheriff," Honey began, "Red's gone! He signed up for the Scarecrow Contest but didn't show up. I even helped him get ready. How could he have disappeared so quickly?" She glanced around again, her face knotted with anxiety.

"Sorry, Honey," Sheriff O'Neil said. "Haven't seen him. We've been kinda busy here." He nodded toward the hay maze. "I can tell you this much—he's not the one lying dead inside."

Honey's face visibly relaxed, but only momentarily. "Then where could he be? Nobody's seen him since I left him in the dressing room tent."

She shook her head, mumbled something, then went off in search of him, worry embedded in her face again.

After she left, I noticed Crystal and Tiffany were huddled by the entrance to the maze. They too looked anxious, no doubt for news as to the identity of the dead body. Tiffany bit her nails while Crystal rubbed her daughter's back.

Paula seemed to have disappeared completely, and I wondered where she'd gone—and why. Apparently this wasn't the photo op she was looking for. Meanwhile, Adam stood alone at a distance, a frown on his leathery face. Several other scarecrow contestants had gathered by the tent, talking and shaking their heads and probably wondering who the dead scarecrow was. But the victim couldn't have been among the contestants. He—or she—must have died before the contest began.

Moments later several of the sheriff's deputies arrived, along with paramedics and the coroner. The deputies continued the job of clearing the festival area of looky-loos while the paramedics and coroner rushed into the maze, guided by J.J. Jake had mentioned that most of the kids who worked at the maze knew its twists and turns by heart and could rescue anyone who became seriously lost. Wish I'd known that earlier.

"There's Honey!" Aunt Abby pointed at Honey and Red, who were headed our way. Red, looking a little dazed, was still dressed as a scarecrow, while Honey was smiling and holding on to Red's arm as if he was keeping her upright.

"You found him!" Aunt Abby said, sliding over on the picnic bench so Honey could have a seat. But Honey remained standing, still clutching on to her scarecrow. Red's costume featured a tattered tux, full of patched holes and stitched tears. He wore a top hat with a large stuffed crow perched on top, and I wondered if that was actually supposed to scare away other crows, or attract them.

"I'm so relieved," Honey said, patting her chest. "He'd gone to the restroom and missed the whole contest! Can you believe it?"

Red blushed and grinned. "Oh well. I won last year. It was time for someone else to take home the prize. I heard you came in first place, young man," he said to Dillon.

Dillon nodded and waved the certificate.

"What are you going to spend it on?" Red asked.

Dillon shrugged.

"Well, save a little for some of my caramel apples," Red said. "They're the best in the West. I've got 'em covered in nuts, sprinkles, candy, coconut, dark chocolate, white chocolate, and anything else you can think of. With your winnings you could sample one of each!" Red seemed either unaware or uninterested in the discovery of the dead body.

Dillon mumbled something unintelligible and Red nodded as if he'd understood him. Before I could kick Dillon under the table for his rudeness, Honey caught her breath.

"The sheriff's back!" she said. She quickly let go of Red's arm and headed for the lawman who'd just appeared from inside the hay maze. We got up and followed her over, eager to hear what he had to say. Tiffany and her mother joined us.

"Murph!" Honey said. "Did you find out what happened?"

"Who is it?" Tiffany demanded, after pulling her finger from her mouth.

Crystal patted her daughter's back.

"Was it an accident?" Aunt Abby asked. "A heart attack?"

"Calm down, everyone." Sheriff O'Neil took a deep breath. "It seems we've had another murder."

"What?" Honey said, her hand covering her mouth. "Who? How?"

The sheriff shook his head, then finally said, "It's weird. His mouth was stuffed with apple seeds."

Honey's eyes widened. "You can't be serious!"

Aunt Abby frowned. "You mean, he choked to death on a mouthful of seeds?"

Honey shot her a look. "Apple seeds are poisonous."

"Was that the cause of death?" I asked.

"No," the sheriff said. "Apple seeds are only poisonous if ingested. Plus, it would take a lot. I think that was symbolic."

"Symbolic? So he wasn't poisoned?" Aunt Abby asked.

"Actually he was stabbed," the sheriff answered.

Honey looked ready to faint and grabbed Red's arm.

"Stabbed? With what?" Red asked.

The sheriff locked eyes with him. "As a matter of fact, it was a sharp-pointed stick."

Red frowned. "What kind of stick? Like a tree branch or something?"

"No, the kind you use in making caramel apples, Red," the sheriff said solemnly.

"Wait a minute," Red said. "You don't think—"

"I don't think anything, right now," the sheriff answered. "But I do have a lot of questions."

Tiffany spoke up. "You keep saying *he*. Do you know who he was?"

The sheriff's frown deepened. "I'm sorry to tell you this, but the victim was our own Nathan Chapman."

Deputy Bonita Javier came over to the sheriff and whispered something in his ear while we stood in stunned silence, watching.

The sheriff nodded. "Adam? Red? My deputy says you saw Chapman about an hour before the contest. Any idea what happened?"

"Sorry, Sheriff," Red said. "I was indisposed." He put finger quotes around the last word.

Adam shook his head. "I haven't seen him since he announced the contest. And then I only heard his voice. You might ask Paula. She seemed interested in him all of a sudden."

The sheriff nodded and looked at the rest of us. "Anyone else see him in the last few hours?"

Tiffany slowly raised her hand, her eyes now rimmed with tears. Her mother tried to pull her daughter's hand back down, but the sheriff wrote Tiffany's name in his notebook. "Crystal?" he said to the woman. "How about you?"

She shook her head. "I haven't seen Nathan for hours. I was in the scarecrow tent, helping with costumes and makeup and what not. Tiffany was in there with me most of the time too, weren't you, Tiff?"

Tiffany turned to her mother. "Mama, I *told* you I saw him, and I need to tell the sheriff. Don't you understand? Somebody killed him!" She began weeping and covered her face with her hands.

"She's sensitive," Crystal said to Sheriff O'Neil, wrapping an arm around her distraught daughter. "If anything bad happens, she dissolves into tears." She guided Tiffany over to a picnic table and sat her down on the bench.

The sheriff looked at the rest of us standing nearby.

"All right, anyone *else* see or talk to Nathan Chapman in the last couple of hours?"

Out of the corner of my eye, I caught a glimpse of Paula backing away from the gathered group. I hadn't noticed her earlier and figured she must have crept up to find out what was going on. Apparently the sheriff saw her too. He looked down at his notebook, then called out, "Ms. Hayashi?"

Paula froze. "What? I had nothing to do with this. I can't hang around here while you people decide who killed that guy."

"But you *do* need to tell the sheriff that you were talking to Nathan earlier," I blurted, then wished I hadn't, noting the stinging look she shot me. Still, he needed to know. I had seen Paula not just talking to Nathan Chapman, but obviously flirting with him.

"Shut up," Paula snapped at me. "You didn't see anything, because I never saw the guy."

I met her vicious gaze and frowned. Why was she lying? "Paula, I'm not the only one who saw you." I glanced at Tiffany, remembering the spat she'd had with Nathan, then decided not to bring her into it. "Willow, the coffee girl, also saw you flirting with him." Willow could give the sheriff her eyewitness account.

"I wasn't flirting!" Paula huffed. "And I certainly didn't hang around and kill him. I had no reason to. He was a hick, just like the rest of you."

Honey murmured something I couldn't make out. The sheriff glanced at his notebook, then said, "You might have had a reason, Ms. Hayashi."

Paula's eyes narrowed. "Oh yeah? Like what?"

"How about that promotion you'll receive at Eden Corporation after your boss's death?" the sheriff asked.

Paula shrugged. "Well, sure, now that Reub—I mean, Roman is gone. But that just means more work for me."

Honey pointed to Paula, her eyes wide. "That certainly gives her a motive to murder Roman!"

"Well, I didn't do it!" Paula said emphatically, but I thought I saw a crack in her tough facade.

"Honey's right. You did have motive," the sheriff said.

"Why? So I could take over his job?" Paula said, shaking her head. "He was on the way out already. It was just a matter of time."

"Maybe you wanted to hurry things along," the sheriff said.

"But why would I kill Nathan?" Paula asked. "I had nothing to gain. Besides, anyone could have stabbed him with that apple stick. They're probably all over the place. Why don't you ask Honey what she and Nathan were arguing about the other night at the bed-and-breakfast. You want a motive? She's got enough for two murders."

Sheriff O'Neil turned to Honey, who looked stricken.

"I . . . I told you," Honey muttered. "We were just discussing the GMO apple situation and trying to figure out what to do about it. Red was thinking of selling, while I was against it. Then Nathan seemed to be weakening. . . ."

Odd. I thought she'd said they'd been discussing the festival.

"Not the way I heard it from Nathan," Paula said,

raising an accusing eyebrow. "He said he told you he was going to sell his land to Eden Corporation, and you threw a hissy fit, told him you'd do anything to stop anyone else who might be thinking of selling. That's the truth, isn't it, little miss innocent?"

"I . . . I . . . would never kill anyone," Honey said. She glanced at Red, who was frowning.

Aunt Abby put an arm around Honey, but the woman shook it off. It wasn't looking good for Honey, but then again, Paula didn't look so innocent either.

"You're just trying to make it look like I killed Roman to cover your tracks," Honey said, turning her wrath on Paula, "and now you're accusing *me* of killing my friend Nathan just because we had a little spat?" She looked back at the sheriff. "It's all lies, Murph. These city big shots come into our county and try to take over our businesses, but they aren't going to get away with it, right, Red?"

Red looked helplessly at Honey. Doubt was written across his face. Did he think the woman he loved was possibly guilty of two murders?

The sheriff dug into his pocket and brought out a plastic baggie. Inside was a red bandanna. He carefully took the bandanna out of the bag, holding it by the tip of one corner. "I found this near Nathan's body," the sheriff said. "Do you recognize it, Honey?"

Honey's face want pale. "It's not mine, if that's what you're implying. Look around. Almost all of the scarecrows use bandannas as part of their costumes." She glanced at Red, who had his hand on the pocket of his plaid flannel shirt. He pulled his hand away quickly. It appeared empty. Had there been a bandanna in his chest pocket?

"Where's your bandanna, Red?" Sheriff O'Neil asked.

Apparently struck speechless, Red just shrugged.

"There was something stuck to this bandanna," the sheriff continued. He held up the plastic bag. At the bottom were two tiny black seeds.

Apple seeds.

"Can I check your pocket, Red?"

"Sure," Red said, stepping forward. He pulled open his pocket and let the sheriff dig around inside. "Nothing, see?"

The sheriff stepped back. "Honey, I need to see your pockets."

"Why?" she said, covering the pockets of her pants with her hands.

"Deputy?" the sheriff said, nodding to Deputy Bonita Javier. The woman went over to Honey and gently slid Honey's hands away from covering her pockets. "Is there anything in your pockets that could poke me—needles, knives, anything like that?" the deputy asked.

"Of course not!" Honey said.

The deputy slowly reached into one of Honey's pockets and came out empty. She reached into the other one, dug around, and again pulled out an empty hand.

Then she held up one finger. A black seed was caught just under her fingernail.

The sheriff looked at Honey, clearly disappointed. "Honey, I'm afraid I'm going to have to take you in for questioning."

Honey looked at Red, her eyes beginning to cloud with tears. "I . . . I . . . I want a lawyer!"

Chapter 17

"I'm not arresting you, Honey," Sheriff O'Neil said. "I just want to talk with you in a more private setting."

Jake stepped up. "Honey, if you want an attorney, you have that right. I can contact one of my colleagues who lives in Sacramento. Just let me know."

Honey looked at Jake, then back at the sheriff. "All right, Murph. I'll come with you. But I didn't see anything or do anything." She turned back to Jake. "Thanks for the offer. I may take you up on it."

Aunt Abby embraced Honey. "Don't worry, dear. Wes will make sure you're okay, won't you, Wes? Will you go with her?"

Detective Shelton looked at Sheriff O'Neil, who nodded.

Honey took Aunt Abby's hand. "Will you take care of everything at the Enchanted Apple while I'm gone? There's apple pie in the fridge. The coffeemaker is ready to go. The rooms have been cleaned, so there's not much to do. Just fill in for me until I get back? You have a key."

"Of course," Aunt Abby said. "And you'll be back in no time." She shot Detective Shelton a look.

While Sheriff O'Neil gave orders to his deputies to close down the festival, Honey hugged Red, wiped away tears, and followed the sheriff to his patrol car. To everyone's relief, she was saved from the humiliation of handcuffs, since she wasn't being arrested. Detective Shelton continued to help clear the area, promising my aunt he'd see her back at the bed-and-breakfast inn after he stopped by the sheriff's office to check on Honey, per Aunt Abby's orders.

The dwindling stragglers scattered for their cars that were parked in a dirt lot several yards away. People continued to mumble about the death of the human scarecrow and some voiced their disappointment that the festival was over, at least for the day. I wondered if it would reopen for its final day tomorrow after all that had happened. If not, someone had hinted that there would be serious financial losses for the Apple Valley merchants who'd invested their time and products in the event. But then, murder always took precedence over anything else.

"Darcy," Aunt Abby called to me. She looked weary. I had a feeling the long day of work, coupled with the discovery of another body and her concern for Honey, was taking its toll on her usual high-energy level. I couldn't help worrying about her.

"Yes, Aunt Abby?"

"Do you mind if I don't join you and Jake for dinner tonight? I'd like to get back to the inn and keep an eye on the place. I promised Honey."

I hadn't planned to invite my aunt and cousin to join Jake and me for his birthday dinner, but now I felt a little guilty about omitting them. "Of course," I said. "Do you need help?"

"Oh no, Dillon will be there. I'm going to whip up some dinner so feel free to join us if you don't feel like going out either. Maybe we can figure out a few things over a nice bowl of my mac and cheese."

I glanced at Jake; he nodded, sensing my feeling of guilt if I just went off and left them. There went our romantic birthday dinner—again.

"That sounds great," I said to her. "We could all use a good dose of comfort food about now. Are you sure you're not too tired?"

"Cooking a big batch of mac and cheese is about the only thing I can think of that will lift my spirits and give me back my energy. And Wes loves my mac and cheese."

"All right, we'll be there as soon as we can. I just have a couple of things I want to check on before I leave."

"Anything you can do to help Honey would be nice," Aunt Abby said. Then she and Dillon hopped onto their electric scooters and rode the short distance to the school bus. I watched as Dillon—still half scarecrow—loaded the scooters and Aunt Abby closed up the bus. Moments later they were on the road back to the Enchanted Apple Inn.

I turned to Jake, who was talking on his cell phone, and figured he was contacting the lawyer friend he'd mentioned. I scanned the area while he chatted, looking for a familiar face, hoping Crystal and Tiffany might still be around, but I didn't see them, nor Paula, Adam, or Red.

Where had everybody gone?

"Sorry about dinner tonight," I said to Jake as we headed for Crystal's temporary wine tent to see if she might be there.

"That's okay. We wouldn't be able to enjoy it until these murders are solved anyway."

"It's hard to believe the two deaths are related," I said, "since Nathan and Roman seem to have so little in common. But it's also too coincidental that two people connected with the festival would be murdered in Apple Valley in such a short time."

"Unfortunately Honey seems to be the primary link between the two," Jake added.

"How so?"

"She argued with both of them," Jake said.

"I'd hardly call her conversation with Roman an argument. A disagreement, maybe. And we don't really know if she argued with Nathan that night." I recalled the two conflicting answers she'd given when asked about her conversation with Nathan.

"She seems to be pretty passionate about the apple industry," Jake added.

"That doesn't mean she's going to kill everyone she

argues with. If I did that, the bodies would be piled higher than a haystack."

"Promise you'll never argue with me?" Jake said, grinning.

"As long as you keep agreeing with me, we'll have no problem."

We stopped our witty repartee as we approached the wine tent. The flap was down, but there was a light on inside. I called out, "Crystal?" so as not to startle her, then lifted the flap and ducked inside, with Jake right behind me.

"What are you doing here?" Crystal said, blinking rapidly. She was sitting on a stool, enjoying a glass of her own wine. "We're closed. The whole festival is closed."

"I know. I was there when Sheriff O'Neil made the announcement," I said. Apparently she hadn't noticed me. "I just wanted to check on you and your daughter, see if you're all right."

"We're fine," she said bluntly and got up. Setting down her empty glass, she began loading bottles of wine into a cardboard carton. "Of course, I won't make half my money back for renting the tent and buying all the supplies, but at least my daughter and I are still alive."

Odd thing to say, I thought. "Uh, yeah. I hope no one else gets hurt." I looked around for her daughter, then asked, "Is Tiffany here?"

As if on cue, Tiffany appeared from the tent's back entrance. She had wiped off her scarecrow makeup and changed into jeans and a "Wise Apple Winery"

T-shirt, but her cheeks were still flushed, her eyes red-rimmed, and she looked as if she was in a daze.

"Tiffany? Are you all right?" I asked.

Tiffany started to say something, but Crystal cut her off. "I told you, we're fine. Tiff just lost a friend of hers. We both did. But she'll be all right. As soon as we pack up here, I'm going to take her home, run her a nice hot bath, and get her to bed. She needs rest, that's all."

Obviously Crystal wasn't feeling the same loss for Nathan as her daughter. But then, Crystal and Nathan hadn't seemed as close as Tiffany and Nathan.

"Is there anything I can do?" I offered again.

"Yes, pack up and go home too. The festival's probably canceled for the rest of the weekend. There's nothing more to do around here."

"Aren't you worried about a killer running around?"

"Tiff and I have no reason to be frightened by some nutcase. I told you, I'm sure it has something to do with that GMO company, and I'm not a threat to them. You heard that Asian lady. She said Nathan was secretly planning to sell his property to Eden Corporation. Somebody around here must not have liked that idea, and it had to be someone who knew about the deal. Someone who was worried she might lose her farm someday too, if the GMOs took over everything."

Her farm? Crystal was clearly referring to Honey.

"You really think Honey did this?" I asked.

Crystal shrugged. "It looks that way to the sheriff. I'm just sorry for Red. He didn't know what he was getting into with her."

"Mama!" Tiffany snapped. "Shut up! You act as if

Dad were stupid. It was you that drove him away. I don't know what you did, but whatever it was, he couldn't live with us anymore and left. He's happy with Honey, so just let it go." Tiffany stormed out of the back of the tent, leaving Crystal standing there with her mouth open.

Crystal pulled herself together, closed her mouth, and resumed packing her wine bottles. "As you can see, my daughter is very upset. If you want to help us, then help Sheriff O'Neil prove that Honey killed those two men so the rest of us can get on with our lives."

I glanced at Jake, who'd been standing by, letting me do all the talking. He gestured toward the entrance flap, indicating we should go.

"Well, I hope Tiffany feels better soon," I said, not knowing what else to say. We let ourselves out of the tent.

After we'd stepped out of hearing distance, I stopped.

"Crystal seems awfully protective of her grown daughter," I said to Jake.

"A bit overinvolved," Jake agreed. "But then, Tiffany's father left the family, which must have been painful. Maybe Crystal feels a sense of guilt about that and is trying to compensate."

"Do you think Tiffany saw Nathan as a father figure? Or do you think they were romantically involved?"

"If she was involved with him, I can see why Crystal might not like the idea of him being so much older."

"Makes sense, but they were behaving too oddly," I said. "I wonder if Dillon can find out more about Tiffany—and Crystal, for that matter. We don't know much about either of them, other than Tiffany is living with her mother, who owns a winery and is divorced."

We started for Jake's truck; then I spotted Adam and Paula in the dimly lit parking lot. Paula was gesturing a lot while Adam was just standing there. I wondered what they were talking about.

"Come on!" I whispered to Jake.

"Where are we going?" he asked.

"Follow me." I led him through the few parked cars that were still in the lot, staying in the shadows and keeping quiet. As soon as we were within hearing range, I ducked behind a van, then pulled Jake down with me.

Jake looked at me as if I was crazy.

Maybe he was right.

"What are you doing?" he whispered.

"Spying on Paula and Adam. Isn't it obvious?" I whispered back.

"Why? I feel like a fool."

"Because I think they're up to something. Shhh! Listen."

I caught Paula in midsentence. ". . . that's why I need you to do this for me, Adam!"

"I don't want any part of it, Paula," Adam said. "You led me to believe everything would be okay, and obviously it's not."

Paula's former light flirtations had been replaced by insistent vocals, while Adam's puppy dog demeanor had morphed into that of a frightened mouse. What was going on between these two?

"But you said you'd help me convince the others to sell, Adam," Paula said. "You can't back down now."

"What are you doing?" a voice called from behind us. We were caught!

I turned to see Red standing under one of the parking lot lights, but he wasn't looking in our direction. He was squinting at Paula and Adam. He hadn't seen us after all!

Paula froze. Adam glanced around the semilit parking lot to see where the voice had come from.

"Is that you, Adam?" Red called. He began heading over to where they stood.

"Now what?" Paula said under her breath. "That's all I need. Honey's doofus boyfriend snooping around. Get rid of him."

Adam frowned at Paula. "How'm I supposed to do that? He's my friend."

"Really?" Paula said, eyeing him. "I doubt he'd be your friend if he knew—"

"Shut up!" Adam said, his face twisted in anger. This was a change. It was the first time I'd seen the usually even-tempered man look and sound upset.

"Hey, what's going on?" Red said as he approached the couple. He scrutinized Paula.

Paula forced a smile. Adam kept his frown.

"Nothing," Paula said. "Just chatting."

"We were talking about—" Adam started to say.

Paula cut him off. "The dead guy. Poor thing. And now they've arrested Honey. You must be devastated." She reached over and placed her hand on Red's arm.

Boy, the woman could really turn it off and on, I thought.

"The sheriff didn't *arrest* her," Red said, shaking off her hand. "He's just questioning her. He's probably going to question everyone who saw Nathan before he got murdered." Red's face fell and he shook his head. "I'm heading to the station right now, see if Honey's all right, if I can take her home." He started to turn and walk away, then looked back at Paula. "Don't think you're fooling anyone, young lady. We all know what you're up to."

"Oh, what's that, Red?" she said smugly.

"You're trying to sweet-talk us all into selling our properties. That's what the other dead guy was trying to do, only he tried it with cash. You're just using a different approach." He eyed her up and down, making an obvious reference to her sex appeal. "But we see right through you. Don't we, Adam?"

Adam started to say something, but Paula interrupted him again. "Listen, carrot top, you better face it. You're about to lose your Honey Bear 'cause she's going to prison for murder. I'll bet they find her fingerprints on that apple stick of yours, and when they do, maybe they'll arrest you as her accomplice."

"Why, you little . . . ," Red sputtered. "If I weren't a gentleman . . ."

"I doubt you are, leaving your wife and kid for another woman," Paula said.

If Red suddenly felt like murdering Paula at this point, I wouldn't have been too surprised.

"You know nothing about my marriage or the reason I left," Red said. "I don't cotton to liars. And you fit in that category perfectly, lady. The sooner everyone realizes it, the sooner you'll be out of here on your butt."

"Oh, it'll take a lot more than a few fires and a couple of murders to get rid of me," Paula said. "In fact, I'll bet you set those fires yourself and tried to make it look like Eden Corporation did it. Funny how only a storage building and an old barn were burned and not the nearby houses. Seems a safe way to gain sympathy while you place the blame on others. I'll bet you and Honey thought that whole plan up, and when it didn't work to drive us out, she took it a step further and murdered my boss. And maybe Nathan found out about it and you killed him too."

"Why, you . . ." Red reached out, ready to grab Paula around the neck.

Paula hustled back behind Adam for protection.

Adam held up his hands, trying to keep Red at bay.

Jake jumped out from behind the car and ran over. I was right behind him.

"Hey! Calm down!" Jake shouted as he approached them. "Everyone, just chill."

I caught up with him in time to see Paula peek out from behind Adam as her cover.

She had her Coach bag open and her hand inside.

Moments later, she withdrew a gun.

Chapter 18

"Whoa, whoa, whoa!" Jake said, raising his hands. "Put the gun down. You don't need that."

Uh-oh, I thought as I felt sweat break out on my forehead. Paula had a gun. Did *she* murder Roman and Nathan? If so, why hadn't she used the gun?

"Back off!" Paula said, wildly waving the gun at all of us. "One of you could easily be a killer and I'm not taking any chances."

"Wait a minute." I raised my hands like Jake. "You think one of *us* did it? Then why do *you* have a gun?"

"To protect myself, obviously," Paula snapped.

"But you said you thought Honey was the killer and now you're accusing us." Out of the corner of my eye, I saw Jake inch closer to Paula. What was he up to?

"I don't know anymore, but I'm not going to stand around and be the next victim, that's for sure. Whoever killed Reuben probably wants me dead too, since we both work for the same company. And the way I figure it, it has to be one of these apple fanatics."

"But what about Nathan? He's not one of your GMO company men. Or is he?" I asked.

"No, he probably just got in the way," Paula answered. "Who knows? Like I said, I'm not going to wait around and find out. I'm outta here."

She started to back up. Adam, standing next to her, didn't move, his face frozen. Red stood with his hands in his overall pockets, looking baffled.

Jake took another step forward. "Paula, wait. Is there something you're not telling us? Something you know that could help us figure out who killed those two men?"

"No, I told you," Paula said. The gun trembled slightly in her hand. "Now stay back!"

This time Red stepped forward, his hands still in his pockets. "Listen, miss, if you do know something, you have to at least tell the sheriff. Honey didn't do this and we need to clear her name before anything more happens."

"Shut up, you old geezer," Paula said, aiming the gun at him. "And back off!"

Red started to pull his hands out of his pockets.

"Don't even think about it!" Paula snapped.

"I was just going to raise my hands," Red offered.

"Okay, but do it slowly. If I see any kind of weapon, I won't hesitate to use this gun."

He continued to withdraw his hands. In one of his hands he held an object.

"Freeze right there," Paula said, waving the gun. "What is that?"

Red slowly held up the round red object for Paula to see. "Calm down. It's not a weapon. Just an apple."

Paula frowned at him, obviously puzzled.

"You always carry around—" she started to say, but Red saw his opportunity and went for it.

"Here! Catch!" he called out. With a lightning-fast motion, he tossed the apple to Paula.

As expected, Paula's reflexes kicked in and she tried to catch the apple coming right at her. In that split-second of distraction, Jake rushed over and knocked the gun from her hand. He bent over and snatched it up, then checked to see if it was loaded. He removed the clip and pocketed it and the weapon. The guy seemed to know his way around a gun.

I let out a breath of air. Red and Adam looked visibly relieved.

"Give me that!" Paula screeched, and lunged for Jake as soon as she realized what had happened. Adam and Red rushed to yank her off, wrestled with her for a few seconds, and then pulled her arms behind her back and held them tight.

"Call the sheriff!" Jake said to me.

But I was already on it.

"Do you think she did it?" I asked Jake on the ride back to the Enchanted Inn. The men had kept Paula under control until Sheriff O'Neil arrived. Jake explained to him what had happened; then the sheriff arrested her— for threatening the lives of others. It was all he could charge her with at the time, but I was hoping he'd find more that would link her to the murders.

Jake shrugged. "I don't know. She certainly had motive. If she killed her boss, she could take his place in the company faster. Then again, maybe it was a crime of passion. Maybe she and Roman-Reuben were having an affair and he cheated on her."

"But she was the flirty one," I argued.

"Doesn't mean he was being faithful to her. Maybe that was her way of trying to get even—flirt with every guy who came along. When that didn't work, she killed him."

"But that still doesn't explain how Nathan Chapman ties in," I said. I thought for a moment. "Maybe Nathan found out she killed Reuben and blackmailed her?" I offered. "He wasn't the most upstanding guy around."

"It's possible."

"But why didn't she just shoot them?" I asked. "Why go to the trouble of using that apple corer and sharp stick to stab them?"

"Maybe to throw everyone off," Jake suggested. "If she made it look like Honey did it, then she figured she'd be in the clear."

"But if the sheriff still doesn't have any evidence to hold her, how is he going to prove she was the killer?"

"That's up to him. Not our circus. Not our monkey."

I frowned at him. "What's this got to do with a circus and monkeys?"

"It's a saying. It means not our problem."

I scrunched my nose. "Huh?"

"Never mind. Listen, I'm starved. I hope your aunt's got dinner ready. I'm sure she'll want to hear the good news about Paula being arrested. Hopefully Honey will be released soon."

I pondered what had happened the rest of the ride to the inn. Something was still bothering me; it seemed to be just out of my reach.

So far, no fingerprints had been found on the weapons. If Paula killed those two men, she had apparently been careful. Gloves? And that meant the murders were premeditated, at least to some degree, rather than in the heat of passion.

And what about the murder in the maze? I doubted Paula knew her way around in there any better than I had. If she'd followed Nathan in and stabbed him, how could she be sure she'd make her escape in time to offer an alibi? Or had she somehow figured out the fastest way in and out?

The old adage "An apple a day keeps the doctor away" sure didn't seem to apply to the recent events. In fact, it was an apple that had caused Paula to lose her gun and end up being arrested. Apples. All those health benefits Honey had mentioned—antioxidants, fiber, vitamins, calcium, potassium—might help reduce the risk of developing such diseases as cancer, hypertension, diabetes, stroke, cholesterol, and dementia, but there appeared to be a new side effect: murder.

I was still convinced that Eden Corporation was the snake in the Garden of Evil. What was it that Nathan Chapman had written in one of his articles? Something like "There's a nasty pest that's threatening the very core of the apple business, and the whole thing is rotten, any way you slice it." If he really believed that, why would he consider selling his farm and his legacy?

I needed Dillon to do a little cyber-sleuthing for me and see if he could find out anything more on Nathan Chapman and Paula Hayashi. Maybe, like Adam and Eve, they'd been tempted by some kind of snake we hadn't discovered yet.

We arrived at the inn to the intoxicating smell of Aunt Abby's gourmet mac and cheese. The dining table set, the wine decanted, and glasses waiting for us. Jake and I took off our jackets, hung them on the antique coatrack by the door, and headed straight for the beckoning drinks.

"Something smells good," Jake said as soon as Aunt Abby appeared from the kitchen. She wore one of Honey's apple-themed aprons and had slipped on a pair of bright red pot gloves. She clapped them together when she saw us.

"Oh, good! You're back! We can serve dinner now. Dillon! They're heerrree!" she called to the kitchen, then gestured with her large mittened hands. "Have a seat. The casserole will be right out. Enjoy a glass of wine. I know Honey would like you to have it."

"Has there been any word?" I asked Aunt Abby, hoping the sheriff or Detective Shelton might have notified her about Honey's possible release.

Her smile drooped. "No. Have you heard anything?"

I glanced at Jake. "Actually there was an incident at the festival grounds after you left."

Dillon appeared from the kitchen carrying a large

green salad. He stopped when he saw the anxious look on his mother's face. "S'up?"

"I was just about to tell your mom that Jake and I overheard Paula talking to Adam in the parking lot."

"Spying on her, eh?" Dillon said, not mincing words. He had a talent for being direct.

"I suppose you could call it that. Anyway, Red showed up and he and Paula started arguing, and then Paula pulled a gun."

Aunt Abby's eyes flashed. "What?"

Dillon looked shocked. "She had a gun?"

I nodded. "It makes me think she had something to do with the murders, but she claims she didn't."

"Then why would she have a gun?" Aunt Abby asked.

"She said it was for protection," I said. "She was planning to leave town, probably because she knew the sheriff would soon realize what she'd gain by killing Roman."

"But what about Nathan?" Aunt Abby asked.

"That's another thing," I said. "She was talking to him a little before he was found dead. She said he told her he was going to sell his farm to Eden Corporation."

"Dude, that doesn't compute," Dillon said. He set the salad bowl on the table, pulled out a large green leaf, and stuffed it in his mouth. "Chapman was, like, the head of the festival or something, right?"

"I agree, Dillon, it really doesn't make sense. That's why I thought maybe you could check him out on the Internet, see if you can find anything more about him. And Paula Hayashi too, while you're at it. Maybe there's something out there we haven't discovered yet, something that might lead to some kind of connection between these murders."

"Yeah," Dillon chuckled, "like a *love* connection. I saw that chick all over Chapman at the festival."

I nodded. "That's what Willow said too. But I think Paula was just using her feminine wiles to get whatever it was that she wanted."

"She's pretty hot," Dillon said. His eyes glazed over for a moment.

"Snap out of it, lover boy!" I said to him.

Aunt Abby clapped her mittens together. "Everyone! Sit down! I'll bring out the casserole before it gets cold and we can talk about all this over my special mac and cheese. There's a secret ingredient in this recipe. I'll bet you'll never guess what it is."

I looked at Jake. He looked at me. We said it at the same time.

"Apples."

After dinner, I helped Aunt Abby clean up the kitchen while Dillon got out his laptop and started searching for info on Nathan and Paula. Jake was talking on the phone to his attorney buddy in Sacramento, in case Honey wasn't released and needed his help. Just as Aunt Abby and I finished, there was a knock on the door. We looked at each other, reminiscent of an old horror movie—"Who could that be at this time of night?"—then Aunt Abby went to the door, with me right behind her.

She opened it to find Detective Shelton standing under the dim front lamp.

"Wes!" my aunt said before embracing him—something I would never get used to. "Did you bring Honey with you?"

A woman stepped out from behind him.

Aunt Abby's face fell when she realized it was Paula Hayashi.

"Sorry," Wes said. "Sheriff O'Neil is still talking to her. But she's fine. Cooperating fully. I'm sure she'll be back soon."

Aunt Abby turned to Paula, who shouldered her way inside. "What are *you* doing here?" my aunt said to her. She turned to Detective Shelton. "Didn't Sheriff O'Neil arrest this woman for illegal gun possession?"

My aunt had really learned her police terms.

"They couldn't hold me. I did nothing wrong," Paula said. She raised an eyebrow. "I know my rights. Satisfied?"

"But she aimed the gun at us," I argued. "That's got to be illegal?"

Detective Shelton shrugged. "She said she felt threatened and was just protecting herself."

"Which is true," Paula added.

"But she could have shot one of us!" I argued.

"The gun wasn't loaded," he answered. "I checked."

Paula gave a smug smile.

"So, what are you doing back here?" Aunt Abby asked her, clearly as irritated with the woman as I was.

"To get my things. I'm leaving." Paula spun around, her black hair shimmering in a cascading wave.

"The sheriff is letting you go?" Aunt Abby asked.

"He knows where to reach me," she replied, and headed up the stairs to her room.

"Good riddance," Aunt Abby whispered when Paula reached the top landing. She turned to Detective Shelton. "How's Honey holding up? Why hasn't she been released?"

"She's all right," the detective said. "I'm sure Murph will let her go soon. Meanwhile, he asked me to give Ms. Hayashi a ride back here."

Jake, still on the phone, covered the mouthpiece and said, "My buddy should be there soon. He'll get her home, I'm sure."

Aunt Abby nodded, but she didn't look appeased. "I hope so. I hate to think of her down there being grilled for something she didn't do."

None of us said anything for a moment. Then Wes broke the silence. "Something smells good."

Aunt Abby perked up a bit. "That would be my apple-pecan pie! It's fresh out of the oven—"

Another knock at the door caused us all to freeze. This one was louder and more forceful. Aunt Abby glanced at the detective. He took charge, stepped over, and opened the door.

Under the pale overhead light stood Adam Bramley.

"Adam?" Aunt Abby said. "What are you doing here?"

Adam removed his cap and stepped inside. In his hand he held what was once an expensive camera. But the lens had been shattered, the guts ripped out, and the strap cut up into pieces.

His eyes narrowed. He glanced around at the five of us, then called out, "Where is she!" He held up the mangled camera, his face twisted in anger.

"Who?" Aunt Abby asked. "Honey? She's still at the sheriff's office."

"No, not her. That witch who's trying to turn us all into her minions. Paula!" He nearly spat her name.

"She's upstairs . . . ," Aunt Abby began.

Adam headed toward the staircase.

"Good," he said, holding up the broken camera. "I have something of hers I want to return."

Uh-oh. He looked as though he was going to do a lot more than just return what looked like Paula's busted camera.

Chapter 19

Detective Shelton lunged forward and grabbed Adam by the arm, swinging him around before the man could take the first stair step.

"Hold up, buddy," the detective said.

Adam shook his arm free and glared at the detective. In the short time I'd known Adam, he'd never shown such emotion. "I'm not your buddy, and you have no jurisdiction here," Adam spat, "so butt out of my business."

Whoa, this was a new side of the man I'd thought was a timid mouse.

"Let's take it down a notch," Detective Shelton said, his low tone soothing. "I get you're pissed about something, so why don't you tell me what happened? Maybe I can help."

Part cop, part negotiator, part therapist—no wonder

Detective Shelton was so good at his job. Out of the corner of my eye, I caught Aunt Abby beaming at the way he was handling Adam.

"This is none of your business," Adam said. He looked at the rest of us as we stared at him in shocked silence. "That goes for the rest of you people. None of you outsiders know anything about what goes on in Apple Valley. All this trouble started when those Eden people came sniffing around, lying about who they were and what they wanted, trying to change our way of life. Now look what's happened. Nathan Chapman is dead because of them." He looked up at the first-floor landing. "Because of *her*!"

"What the hell is going on down there?" Paula stood at the top of the staircase, straining to look down at the small crowd. Her eyes flashed when she saw what Adam held in his hand. "Oh my God! Is that my Nikon? What have you done to my two-thousand-dollar camera, you jerk!"

Paula headed down the stairs dragging an Yves Saint Laurent suitcase. When she reached the bottom, she let go of the luggage handle and held out her hand for the camera. Adam plopped the broken pieces into her open palm.

"There you go," he said with a strange grin right out of a horror movie.

Paula looked livid as she absorbed the condition of her expensive camera. "Why, you son of a . . ." She raised up the jumble of metal and plastic and swung it toward Adam's head. He ducked just in time and bits of the camera flew past him, hitting the far wall. The pieces clattered to the floor in a heap.

"Detective!" Adam pointed an accusing finger at Paula. "She just tried to kill me! Arrest her!"

Ah, so now he wanted the law involved.

"Like you said, I don't have jurisdiction here," Detective Shelton said, repeating Adam's words back to him. "And she didn't hit you, so I think we should just let the woman go ahead and leave."

"The sooner, the better," Adam said with a snarl.

Paula shot a daggered look at Adam. "You need to get a life. You've been drinking too much of your own apple hooch and it's made your brain wormy. And by the way, you're going to pay for my camera. My lawyer will see to that."

"Go ahead and try, witch," Adam countered. "You can't prove I did anything to it. Maybe I found it after some vandals had gotten to it, and I was just trying to return it to you, like any good citizen would do. Not that you'd know about that."

Paula shook her head. "Wise up, old man. Eden has spent over a decade developing the Eden Apple and it'll be on the store shelves all over the country. That's because they're perfect. All you have to do is look at them. And it's people like you and Honey who are the bad apples, spoiling the barrel for the rest of us."

With that, she grabbed her suitcase handle and high-heeled her way through the open front door. I caught a glimpse of her unlocking her late-model Volvo just before I closed the door.

"Wow," I said, suddenly feeling exhausted from all the drama. "I need a glass of wine."

"Why don't we all go back to the dining room?" Detective Shelton said. "Adam, you too."

It was more of a command than an invitation, but the detective said it so smoothly Adam didn't seem to notice. He headed in, the detective ushering his way.

"I think there's a bit more pie, Adam," Aunt Abby said, playing the role of hostess in Honey's absence. He gave a single nod and Aunt Abby ducked into the kitchen. Jake and I sat down at the table opposite Adam and Detective Shelton while Dillon quietly slipped out and headed for the stairs. I hoped he'd remember to do the research on Paula I'd asked for, as well as Honey, Red, and Adam. Maybe he'd come up with something so we could end this nightmare.

"Adam," the detective said, "you want to tell me what happened between you and Paula Hayashi?"

Before he could answer, Aunt Abby brought in the warm pie slice and a fork for Adam. The rest of us poured ourselves some wine—all but the detective, who accepted a cup of coffee from Aunt Abby. Adam took a bite, then nodded, either as a thank-you for the pie, a response to how much he enjoyed it, or as an answer to the detective's question regarding what had happened between him and Paula.

When he finished the first bite, he said simply, "She played me."

"How so?" Detective Shelton asked.

Adam glanced over at Aunt Abby, who'd taken a seat at the end of the table; then he looked at Jake and me. "You all saw her. She came on to me right off the bat. Pretended she wanted to know about my farm and the apple business for some phony article she and that Roman character were supposedly doing. She said she'd be taking pictures of me picking apples, driving the tractor, having a glass of apple cider. She promised it would be in this big glossy magazine and all over the Internet."

"We *all* believed her and Roman," Aunt Abby said. "We had no reason not to. We were duped too."

"Yeah, but she made a fool out of me. She acted like she really liked me. I shouldn't have been so stupid. I mean, what would a young, pretty city woman like her want with an old country guy like me? But like an idiot, I fell for that snake in the grass." Adam pushed the unfinished pie away, as if he couldn't stomach any more.

"We've all been there, Adam," the detective said, obviously trying to show empathy for the guy. "When you talked with Paula, did you learn anything that could help with these murders? Anything that might give Sheriff O'Neil a clue?"

Adam wrinkled his brow and thought for a few seconds, then shook his head. "Not that I can think of. She asked me a bunch of questions about the farm, how I processed my apples, what I thought the place was worth. Things like that. I thought it was all background stuff she was gathering for the story. Now I think she was trying to feel me out about whether or not I might be in a position to sell."

"Did you give her any indication you would?" Jake asked.

"No," Adam answered. "Although I did mention I was worried about the drought we're in. If it continues, my farm and a bunch of other farms around here could be in trouble. She seemed real interested in that, but she never asked me directly if I would sell the place. If I didn't know better, I'd figure she had something to do with the drought, just to run us apple people out of business. But of course, she can't control the weather."

"But she might have planned to capitalize on that," Jake said. "How bad has the water shortage been?"

Adam shrugged. "Bad. We farmers are trying to stay optimistic, but it's getting harder as the drought lingers on. We had this festival to kick off the season and get the tourists up here, but if some of the apple farms have to close—or sell—the tourists will stop coming. One of my wells is completely dried up for the first time in twenty years. I lost some of my crop because of that. Some of the trees are still producing, but the apples are hardly worth picking because they're undersized. I've had to let some of my workers go, and they have families to feed. Yeah, sure, I'm worried, but I'm not giving up."

"Isn't there anything you can do?" I asked, after watching his face tighten as he spoke about his problems.

Adam played with the pie, mashing it into mush. "Actually it's worse than just not having enough water. With the drought, the trees have a harder time fighting off pests and disease. The roots are stressed and the limbs are dying. It's like I'm growing an apple graveyard out there. That's why I'm so angry with these GMO people. They swoop down the minute we have problems and don't offer to help. They just want to buy us out and get rid of us. We small-scale farmers can't compete with the big corporations."

"But people still want organically grown fruit," Aunt Abby offered. "Now more than ever."

"Yeah," Adam said, "but only if it's available. Those GMO apples are taking up more and more shelf space."

Detective Shelton, who'd been listening intently as Adam shared his woes, cleared his throat. "Adam, do you know of anyone who might have wanted to kill Nathan Chapman?"

Adam shook his head. "To tell you the truth, I thought maybe Nathan might have killed Roman."

That made me sit up. "Why?" I asked, beating the detective to the punch.

"Because he hated those Eden Corp people more than anyone. After all, he was head of the Apple Festival, and if there was no more festival, there was no more need for Nathan Chapman."

"But Paula said he told her he was thinking of selling his farm to Eden Corporation. Maybe he wasn't that interested in the festival anymore."

"That's bull. The festival—and representing his family's legacy—was everything to him."

"Was he really descended from Johnny Appleseed's family?" Aunt Abby asked. "Are you sure it wasn't just something he made up to impress the tourists?"

"Why would he make up something like that?" Adam said, frowning.

"I might know why," came a voice from the hallway.

Dillon entered the dining room, holding his open laptop in one hand. He sat down at the other end of the table.

"What have you got?" I asked Dillon, mentally crossing my fingers that he'd uncovered something significant that would help free Honey and identify the killer.

Dillon didn't answer at first. He set down the laptop and tapped on the keyboard. Finally he began reading from the screen. "Okay, well, it's a little confusing, but I found out that Johnny Appleseed had two brothers named Nathaniel—one born in 1776, two years after John, and the second one in 1781. Weird, huh?"

"Very weird," I said. "Why would the parents give two of their sons the same name?"

"I'm not sure," Dillon said, squinting at the computer screen, "but they had two different mothers. John's father—also Nathaniel—was married to Elizabeth in 1770 and then he married Lucy Cooley in 1780. I'm guessing the first wife died."

"You're probably right," I said. "That happened a lot back then. Women often died in childbirth, or she could have contracted a contagious, deadly disease."

"Yeah, so anyway, the second Nathaniel Cooley was actually John's half brother from another mother, born in 1781. He's the one who joined Johnny Appleseed in spreading the word of apples, but he quit after a while, went back home to Ohio, got married, and had a bunch of kids. Guess what he named his son?"

Dillon looked up from the screen to see if we were following.

"Nathaniel," I said. "So you've been to Ancestry-dot-com, but where is this going?"

"I'm getting there," Dillon snapped. "And this is way beyond that simple site. So this Nathaniel the fourth, middle name Cooley, was born in 1810, along with four other kids. He lived to the ripe old age of ninety."

"Wow," Aunt Abby said. "Hope I live that long."

Detective Shelton smiled at her.

Dillon continued. "Okay, so they had nine kids, including three boys, one named John Chapman, but no Nathaniels this time."

"Again, what does all this have to do with murder?" I asked, growing impatient.

"Dude, the Nathan Chapman that ran the festival and was killed, he claimed he was a descendant of Johnny Appleseed Chapman's family, right? Johnny Appleseed never married or had kids, but his half brother, Nathaniel, did, and *his* son, Nathaniel, named one of his three sons John. That's probably the one Nathan claimed was his great-great-great grandfather."

"Okay," said Aunt Abby, "you lost me halfway down the family tree."

"Nathan Chapman really *was* a descendent of a John Chapman," I summarized for my aunt, "just not *the* Johnny Appleseed Chapman."

"Not exactly," Dillon said.

"What do you mean?"

"All three of Nathaniel's sons died before the age of three, including the one Nathan claimed was his relative."

"Whoa! I'm so confused," I said. "What does all this mean?"

Dillon smiled condescendingly. "It means that the present-day Nathan Chapman, who's supposed to be a descendant of the John Chapman family, really couldn't have been."

"So he lied about being related to the Chapman family?" Detective Shelton clarified.

Dillon nodded. "Dude, not only that, but listen to this. Nathan Chapman isn't even his real name."

Aunt Abby blinked. "You're kidding! How do you know?"

Dillon shrugged nonchalantly. "It's what I *do*, Mom."

"That's true! You're a genius, Dillon!" Aunt Abby practically squealed.

"I think we're getting off track here," the detective said. "If his name's not Nathan Chapman, then what is it?"

Dillon looked at Adam. "Ethan Bramley."

Everyone turned to Adam. His face was as red as the apple place mat in front of him.

"He's your *brother*?" Aunt Abby said to him.

Adam looked down at his mangled pie. "Half brother."

"Oh my God," I said, almost speechless.

"Unfortunately yes," Adam said, looking down at his mashed dessert. "You guys can probably figure out why I chose not to share that information with anyone. My half brother was a liar and a cheat and knew absolutely nothing about family."

"In fact," Dillon added, "he was an ex-con."

Adam looked up, his face even redder than before. He sighed. "It's true. He was in prison for a while. Now can you see why I didn't want anyone to know we were related?"

"What was he in prison for?" Detective Shelton asked.

Adam cleared his throat. "Manslaughter. He accidentally killed a guy in a bar fight over some woman. He didn't mean to, but they sent him to Folsom anyway."

"But he owned the farm adjacent to yours, didn't he?" Aunt Abby asked. "I think Honey told me that."

"It's actually my property," Adam confessed. "Was, anyway. I gave it to him so he could start over, make a good life. What a mistake. I had to hire a bunch of guys to work the place after he started running around again, drinking and gambling and chasing women. The only reason I helped him was that he was family, and that means something around these parts to most people."

I was slowly putting one and one together, if not two and two. "So all this time you've been covering for your half brother, working both farms, spending your own money on extra hired help. Then Paula Hayashi comes along and pays you some attention and you think maybe she likes you. And then you catch Nathan flirting with her and . . . and you didn't like that, did you, Adam?"

Adam stood up suddenly, nearly knocking his chair back. He jabbed a finger at me. "You listen here, lady!"

"Hold up," Jake said, raising a hand.

Detective Shelton stood up next to Adam, no doubt ready to act if needed.

"Hey, my so-called brother went through women like they're candied apples," Adam spat. "He'd had half the women in this town. I was ashamed of him, but I tolerated him for the sake of my parents and because he needed me and because that's what we Bramleys do. But if you're implying I killed him just because he was flirting with that witch, you're dead wrong."

Jake looked up at Adam. "Now that he's dead, what happens to the farm?"

If looks could kill, Jake would have been a dead man. Adam stared at him so long I thought he might be having some kind of seizure. Finally he blew out a breath of air and spun around, this time knocking his chair over. He stomped out of the house, leaving the rest of us staring at the slammed front door.

Chapter 20

"Well, that was quite the bombshell," I said, breaking the silence.

Detective Shelton righted Adam's overturned chair and sat down in his own.

"Nice work, Dillon!" Aunt Abby congratulated her son, and patted him on the back. "He's quite the white hat, you know."

"White hat?" I said, frowning. "You mean he's a good guy, like in the movies?"

"Mo-om!" Dillon whined. "Don't say that! I'm not any kind of hat—white, black, or gray. That's a stereotype."

"Black hat? Gray hat?" I repeated, even more confused.

"It's better than calling you a hacker," Aunt Abby whispered to him, adding a final pat.

"Mom, a hacker isn't necessarily a criminal, you know." He shot a glance at Detective Shelton.

"Would you two please explain what you're talking about!" I demanded.

Dillon rolled his eyes, then took a deep breath and began speaking to us as if we were school children. "A black hat is just a media term that stands for hackers who break into security systems either to steal information or to insert malware. What they do is usually illegal."

"Always illegal," Detective Shelton quietly interjected.

Dillon avoided his gaze. "White hats break in to show companies that their systems are weak."

"Like you did at the university," Aunt Abby added.

Dillon glanced nervously at Shelton. "Hey, I paid for doing that, even though I wasn't doing anything wrong. I only used open sources—I didn't hack. Only UC Davis didn't see it that way because I didn't tell them ahead of time."

Detective Shelton shifted in his seat. We were in a gray—hat—area here and I felt the cop's discomfort.

"So, what's a gray hat, anyway?" I asked. "Someone who breaks in and can't decide to use their power for good or evil?"

"Ha-ha," Dillon said, not even close to laughing. "A gray hat is someone who may *technically* commit a computer crime, but he doesn't do it for personal gain. That's what I did when I broke into the campus computer. Since I didn't tell them ahead of time that I was going to do that, they accused me of wanting the information for my own use. But that wasn't true."

"But it's still illegal," the detective said, still eying Dillon.

"Technically," Dillon reiterated without looking at him.

"So the stuff that you dig up on the Internet, like what you found on Nathan Chapman, or whatever his name is," I said, "is that white, black, or gray?"

Dillon shrugged again. "Gray, if you want to call it that. What *I'm* trying to do is find out stuff to help Mom's friend who's been accused of a crime. That's why I'm checking out other people—to find out if they're hiding anything that might be suspect."

"They call that invasion of privacy," Detective Shelton interjected. "A misdemeanor or a felony, depending . . ."

Dillon groaned. "Not if I use public sources that are available to anyone who cares enough to dig around. If I use the Internet to find out stuff without authorization, then yeah, I guess I'm guilty of invasion of privacy. But like I keep telling you guys, I'm just trying to help Mom's friend by finding out the truth. I'm not disclosing the information to the public."

"He's right," Jake said, the attorney in him revealing itself. "Dillon's not using the information for publication, to offend, with malice, or put the person in a false light." I could just picture him in court, wearing a suit and tie and reciting all that legal lingo. I had a feeling the female jurists hung on his every word. "But they could still sue you."

"So sue me," Dillon countered. "Anyone can sue anybody, these days. You know that. But if it's the truth, they won't win." He shot a look at the detective.

"All of this is debatable," the detective said, "but that's not important at the moment."

"True," I added. "We've just learned that Nathan

Chapman wasn't who he claimed to be and in fact was half brother to Adam Bramley, who was covering for him."

"And now Nathan's dead," Aunt Abby said as she rose from the table. "Anyone want more pie or coffee?"

I smiled at her non sequitur. "None for me," I said, "but if there's more wine . . ."

She nodded and headed for the kitchen.

"So, what do we know?" I asked the others while we waited for Aunt Abby to return. "Did someone find out who Nathan really was and then killed him?"

"That seems unlikely," the detective said, "unless he threatened them and the killer murdered him to protect him—or her—self."

I tried coming in from another angle. "All right, then maybe he was murdered because he was planning to sell his property. Maybe his half brother, Adam, killed him when he heard about his brother's plans. After all, he was the one who had the most to lose if Nathan sold the farm. Adam wouldn't inherit it back, assuming he's in Nathan's will."

"But we still have the murderer of Roman Gold, aka Reuben Gottfried, to ID," Jake said.

Aunt Abby returned with a tray filled with two coffee cups, two glasses of wine, a cup of tea, and a Red Bull. She set the coffees in front of Detective Shelton's and her own place, then came around the table and handed Jake and me our wine, before giving Dillon the energy drink.

"You know," Aunt Abby said as she took her place at the table with her tea. "We've learned so much about all these people and yet Honey is still at the sheriff's office and we still don't know who killed those two poor men." She topped off her summary with a sip of the fragrant hot drink. Was that apple I detected?

I took a swallow of wine and let the cool liquid begin to work its magic on my tense muscles.

"Dillon," I said after licking my lips. "Would you put on your gray hat again and see if you can find out more about Red Cortland, Honey's friend? It seems odd that he disappeared around the time of Nathan's murder. And while you're at it, check out Crystal and Tiffany, see if they have any secrets that might embarrass them somehow."

Detective Shelton sighed. "I'm going to pretend I didn't hear that," he mumbled into his coffee.

Dillon picked up his laptop and soda and headed up the stairs without saying good night.

Aunt Abby yawned. "You two should get to bed," she said to Jake and me. "Wes and I will wait up for Honey. I'm sure she'll be home soon."

"I hope so," I said, but having my doubts. I rose with my wine in hand and turned to Jake. "You coming?"

"Do you mind if I wait to hear from Casey, my lawyer friend?" he said, remaining in his seat. "He should be at the station by now, so I should know something soon."

"Keep me posted," I said. But before I reached the stairs, I glimpsed car headlights through the front window and stopped. "Someone's here!"

"Honey!" Aunt Abby got up, rushed to the door, and opened it.

I joined her and peered around to see Sheriff O'Neil's squad car. He opened his car door, lighting up the inside, and stepped out. I strained to see if anyone else was in the car, but the sheriff closed his door, turned, and faced his anxious greeting party.

"Where's Honey?" Aunt Abby asked, her face fallen.

The sheriff shook his head slowly. "Sorry, folks. We're going to have to keep her awhile longer."

"That's ridiculous!" Aunt Abby peered up at him, confused. "Why? What about her lawyer?" She glanced at Jake.

"He's there, but we've had to formally charge her. She won't be going home until the judge sets bail on Monday."

"That's absolutely crazy!" Aunt Abby was nearly beside herself. "She didn't do anything!"

"I'm afraid that's not what the evidence says," Sheriff O'Neil said.

"What evidence?" Aunt Abby asked. "The apple corer? That apple stick? Anyone could have used those things to make her look guilty."

"Actually there's something else," the sheriff said.

"What is it?" Aunt Abby demanded. "A smoking gun?"

The sheriff shook his head at my aunt's sarcastic statement. "Remember the seeds we found in her pocket?"

"Yeah, so?" Aunt Abby said. "They were just a bunch of apple seeds. That doesn't make her a murderer."

Sheriff O'Neil sighed. "Forensics looked at the seeds we found in Nathan Chapman's mouth under a microscope, then did some testing. They matched the seeds in Honey's pocket." He looked at Aunt Abby and added, gravely, "Both seeds came from Honey's apple orchard."

"Well, I'm not leaving the inn until Honey is cleared and back here where she belongs," Aunt Abby said to Sheriff O'Neil after we'd settled back at the dining table and caught him up on Dillon's discovery. I had a feeling this was going to be a long night for all of us— but worse, of course, for Honey.

"You're barking up the wrong apple tree, Sheriff," Aunt Abby continued, fiddling with her tea bag as she spoke. "You need to take a closer look at Adam Bramley. We just figured out that he had the most to lose."

"How so?" the sheriff asked, glancing around at us.

"Isn't it obvious?" Aunt Abby said, her eyes flaring. Detective Shelton laid a hand on hers to calm her down. She took a deep breath and started again, counting out each point on her fingers.

"First, Adam could have killed Roman for trying to buy out his half brother. Second, he could have killed Nathan or Ethan or whatever his name is, because he wanted his land back and because he was flirting with Paula. And third, he has a violent temper. We all witnessed it tonight. I think he's your killer." She rested her case.

I knew she was jumping to conclusions, but her argument made some sense.

"Look, Abby, I understand your concern for your friend—Honey's my friend too—but we don't have enough evidence to arrest Adam Bramley. His finger-prints aren't on the weapons. He's not the one who had apple seeds in his pocket—"

"But he has no *alibi*," Aunt Abby said, interrupting him. "Like I said, take a closer look. My son did, and he found out all kinds of motives for murder."

"By the way, where is your son?" the sheriff asked, looking around. "I have some questions for him too. He seems to know a lot about all this. I'd like to know where he's getting his information."

"From the Internet," Aunt Abby said, almost defi-antly. "It's all there for anyone to find, even you, if you know how to look."

Detective Shelton shook his head. He knew there was no point in stifling my aunt.

Sheriff O'Neil frowned and started to respond, but this time I cut him off. We were going nowhere with all this. "I think we're forgetting about Paula Hayashi. She could have killed Roman to hurry up her promotion at Eden Corp. Or maybe that wasn't going to happen because Roman had something on her that would hurt her chances of making CEO. And remember, Roman was right across the hall from Paula, and she had easy access to his room. She could have made it look like Honey murdered him by grabbing the corer from her display case and using it to kill Roman."

"Still," the sheriff said, "you've got no proof. And why would she kill Nathan?"

That stopped me. Paula had been flirting with Nathan, it was true. But had he rebuked her and made her mad? Not if he was the player everyone said he was. And even if he had, that was hardly enough motive to kill him. She seemed to move in and out of relationships without a backward glance.

"We're going around in circles," Jake spoke up. He'd been quiet, like Detective Shelton, but then the two men tended only to speak when they had something to say, unlike my aunt and me. We just tossed out theories left and right.

"Well, to my mind, those circles all lead back to Honey," Sheriff O'Neil said. "As much as I hate to think of Honey killing those two men, I don't have any other viable suspects. I need solid evidence. And the evidence I have—the apple seeds, for instance—connects her to the crimes."

Jake's phone rang. He checked the ID, then took the call. We listened as he talked to the person on the other end.

"Hey, Casey, thanks for calling. Any news? . . . How much? . . . I'll check . . . Want to stay here at the inn tonight? . . . Okay, have a safe trip back. Thanks again, and let me know."

He was about to hang up when Aunt Abby whispered, "Ask him how Honey's doing."

"Casey, how's she holding up?" Jake listened, said something, then hung up.

"Well? How is she?" Aunt Abby said.

"He says she's all right, thanks to the sheriff," Jake said, glancing at Sheriff O'Neil.

Aunt Abby shook her head. "I doubt it, since this is all his fault."

Detective Shelton took Aunt Abby's arm. "Abby,

you know it's not his fault. He's just doing his job. This work is not always pleasant, but I was there with Murph, and believe me, he's doing all he can to make her comfortable during this ordeal."

"Like what? Spraying for bedbugs and giving her a horsehair blanket? Serving her croutons to go with her ration of tap water?"

"Aunt Abby—" I started to protest.

"No," Detective Shelton said patiently. He'd obviously handled upset citizens many times and knew how to deal with an indignant Aunt Abby. "Murph brought her pillows and blankets from his own home, ordered takeout from the local pizza parlor, and even served her some of Crystal's sparkling apple cider. And he lent her his iPad so she could stream a movie."

"Hmmmph," Aunt Abby grunted, crossing her arms. "Well, like I said, I'm not leaving here until I've done all I can to prove Honey's innocence and get her out of there." She rose from the table. "I'll see you all in the morning. Breakfast will be at seven. I want to get an early start on finding the murderer. Good night."

With that she turned and headed up the stairs. We all got up. Detective Shelton glanced at Jake and me, then shook Sheriff O'Neil's hand and told him he'd come by the office in the morning.

Sheriff O'Neil also bade us good night and, with hat in hand, left.

I locked the door after him, shut off the lights, and took Jake's proffered hand. I followed him upstairs to what I was sure would be a night of tossing, turning, and troubled sleep.

* * *

I awoke in the middle of the night, roused by sounds outside my door.

Footsteps, to be exact.

I could hear the old floorboards of the inn creaking with each step. I sat up and stared at the door. A light underneath flickered past.

Someone was out there!

I shook Jake, but he didn't budge. His soft snoring continued, uninterrupted. Figuring it was that last glass of wine that put him in such a deep sleep, I threw off the covers and tiptoed to the door. Checking to make sure the door was locked, I pressed my ear against it and listened for any sound coming from the other side.

The creaking footsteps faded away. The light I'd seen underneath the door was now gone.

I stood still, listening, then heard another creak, this one more distant.

It had come from the staircase.

"Jake!" I called softly, not wanting to alert the intruder, but Jake was out cold. And there was no way I was going into my aunt's room to wake Detective Shelton. Besides, I hated the thought of being one of those scared women who woke their sleeping mates every time they heard a sound.

Moving as slowly and quietly as I could, I turned the lock, praying it wouldn't make a loud click and alert the possible intruder. I got ready to open the door, figuring if I spotted someone, I'd scream and wake Jake and the rest of the house.

No one was there.

I glanced around for something to use as protection before heading out. My room lacked the antique tools that were displayed in the dining area, displaying only pictures of varietal apples that hung on the wall.

Think! I told myself. *Before the intruder gets away!*

I thought about all the stuff I had in the bathroom. My razor—what? Slit his wrists? My hair dryer? Heat him to death? My shampoo? Make his eyes water? Crap! Whatever happened to the days when we carried hat pins and used hair spray as Mace?

I spotted my cell phone lying on the dresser.

Yanking it from the charger, I tapped on the app selections, then typed in "police siren." Choosing from a dozen variations, I picked the free one and watched it load, which seemed to take forever. My spur-of-the-moment plan was to creep downstairs with my thumb ready to press the button for the siren as soon as I confronted the intruder. Not only would it scare him, but it would bring the others running.

As soon as the app was loaded, I gently twisted the doorknob, trying to keep it from making any sound. It was a trick I'd learned when I was a kid playing hide-and-seek. If I opened a door slowly, it tended to creak, but if I jerked it open fast, it didn't.

It worked—no sound.

Using the dim light from my cell phone, I headed down the hall to the stairs, walking along the floor as close to the wall as possible to prevent more creaking— another trick I'd learned as a kid while trying to hide. Step by step, I made my way down the stairs, keeping my thumb hovering over the siren app button and an eye for anything that moved.

I spotted a subdued light in the kitchen.

Whoever it was had to be in there!

I tiptoed down, ready to hit the police siren app at any second.

As I approached the kitchen, I realized the dim light was coming from the open refrigerator. Suddenly the intruder spun around.

He was holding something metallic and sharp in his hand.

"I've got a knife!" he yelled.

I jumped a foot, screamed, and reflexively hit the police siren. The shrill, pulsing noise filled the house. It was loud enough to wake the dead—or dead asleep.

Seconds later, Jake, Detective Shelton, and Aunt Abby were standing beside me.

The detective switched on the kitchen light, spotted the intruder, and pointed his gun at him. The man, wearing a black hoodie and what looked like pajama bottoms, lowered his weapon—a pie server.

"Dillon! What the hell?"

Chapter 21

"What?" Dillon stood with his mouth open. "I was hungry! Is that a crime?"

"Oh my God, you scared the crap out of me!" I stared at him in disbelief. "Slinking around in the middle of the night when there's a murderer on the loose. Are you crazy?"

"I wasn't slinking," he argued. "I was being quiet so I didn't wake anyone."

"Why are you awake at this hour, anyway?" I asked. "It's two a.m. You're usually comatose all night."

"Like I said, I was hungry." He gestured at the half-eaten apple pie on the counter with the pie slicer. "I was about to cut myself a piece when you came creeping around. Besides, I couldn't sleep."

"Why not, dear?" Aunt Abby came forward. "Are you all right? Do you need some hot milk?"

"No, Mom, I don't need hot milk. I haven't wanted

hot milk since I was five. I've been on the computer, digging around, trying to save your friend. I was going to wait until morning to tell you, but now that you're all up . . ." He glanced at each of us.

"What did you find?" I said, the little hairs on my neck tingling. "More of Adam's secrets? Nathan's? Roman's? Paula's?"

"Dude!" Dillon held up his hands, including the one that still held the pie server. "Calm down. Let me get my pie, and I'll tell you."

"I'll make coffee," Aunt Abby said, then added, "Decaf."

I shambled off to the dining room to wait for Dillon. The room seemed to have become our mystery-solving meeting place. When I noticed Jake and Detective Shelton weren't following me, I quickly realized why. No man could resist Aunt Abby's pies, not even at two in the morning. Finally the three guys entered the dining room, each one holding plates of warm apple pie.

Dillon put his plate and laptop on the far end of the table and sat down in his usual spot. Jake took the seat next to me. Detective Shelton settled on the other side of us, leaving an empty chair for Aunt Abby.

"So, what did you find out?" I asked before Dillon could take a mouthful. He ate a bite anyway before beginning.

"Okay, I looked up Red Cortland first, even though I don't think he's a killer. He doesn't seem the type."

"There is no 'type,'" Detective Shelton interjected.

Dillon ignored him. "But then I figured he had a lot to lose like the other farmers if Eden started eating up all the properties around here. He could have killed Roman to help keep the company away, so I checked him out."

"And . . . ?" I asked, growing impatient with the meandering way Dillon told a story.

"Dude, chill." He took a breath. "Okay, I found out his divorce from Crystal was pretty messy. I managed to get a hold of the court documents—they're open to the public," he added, shooting a glance at Detective Shelton, "and Crystal made all kinds of accusations, things like he walked out on her with no explanation, he rarely sees his daughter, yada yada."

"A contentious divorce," I summarized. "That's not uncommon. But what does that have to do with killing Roman or Nathan? It seemed like Nathan was one of Red's friends." I thought about the argument he and the other men had had with Honey that first night we'd arrived. Maybe they weren't such good friends after all.

"I'm not done yet," Dillon said, then helped himself to another mouthful of pie. Aunt Abby entered with a tray of coffees and passed them out to everyone, waitress-style. When all were served, she joined us.

I waited for Dillon to finish his latest bite. "So, anything else?"

"What did I miss?" Aunt Abby interrupted.

I sighed. "Nothing. Dillon found Red and Crystal's court papers and a few angry comments from Crystal, but there were no surprises there. I'm hoping he has more." I looked at him.

Dillon smiled. His eyes twinkled, just like his mom's when she was hiding something.

I leaned in. "Dillon?"

"Okay, well, I noticed something in the court report that made me curious."

"What was it?" Aunt Abby asked before sipping her coffee.

"There was a file marked 'sealed,'" Dillon said.

"Sealed? Did you get inside?" I asked.

Dillon shrugged. "Dude, I'm not a magician." He took another bite of pie.

"That's it? That's all you have to tell us?" I said. "You couldn't get into the sealed file?" I was tired, crabby, and completely exasperated at this point, and I just wanted to go to bed.

"Well, not yet, anyway," he said, his mouth still full. He swallowed, then added, "But I will." He stared down at his pie, not daring to look up at the detective.

After being pumped up with anticipation, I felt deflated by Dillon's lack of anything solid. He certainly was confident about his skills, but if he hadn't been able to break into the sealed file already, why did he think he could eventually?

I rose from the table. "I'm going back to bed. Thanks for trying, Dillon. Let me know if you find out anything else. But next time, wait until morning."

"No probs, Darce," Dillon said. "Just so you know—medical files aren't easy to access, but there may be a back door."

Out of the corner of my eye, I thought I saw Detective Shelton wince.

"Was the sealed file a medical file?" I asked Dillon.

Dillon nodded and finished the last bite of pie.

When he didn't volunteer more information, I asked, "What kind of medical file?"

"Won't know that until I break . . . er, get in."

"Whose file was it? Red's or Crystal's?"

"Red's."

I thought for a moment. Why would a medical file be important in a divorce case? And why was it sealed? True, medical information is confidential, but Dillon had had no trouble finding out the details of the divorce, so why the secrecy with this file?

"Now I see what kept you up all night," Aunt Abby said, patting his arm. "Trying to get more information for Honey's case. I'm sure you'll figure it out, dear. And we're all very grateful."

Detective Shelton shook his head and rose from the table, having finished his pie and coffee. "I just want to go on record: I heard nothing. I know nothing. And I don't want to know anything about any illegal activity. Good night, everyone."

"Hey, I haven't done anything illegal," Dillon called out, then added, "Yet," under his breath.

"I'll be right up, sweetie," Aunt Abby called to Detective Shelton as he headed for the stairs.

Jake rose, collected the pie plates, and took them into the kitchen while Aunt Abby gathered the empty coffee cups and followed him. Dillon remained at the table, punching keys and frowning at the results.

"You need to get some sleep," I said to him. "You've done enough for tonight. You can try again in the morning."

Dillon didn't appear to hear me. He continued clicking and frowning and clicking again, occasionally chewing on his nails between what I guessed were failed attempts. I knew what it was like to be driven. I felt the same way about this murder situation, and I was frustrated we hadn't come up with anything substantial to help Honey.

Tomorrow was Sunday, giving us only one more day to clear her name and find the killer before we had to return home and get back to our jobs at the Fort Mason food trucks. If Abby didn't show up at her usual spot, she could lose her place, and that meant she'd lose a considerable amount of business. Still, I knew she wouldn't leave until all this was settled. When it came to helping her friends, she was stubborn that way, much like her son.

And much like me. Apparently it was in our blood.

The thought of blood made me think of Red's sealed medical file. What was up with that?

I slept soundly for the first time since I'd arrived at the inn and awoke to find Jake missing from the bed. I checked the time—eight a.m.—got up, and looked for him in the bathroom, but when I found it empty, I figured he'd already showered, changed, and gone down to breakfast. I jumped in the shower, cleaned up in record time, then got ready to meet the others downstairs to see if there was any news.

As soon as I entered the dining room, I stopped. The hairs on the back of my neck stood up.

Dillon lay slumped over his laptop.

It wasn't until I noticed the rivulet of drool, not

blood, coming from his mouth that I let out a breath of air. Thank goodness. Maybe we didn't get along all that well. Maybe he dressed like a teenage boy and ate everything in the house and wore a rat on his shoulder just to bug me, but I really didn't want anything to happen to him. Besides, he made life interesting.

I glanced around, found a small pillow on one of the couches in the parlor, and brought it over to him. Gently, I lifted his head, moved the laptop away and substituted the pillow, then carefully laid his head back down. I looked at the computer screen to see if he'd left any clues to his late-night searches, but it had turned into his screen saver, an electronic maze filled with colorful chomping heads in continual movement. Retro Pac-Man.

I checked the kitchen, smelled coffee, and noticed the pot was half-full, but there was no sign of Aunt Abby, Jake, or anyone else. Pouring myself a cup, I headed for the parlor to look for Jake and spotted him through the sliding glass door that led to the garden. He was sitting in a white wicker chair on the stone patio, talking to Sheriff O'Neil and Detective Shelton.

I slid open the door and let myself out, closing it behind me so as not to wake Dillon.

"What are you guys doing out here?" I asked, helping myself to one of the empty wicker chairs that encircled a pond filled with lily pads. "Jake, why didn't you wake me?"

"You needed your sleep," Jake answered. "I didn't want to disturb you."

I looked at Detective Shelton. "Where's Aunt Abby?"

"She's gone to the station to see Honey," Sheriff

O'Neil answered instead. "I told her Honey needed a few things and your aunt offered to pick them up and take them to her."

I nodded, yawned, and sipped the coffee, hoping it would make me more alert after being up half the night. I was still feeling the hangover effects of the deep sleep I'd been in and wasn't quite ready to fully wake up.

"How *is* Honey?" I asked the sheriff.

"Bonita—Deputy Javier—said she had a good night," Sheriff O'Neil replied. "Red visited and they watched some cooking show on TV."

Wow, I thought. Too bad the city jails weren't more like the country jails.

The men were quiet for a few moments as they drank their coffees, but I sensed there was something unsaid going on between them. I glanced at each one, then frowned. "Has something happened?"

Before anyone could answer, Jake looked at something behind me.

I spun around to see what had caught his attention, then gasped at the disturbing visage before me.

"Dillon!"

Dillon stepped out through the sliding glass door looking as if he'd been run over by a tractor. His hair stuck out on one side, while the other side was smashed down to a matted mess. His right cheek bore the imprint of the keyboard he'd lain on when he fell asleep, and dried drool had left a slimy sheen on his chin. The two-day stubble only added to his frightening appearance. I was glad no children or animals were staying at the inn. They'd have been scared out of their wits.

"S'up?" he said, lumbering toward us like the undead. He dropped into another wicker chair and reached for my coffee that I'd set down on the small table next to me. Before I could grab it, he'd snatched it up and chugged it like water.

Sheriff O'Neil stared at him while Jake stifled a grin. Detective Shelton just shook his head, giving me a brief thought. What if the detective ended up marrying my aunt and Dillon became his stepson? Yikes.

And worse—would that make him my uncle Detective?

"Are you all right?" I asked Dillon after he finished my coffee. He sat back and leaned his head against the chair.

"Yeah," he said. "Didn't get much sleep. Tried to find out what was in that medical file."

The three men shared a look. I was sure something was going on between them.

"What's up with you three?" I asked.

After a moment of silence, Jake said, "The sheriff may have learned something about that file."

Dillon frowned. "You did?" he said, eyeing the sheriff.

I leaned in. "What did you find out?"

Sheriff O'Neil shrugged. "Nothing yet. After Wes told me about Red's medical file, I called a friend of mine—a nurse—and collected on a favor she owed me. She's going to check it out, let me know what's inside. I'm waiting for her call back." He patted his pocket, where I guessed he kept his cell phone.

"Good," I said, although I didn't hold out much hope

for finding an answer to the murders in a medical file. Still, the information might lead to something.

"However," the sheriff added, "it may not be admissible in court."

Dillon groaned. "Dude, I spent all night trying to get in there and all you had to do was make a phone call? And it *still* might not work?"

"Hey, Dillon," I said to him. "If it hadn't been for you, we wouldn't have known about the file."

"Well, don't get your hopes up," Sheriff O'Neil added. "It may be nothing, but I thought it was worth checking out."

Dillon laid his head back down and closed his eyes. "Bet you didn't find the e-mail Red sent to Nathan Chapman—or whatever the dude's name is."

"E-mail?" I repeated.

"What e-mail?" Sheriff O'Neil asked.

Dillon shrugged nonchalantly. "I printed them out. They should be in Honey's office."

Sheriff O'Neil got up and headed inside. A few minutes later he returned with a sheet of paper in his hand.

"Why didn't you tell me about this?" the sheriff said, standing over Dillon.

Dillon's eyes fluttered open. "Dude, I just did."

"Don't call me 'dude,'" Sheriff O'Neil said. He sat down, held up the paper, and read it aloud. "'Stay away from her or I swear I'll kill you.' That's from Red," the sheriff explained. "Then Nathan responded, 'Get off my back!' That's it. They're dated before the first murder."

The sheriff looked up at us. The detective, Jake, and I were stunned into silence.

Dillon lifted his head and said, "Sounds like Red had some kind of motive to kill Nathan."

"But Red loves Honey," Sheriff O'Neil said. "He'd never let her take the rap."

Detective Shelton frowned. "And it still doesn't give us a link to Roman's death."

"So, what do you think it means?" I asked, puzzling over the brief e-mail exchange. "Red says, 'Stay away from her.' Who's *her*? Tiffany? Honey? Paula?"

"I think we have to be careful about taking these messages out of context," Jake said. "We don't know what went on before or after this. And a lot of people say they're going to kill someone and don't mean it."

I knew, with his background as a lawyer, Jake was being cautious, but these e-mails sounded pretty incriminating. "What are you going to do, Sheriff?" I asked.

"Arrest him," Dillon answered for him. "Let Honey go and we can get the heck out of Dodge."

The sheriff's cell phone rang. He pulled it out of his pocket and answered with "Sheriff O'Neil." He listened, said, "Uh-huh," a couple of times, then thanked the caller and hung up.

"I probably shouldn't tell you this," Sheriff O'Neil said, sighing, "but with these murders, I have a feeling it's going to come out eventually."

"Was that the nurse? What did she say?" I asked, anxious for any news that might help free Honey, even something from a medical report.

"Yes, that was the nurse. It appears Red contracted an illness as a teenager, a viral disease called epidemic parotitis, to be exact."

"What's pertonitis?" Dillon asked.

"*Parotitis*," the sheriff corrected him, enunciating the medical term. "It's essentially mumps."

Dillon frowned. "What's mumps?"

"Years ago, it was a common childhood disease," Jake explained. "Very contagious, but not usually fatal. I had a court case once where a man wasn't vaccinated because his backward doctor didn't believe in vaccines, so my client sued him when he caught the disease and ended up with testicular edema."

"I know what that means—swollen testicles? Ouch," Dillon said, covering his crotch with his hands. "Sounds painful. How do you know when you have these mumps?"

"You get a fever, headache, lack of energy, dry mouth, sore face . . ." Jake listed off the symptoms.

Dillon felt his forehead, then ran his hand over his cheek. "My cheek is kind of sore, and my mouth is kind of dry, and my balls . . ."

"Dillon!" I nearly shouted. "You don't have it. Your mouth is dry from your mouth breathing, and your cheek is sore because you slept on your laptop, and we're not going to discuss your testicles. I'm sure your mom had you vaccinated for mumps, measles, chicken pox, all that stuff—just like my mom did."

Dillon placed his fingers on the sides of his neck, obviously convinced he was coming down with the mumps.

"So that's it? Red had mumps?" I summarized. "That really doesn't help us with a motive for murder."

"Actually," Sheriff O'Neil continued, "he caught something called mumps orchitis during puberty. . . ." The sheriff glanced at Jake and Detective Shelton. They both solemnly shook their heads.

"What's wrong?" I asked. "Is that bad?"

The sheriff took a deep breath. "Mumps during or after puberty can cause infertility."

That little tidbit of medical information quickly sank in.

"Oh my God. Red Cortland could be infertile. And that would mean Tiffany wouldn't be his biological daughter."

Chapter 22

"So what?" Aunt Abby said. She stood in the doorway, flushed from her visit to the sheriff's office or the cold weather outside. "Maybe Red and Crystal adopted her. Or maybe Crystal got artificially inseminated. Times have changed. It's not a big deal anymore, even though back then it was."

I pull up a chair for her. "How's Honey?"

Aunt Abby shrugged. "Okay, I guess, if you like jail." She shot the sheriff a look. "So, what's the big deal about Red being infertile?"

"Nothing," I said, "if he's always known he's infertile. But what if he didn't know back when they wanted to start a family?" I turned to Sheriff O'Neil. "When was the test done?"

"According to the file, Red didn't have the test until last year for new health insurance. They did a prostate exam and that's when he found out about his infertility."

"Last year?" Aunt Abby repeated. "Wasn't that about the time he left Crystal and got a divorce?"

"She's right," I agreed. "Crystal said Red just walked out on her and Tiffany one day about a year ago."

Jake nodded. "Come to think of it, Crystal acted like she didn't know why he left so suddenly."

We were silent for a moment. Some of the loose ends were beginning to come together.

"So if Red didn't know he was infertile until a year ago and he realized Tiffany wasn't his biological child, he could have been so angry he just up and walked out," I summarized. "After all, Crystal had to have been lying to him for all these years."

"Which brings up the question," Sheriff O'Neil said, "who is Tiffany's biological father?"

"Maybe someone knew the answer to that and was killed because of it," Aunt Abby suggested. "Like Roman or Nathan."

"I doubt Roman was around twenty years ago when this happened," Jake said. "But maybe you're right about Nathan. Maybe he found out who the father was and tried to blackmail Red."

"And Red killed him to keep him quiet," Aunt Abby added, her eyes wide. "If that's true, poor Honey!"

The sheriff shook his head. "I've known Red all my life and he just doesn't seem the rotten apple in this case. I think we're barking up the wrong tree."

Again with the fruit metaphors.

"There's still no connection between the two vics," Detective Shelton added, after sitting quietly for several minutes. "My gut says whoever killed Roman killed Nathan. Maybe Red killed them both for reasons that have nothing to do with his infertility. Like you said, Abby, these days the condition itself isn't that big a deal. There has to be more to it."

"Maybe if we find out who Tiffany's real father is, that would tell us something," I suggested.

"It won't be easy," Sheriff O'Neil said. "If Crystal had an affair, I doubt she's going to tell us about it, and if she was artificially inseminated, those records are sealed too, per the donor's wishes."

"Murph," Detective Shelton, said, "maybe talk to Red again now that you know about this and see what he has to say. Maybe he'll tell you something you just can't learn from a medical file."

The sheriff rose. "I'm on it. I'll stop by his farm and confront him, see if I can get him to tell me if he suspects anyone in particular who might be the father. And while I'm at it, I'll try to find out if anyone was blackmailing him about it. Although I think it's a long shot."

The sheriff headed out. I looked at Dillon, who'd lumbered into the dining room and retrieved his laptop while we were talking. He was busy keying away.

I leaned over to him. "Dillon, what are you doing?"

He didn't answer, just continued typing rapidly.

"Earth to Dillon?" I said.

"What?" he snapped.

"I said, what are you looking for?"

He held up one finger to indicate *"Wait a minute,"* then went back to typing. I shrugged him off and turned to Aunt Abby. "Any ideas about what to do next?"

"Not until we hear back from Sheriff O'Neil," Aunt Abby said. "But I suspect Red is the key to this. I know Honey loves him, but a man who can simply walk out on a family because he isn't the father of their child isn't someone I'd fully trust. Maybe one of his friends knows something more that could help—like Adam." Aunt Abby turned to Detective Shelton. "Feel like taking a ride, Wes?"

He caught her drift and nodded. "I suppose." He turned to Sheriff O'Neil. "All right with you, Murph?"

"Of course," the sheriff said.

"Good," Aunt Abby said, rising from her chair, "because I can't just wait around for something else to happen. Time is running out."

"Are you sure you'll be okay?" I asked my aunt. "He could be dangerous if you confront him."

She smiled at Wes. "I'm not worried."

"All right." I turned to Jake. "Then how about we go back to the festival grounds? Maybe some of the vendors will still be there packing up their stuff. And maybe one of them saw something that might help."

"Sounds like a plan," Jake said.

I had a thought. "Aunt Abby, Dillon, can we borrow your scooters?"

Before Dillon could say no, Aunt Abby answered for both of them. "Of course! Good idea. You can cover more ground that way. Besides, they're really fun!"

Jake, Aunt Abby, and I headed upstairs to gather a few things, leaving Dillon working on his laptop. Detective Shelton also remained behind to make some calls. While we were in our room, Jake phoned the attorney he'd sent to help Honey, then left a message when the call went unanswered. We met Aunt Abby and Detective Shelton downstairs before they headed off to visit Adam Bramley.

"Be careful!" I called after them, then felt like an idiot stating the obvious to the San Francisco homicide detective.

While Jake loaded the two scooters into his cream puff truck, I decided to check up on Dillon one last time to see if he'd found out anything more. I stood over his shoulder and tried to read his computer screen.

He turned around and gave me an annoyed look. "I hate when people do that," he said.

I stepped to the side. "Sorry. Find anything?"

"Working on it," he said.

"Like what? More about Roman? Or Nathan? Or Red?"

"Nope," he said.

"Then what?"

"Ever heard of Cryo-Baby?"

I made a face. "Sounds like a baby doll that cries real tears."

"It's a sperm bank."

I blinked. "You're hacking into the records of a sperm bank?"

"I'm not in yet, but I found the only one located in the Apple Valley area. It's called Cryo-Baby. It's where people go to donate sperm and receive infertility treatments."

I sat down next to him. "You're kidding! So, did you find out who Tiffany's father is?"

"Like I said, not yet. But I'm learning all kinds of

things. Do you know how much money a guy makes from donating sperm? Like a hundred bucks!"

I shook my head. "You're not thinking of donating, are you?"

"Why not? My sperms would make some real smart kids."

"It's sperm, not sperms, and I don't think you'd qualify."

"Would too. They give you a complete sperm analysis. I'd pass all that. And there's a whole section on physical appearance. With my awesome hair and eye color and height and weight, not to mention my IQ, I'd fall into the 'high demand' category."

"Yeah? What about your arrest record?"

Dillon shrugged. "A little glitch."

"So you think you can break in to the bank and find out who might have donated sperm twenty years ago, when Tiffany was conceived? Although it sounds like a needle in a haystack, even if you do get in."

"Maybe. Maybe not." Dillon was not one to give up easily when it came to hacking. He loved a challenge, the more impenetrable, the better. He seemed to take special pride in every new success. "We'll see."

"Darcy?" Jake stood at the front door, waiting for me. "You ready?"

I got up from the table, gave Dillon a pat on the shoulder, and followed Jake out to his truck.

We arrived at the festival grounds and unloaded the scooters. Jake showed me how to make mine go: "Step onto the floorboard, turn the knob on the right handlebar to accelerate, let it go to slow down, and grasp the handle on the left to stop. It's simple."

Yeah, right. I'd never ridden a scooter before, let alone an electric one. But if my sixty-something aunt could do it, then surely I could too. I released the kickstand, stepped on, got myself semibalanced, and turned the knob.

Whee! Off I went!

After practicing a few wide figure eights, I pulled up alongside Jake, then followed him down the path to where the vendor tents still stood. Most of the vendors had packed up, leaving behind empty tents, but a few still remained to finish up gathering their goods. I asked the Apple Spices guy and the Apple Butters lady if they knew anything about Nathan Chapman, aka Ethan Bramley, but they had little or no information to offer. Both said the man they knew as Nathan seemed to be a "nice guy," "very sociable," "popular with the ladies," and the woman went so far as to say he "seemed to prefer coeds to cougars."

We scootered over to see if Crystal and Tiffany were still around and found Crystal packing up bottles of wine while her frowning daughter wrapped glasses and put them in boxes.

Crystal looked up when we came to a stop in front of her open tent.

"Sorry, we're closed," she said when she saw us. Did she really think we were there to drink wine? At ten in the morning?

"I see that," I said, dismounting the scooter. I lowered the kickstand.

Jake's phone rang. He got off his scooter, tapped the kickstand, then stepped aside to take the call out of hearing distance.

Crystal seemed surprised when she looked up again and saw me still standing there.

"Can I help you?" she asked.

"Yes," I said. "I wanted to ask you about something."

"Well, make it quick. I need to get back to the winery and at least try to get some kind of sales numbers today. Now that the festival has come to an abrupt halt, I'm losing money every hour."

"Sorry to hear that," I said. "I wondered if you had heard anything more about Nathan's death."

Out of the corner of my eye, I saw Tiffany freeze at the sound of Nathan's name. She shot her mother a look I couldn't read.

Crystal seemed to ignore her daughter. Instead, she ran her fingers through her brassy blond hair, revealing an edge of gray tinged with red. *Time for a touch-up*, I thought.

"No—why would I? I'm not a cop; I'm a winemaker."

Tiffany fumbled a glass and it hit the soft ground. She quickly snatched it up and examined it, then tossed it in the trash.

"Tiff, you gotta be more careful," her mother said. "Those engraved glasses don't come cheap."

Tiffany stared at her mom, her eyes narrow slits. She spun around and left the tent by the back entrance.

Crystal sighed. "That girl. She'll be the death of me yet."

"She seems lovely," I said, slowly leading up to the bigger questions I was about to ask.

Crystal smiled. "Yeah, she got my looks, thank goodness. Red's not exactly George Clooney, with that wild red hair and freckles."

That was a little conceited. And harsh. Was Crystal trying to convince me that Red was her biological father?

"Odd that she didn't get his red hair," I said pointedly.

Crystal stopped packing and eyed me. "Recessive gene, I guess."

"Yes, I remember learning about red hair in my biology class. Doesn't it take two redheaded parents to make a redheaded child? In fact, it's a biological imperative, isn't it? But you're blond, so Tiffany only had a fifty-fifty chance of being a redhead."

Crystal patted her tousled hair self-consciously. "Yeah, the blond comes from my Norwegian heritage."

Or a bottle of Clairol to hide the fact that you're a redhead too, I thought. Time to get to the point.

"Crystal, I'm trying to find out what I can to help Honey get out of jail. Did your husband—ex-husband— did Red get along well with Nathan?"

Crystal frowned at my bluntness. "I have no idea. You'd have to ask Honey about that, now that he's taken up with her. Of course, it won't be easy, since she's in jail." She gave a nasty little laugh.

"Sheriff O'Neil said he heard Red and Nathan arguing one night at Honey's place." I decided not to mention Adam. "Any idea what they might have been talking about?"

Crystal's eyes narrowed. She seemed surprised to hear this. "No . . . Why? Are you suggesting—"

"I wasn't suggesting anything, just wondering. Honey is a dear friend of my aunt's, and Aunt Abby is sure Honey is innocent."

Crystal laughed again. "Honey is hardly innocent. The woman is a husband stealer, and now she's most likely a murderer. I'll bet she killed that guy from Eden Corporation who was staying at her inn because he wanted to take over her property. He probably set fire to the place, hoping to burn it down so she'd have nothing and would have to sell. I figure she must have found out."

"Then what about Nathan? Why kill him?"

"Probably because he found out the truth—that she murdered Roman." Crystal shrugged. "Listen, I don't know. It's none of my business. And I really have to pack up and get out of here."

I was getting nowhere. I thought for a moment, then remembered her argument with Nathan when she saw him with her daughter. "One more thing," I said, Columbo-style. "Did Nathan and Tiffany have some kind of relationship?"

Crystal's face colored and she frowned. "Heavens, no! Where did you get an idea like that? Sure, they were friends, but that's because Nathan was a friendly guy, and my Tiffany happens to be nice to everyone. Tiff would never really be interested in a man old enough to be her father. Now, if you want to know who Nathan Chapman was involved with, go ask that

Paula woman. They looked pretty hot and heavy the last time I saw them."

Was she telling the truth, I wondered, or just trying to distract me?

I spotted Jake still talking on his cell phone and headed over. He looked deep in conversation with someone on the other end, and figuring it was the lawyer he'd sent to help Honey, I was dying to hear what they were talking about. I waited, glancing around the area, and saw J.J., Dillon's friend, exiting the cordoned-off hay maze. He was looking at something on his cell phone. A picture? Of the crime scene? Kids seemed to take pictures of everything these days to post on the Internet. I wouldn't put it past him.

I called to him, but he didn't appear to hear me. I was about to head over to see if he might know something more when Willow appeared and he joined her. As soon as Jake ended his call, I asked, "Was that your lawyer friend?"

Jake shook his head. "That was Murph. He'd just finished talking to Red."

I raised my eyebrows. "Did he find out anything more?"

"He said he confronted Red about the infertility issue. Red confirmed that he didn't learn about being infertile until he went for the prostate exam last year. But he'd suspected Tiffany wasn't his when she didn't turn up with red hair. He knew Crystal colored her red hair blond, but didn't know it was red underneath. She'd been bleaching it since high school, saying she always hated red hair. When he had his prostate exam and found out the truth, he decided he couldn't live with Crystal anymore. He figured she'd been lying about other things, not just about Tiffany."

"Wow," I said, taking it all in.

"The sheriff said Red suspected Crystal might have had an affair," Jake continued, "but when he confronted her, she swore to him she'd had herself artificially inseminated. When Red asked who the father was, she said she didn't know—the records were sealed. He still doesn't know if she told the truth or not."

"How would he be able to find out?"

"I suppose he could go to the fertility clinic and get a court order to see if they have a record of the sperm that impregnated Crystal. Then get a DNA test. But even that would be difficult."

I wondered if Dillon had found anything more. Surely he'd call when—and if—he did.

Jake went on. "Crystal told Red she'd only lied because she knew how much he wanted children and didn't want to hurt his feelings. Sounds weak to me, but that's apparently what she told him. She knew Red had had the mumps when he was a kid and when she didn't get pregnant after a while, guessed maybe he was infertile. She told him she went to the sperm bank and got artificially inseminated and never told him the truth."

"But why would she do that?"

Jake shrugged. "Who knows? People get weird ideas all the time. Believe me. That's one of the reasons I decided not to get back into practicing law. Too many strange lawsuits."

"Does Tiffany know the truth?"

"Red said Crystal begged him not to tell her because it would be devastating for her to learn he wasn't her biological father. But he was so uncomfortable with the lie that he pretty much avoided seeing Tiffany after he left Crystal."

My cell phone chirped. Dillon was texting.

"S'up?" I answered.

I got in, Dillon texted.

I took in a breath. "Find out who Tiffany's real father is? Someone we know?" I glanced at Jake, my eyes wide with excitement.

Yep, Dillon texted back. Crystal's baby daddy is—was—good old Nathan Chapman.

Chapter 23

"I've got to talk to Crystal," I said. "I want to see her reaction when I tell her I know that Nathan is Tiffany's father."

"Are you sure that's a good idea, Darcy?" Jake asked. "What if Tiffany is there with her? You don't want her to find out like this, do you?"

That stopped me for a moment, but then I had an idea. "Jake, maybe you could distract Tiffany? That way I can confront Crystal without her overhearing or walking in on us."

"How am I supposed to do that?" Jake said, frowning. "I don't even know her."

I thought for another moment. "How about this? Tell her you're helping the sheriff and he asked you to check out the hay maze to see if anything was left behind as a clue. You don't know your way around in there like she does, so you need her help to guide you in and out."

Jake shrugged. "That could work," he conceded. "But you be careful. What if Crystal is the killer? If she thinks you're a threat, you could end up like Nathan and Roman."

"Not out here in front of the other vendors who are still packing up," I argued. I glanced at the little old lady in the Apple Sauced booth directly across from Crystal. I doubt she'd be able to come to my rescue, but there had to be others within hearing distance if I started screaming. "I'm pretty sure I'm safe. But you should be careful too. It could even be Tiffany who's behind all this."

Jake rolled his eyes. "That's a stretch, don't you think? She seems so timid."

"You never know," I said. "And we've seen her temper erupt."

The phone rang. I checked the caller ID—Aunt Abby.

"Aunt Abby? Are you all right?"

"Of course, Darcy," my aunt answered. "Wes is taking good care of me." I could almost see the adoring smile on her face.

"Did you learn anything from Adam Bramley?" I asked.

"Who was it said 'Everyone has secrets'?" she answered coyly. "Was it Shakespeare? Or am I thinking of Maroon Five?"

"I think everyone's said that at one time or another," I said. "Now, what did you find out?"

"Well, I noticed that Adam kept looking at Honey when he was over the other night. Before that Paula woman started flirting with him. I had a feeling there was something behind those looks, so I outright asked him. And guess what? I was right."

"You mean, Adam has feelings for Honey?" I asked, flabbergasted at the news.

"Apparently Adam and Honey went out after Honey's husband passed away. Adam even went so far as to ask her to marry him, suggesting that they merge their farms. But she refused. When he kept asking, she finally admitted she was in love with someone else, but he was already married. He later learned Honey was actually seeing this married guy in secret."

"A married man?" I took in a breath. "Do you think it was Red? Were they having an affair before he left Crystal?"

"That's my guess," Aunt Abby said.

"Did you find out if Adam has any connection to Roman or Nathan that would make him a suspect?"

"No," Aunt Abby answered. "He said he only met Roman for the first time that night when he stopped by the inn. And he said Roman never tried to buy his property from him."

"That's because he had Paula to do it," I offered.

"Poor guy," Aunt Abby said. "He's still bitter about how Paula led him on. He needs to let go of these women who aren't interested in him."

"I wonder if he was bitter after finding out Honey wouldn't marry him because she loved someone else— in fact, one of his good friends—Red."

"Oh, Darcy, do you really think he'd go to the trouble

of trying to frame Honey if he still had feelings for her? Wouldn't he go after Red instead?"

"I don't know," I said. "Maybe he wanted to hurt both of them. Remember, Honey and Red both were victims of fires. Maybe he set those fires to threaten them or destroy their farms." I paused for a moment, thinking. "But, then, why would he kill Nathan?"

"Wes looked up Adam's background before we got there to see if he had a police record," Aunt Abby said.

"And?"

"No record. But Sheriff O'Neil said Adam and Nathan got into a fight one night several months ago over a woman after closing down the local bar. They were both drunk. The sheriff locked them in the drunk tank overnight and let them go the next morning when they were sober. No charges were filed, but they were given warnings."

"Who was the woman?"

"The sheriff said neither of the guys could remember her name. They were pretty drunk. She was probably just some local gal."

"So at least it wasn't Honey," I summarized. "Great job, Aunt Abby. Thanks for the info."

"I wish I had more," Aunt Abby said, "but Adam clammed up after telling us that much. He's a sad man. I feel sorry for him. And with his half brother dead, he seems to be a mess." She sighed. "Did you learn anything on your end?"

I filled her in on Dillon's news. "I was just about to confront Crystal about Tiffany's paternity and watch her reaction. Maybe she'll reveal something more about Nathan that will help."

"All right," Aunt Abby said. "Wes and I are going to the jail to talk to Honey about Adam. Maybe she'll have something to add that Adam didn't choose to share."

I was going to say "Be careful" again, but knew it was just habit. Aunt Abby was going to visit her friend in jail, accompanied by a detective. What could go wrong?

With Aunt Abby, anything.

After I told Jake what my aunt had said, we headed over to Crystal's tent. She seemed to be nearly finished with her packing. Sealed boxes were piled around her, with only two remaining open. Tiffany stood behind her, looking at her cell phone.

Jake stepped up. "Hi, ladies," he said cheerily. "Sorry to bother you, but I'm an attorney and I'm trying to find out more about Nathan's murder to help the sheriff."

Good call, I thought, mentioning he was a lawyer but not specifying any details. And it sounded so official, I doubted Crystal would argue with his upcoming request.

Crystal studied Jake. Her face was creased with worry lines—or was that stress? Or annoyance?

"I don't see how we can help," Crystal said. "I've already told Murph everything I know, which is basically nothing. As soon as my daughter and I finish these last boxes, we're heading back to the winery, so if you'll excuse us . . ."

Jake turned to Crystal's daughter. "Tiffany, I wondered if you'd take me through the maze to where they found Nathan's body. You know the layout of the maze, and I'm sure I'd get lost going by myself. Could I just borrow you for a few minutes to show me the way?"

Tiffany looked at her mother. Crystal made a face, then shrugged. "Ten minutes," she said. "Then we're leaving, so make it fast."

Tiffany nodded, then tucked her cell phone into her jeans pocket and silently followed Jake toward the hay maze.

As soon as they were out of sight, I turned my attention to Crystal. I didn't know whether to lead up to my question or just blurt it out. I finally decided not to beat around the bush. "Crystal, I understand Tiffany isn't Red's biological child."

She reared back, looking at me as if I'd slapped her face. "What?" She glanced around to see if anyone had heard me. The only person nearby was the elderly woman across the way. "Of course she's Red's daughter! How dare you say something like that! That's how ugly rumors get started." She took a menacing step toward me.

I took a step back. "Listen, Crystal, I know you're very protective of your daughter. That's why I had Jake take her into the maze—so she wouldn't hear this. But I'm guessing she already knows her real father. And I'm going to do what I can to help clear Honey, and I think you're connected in some way."

"That bastard," Crystal mumbled, and then her eyes narrowed. "Did Red tell you this? He promised that if I didn't take every last penny from him—including the farm—he'd never breathe a word to anyone. It's bad enough Tiffany knows now, without the whole town finding out."

"No, Red didn't tell me."

Crystal stared at me curiously. "Then how did you find out? No one else knows. No one."

"I can't reveal my source," I said, pulling out the classic reporter line, "but I also know who Tiffany's real father is."

Crystal went pale. "You couldn't possibly . . ."

"It was Nathan Chapman."

Crystal's eyes teared up. She turned away, but I saw her wipe her eyes with the back of her hand.

I suddenly felt sorry for her—and a little guilty. This was the first time she'd shown any vulnerability.

"When did you find out Nathan was her real father?" I asked gently. I glanced around, worried Tiffany and Jake might be back before my conversation with Crystal was over, but there was no sign of them.

"Last year, by accident," Crystal said, sniffling. "I was at the local bar with a friend, and Nathan came in. He was drunk. He's always drunk. He started hitting on my friend, and I told him to cut it out. He got mad and began bragging about all the women he'd had—and even some he'd had and didn't even know it."

I frowned, puzzled.

Crystal shook her head. "Like I said, he was drunk, not making any sense. I asked him what he meant. He told me he used to be a regular at the Cryo-Baby clinic, donating his sperm twenty years, so he could 'spread his seed like Johnny Appleseed.' He actually said that."

"And you were a client at the clinic about that time."

She nodded. "How did you know?"

I ignored her question. "What did you do?"

"I freaked out, of course. I had this sudden horrible idea that his sperm might have been used to conceive Tiffany. After I thought about it, I was convinced. She had his hair color, his smile, his eyes. I went to the clinic and demanded to know the truth. It took some convincing—and the threat of a lawsuit—to get them to confirm it. Nathan was the father."

"Did Nathan tell Tiffany?"

Crystal nodded, tearing up again. "He started hanging around lately, paying special attention to her. I thought at first he was flirting with her, but then I suspected he wanted to be some kind of father figure all of a sudden. I went to see him, ordered him to stop trying to get involved in Tiffany's life. "

"And did he agree to stop?"

"Only after I threatened to tell everyone in town he was a fake, a liar, and a cheat—and that he used a sperm bank."

"So you knew the truth about him—that he wasn't related to Johnny Appleseed at all and his name really wasn't Nathan Chapman."

She nodded. A fresh stream of tears flowed down her cheeks. She pulled a tissue from her pocket and blotted her face. "I finally had a private investigator check him out. I needed the leverage. After I told him I knew about his past and his real identity, he promised he'd back off."

"Do you think he ever told Tiffany the truth?"

Crystal's eyes flashed. "I don't know. She's been

acting strange lately. Always angry at me. But I think the truth would destroy her. I want her to keep believing Red is her father."

I thought for a moment. Although Crystal might have had a reason to kill Nathan to protect her daughter, she didn't seem to have a reason to kill Roman. And if Tiffany knew Nathan was her father, and killed him to keep the secret, again, why kill Roman?

"What are you going to do now?" I asked Crystal as she gave a last sniff and stuffed the tissue back into her pocket.

"What do you mean?" Crystal said. "Nothing. Nathan is dead. Hopefully Tiffany doesn't know he was her biological father." She shrugged. "Life goes on."

"But what about the killer who may still be roaming Apple Valley?" I asked.

"Like I said before, I think they have the right person in jail. Look at all the evidence. But that's not for me to decide. That's Murph's job. Meanwhile, I'll keep my doors locked, just in case."

Chapter 24

Crystal looked over at the maze, then at her watch. "What's taking them so long?"

"Maybe Jake found something important," I offered.

She finished taping together the last box, leaving an extra bottle on the table.

"Might as well drink this apple cider, since it won't fit in the box," she said. "Would you like some?"

"Uh, sure," I said, figuring I'd stick around until Jake and Tiffany returned. I still had a few more questions I wanted to ask about Nathan that Crystal might be able to answer.

Crystal glanced around. "The glasses are all packed up. Would you mind getting us a couple of paper cups from Violet over there?" She pointed to the elderly woman across the way. "It looks like she hasn't packed everything away yet."

I nodded and headed for the Apple Sauced booth,

where the woman with a wrinkled, apple-doll face had been selling applesauce "in ten flavors!" according to her sign. As I approached, she was meticulously putting plastic spoons in a large box—one at a time. The paper cups she used to hold individual servings of her "sauce" were still sitting on her table. I glanced at the list of flavors—everything from apple strawberry, apple blueberry, and apple mango, to apple peach, apple cherry, and even apple chocolate. How had I missed that one?

"Hi, could I steal a couple of paper cups from you?" I asked her.

She leaned over and cupped her ear. "Pardon me?"

"I said, could I have a couple of your paper cups?"

"Of course," she said. "That's about all I have left."

"Sold out, eh?" I said a little louder. I took the proffered cups from her gnarled hand.

"That I did," she said as she continued to load plastic spoons into the box.

I thanked her and returned to Crystal, who stood watching me.

"Thanks," she said, taking them from me. She set them on the table.

"That's Violet Melvin," Crystal said as she opened the bottle of cider. She waved and smiled at the elderly lady, and I glanced back. Violet Melvin waved in reply. "She's a sweetheart," Crystal continued. "Each year she comes up with a new applesauce flavor. Did you get to try her latest—the chocolate one?"

I turned back to Crystal, who held out my filled cup. "No, is it good?"

She angled her head. "Different. Last year she sold peanut butter applesauce. Now, that was good."

Crystal slipped into silence as she recapped the apple cider. I sipped my tangy drink, wondering what was taking Jake so long. . . .

Moments later I felt a sudden rush of blood to my head, as if someone had poured sand over me. I blinked, trying to clear away the sensation. In a wave of dizziness, I swooned and caught myself on the table, using it to steady my suddenly tingling legs. I tried to set down the cup but managed to spill the rest of the cider all over the table.

"Oh, I'm so sorry!" I said. Although I was seeing double, I could tell the cider had spread all over her personalized Wise Apple Winery tablecloth.

Crystal looked up at me. "Are you all right?"

I looked down at the table, trying to focus, and noticed a blur of white in the cider spillage. I blinked again and the white blur became white specks.

With a sudden realization, I glanced up at Crystal.

"You look pale," she said, reaching out. "Can I get you something? Do you need to sit down?"

"You . . . you . . ." I tried to talk, but my tongue felt thick and numb.

"Here, let me help you," Crystal said, coming around the table.

"You put . . . something in my drink. . . ."

My thoughts were a jumbled mess, but my fight-or-flight instinct still managed to kick in. There was no way I could defend myself against Crystal in this condition, so flight won.

I backed away from her, looking for help. Violet Melvin had disappeared. I scanned the area for an escape route and spotted the scooter, but I didn't think I could drive the thing in my condition. Instead, I bolted, running as fast as my wobbly, unreliable legs could carry me.

"Stop!" I heard Crystal call.

I glanced back. Crystal stood on the scooter, her hand on the accelerator handle.

Uh-oh. She'd catch up with me fast on that thing.

I kept running, sensing she was right behind me but afraid to look. She would reach me in seconds if I didn't think of something—fast. I had to find a safe place. The vendor tents I passed were empty—or if they weren't I couldn't tell. Everything looked blurry to me.

I spotted the hay maze looming ahead. There was no way Crystal could follow me in there with the scooter. It was my only chance.

Plus, Jake was inside! If I could reach him, he'd be able to handle Crystal easily.

Unless she had some sort of weapon.

And would I be putting Jake in jeopardy if I managed to find him?

Just as I reached the entrance to the maze, I glanced back. Crystal was only a few feet behind me, close enough that I could make out the scowl on her face. Her expression told me everything.

I was going to be her third victim.

I ducked under the crime scene tape and dashed into the hay maze. She couldn't follow me if she stayed on the scooter. The turns were too sharp to maneuver easily. My mind felt foggy, but it was clear enough to know

I needed to keep moving if she decided to follow me on foot. Surely I could lose myself in here again—and keep away from Crystal—at least until I found Jake.

I had to reach him before Crystal did.

I thought about screaming Jake's name, but I knew Crystal would hear me and figure out where I was, so I kept speeding along, darting around corners, twisting and turning, as quietly and quickly as I could. I prayed I'd run into Jake before Crystal ran into me.

I'd been running around like a mouse in a maze for what seemed forever when I tripped over something. I landed facedown on the not-that-soft hay-covered path with a thud. "Oof." I grunted, then felt my chest tighten as the wind was knocked out of me.

I couldn't breathe!

Panicked, I struggled to get up, dizzy from running and the effects of the drug Crystal had put in my cider. I looked down and saw what had tripped me— a man's shoe.

Nathan's? No. I wasn't thinking clearly.

I looked up and realized the shoe had fallen from one of the many scarecrows set up on hay bales inside the maze. This one, towering over me atop a high bale, resembled the scarecrow from *The Wizard of Oz*. I picked up the shoe, thinking I might be able to use it as a weapon against Crystal if she found me, and was about to race on.

And then I smelled smoke.

This time there was no mistaking it. The smoke was coming from somewhere inside the maze. The distinct smell of burning hay proved it.

Oh no! Crystal had set the maze on fire!

But why would she do this now? To kill me, obviously. What about her daughter? Didn't she remember that Tiffany was in here too?

Then it dawned on me. Crystal wasn't worried about Tiffany—the young woman knew her way around the maze like the back of her hand. And no doubt Crystal did too. She'd probably been inside many times herself. But she knew I didn't have a clue how to get out. I only hoped Jake would be able to escape in time with Tiffany before the fire consumed the entire maze.

Meanwhile, he didn't even know I was in here.

I was trapped, with no sense of where to go. All of these bales of dry, bundled hay could go up like a match in minutes.

I started screaming, then stopped myself.

I had to think.

I looked up at the scarecrow overhead. He seemed to be mocking me from his high perch. I grabbed a hunk of straw, lifted my leg, and tried to get a foothold between two stacked bales. The bales wobbled as I pulled on them, but I had no choice. In spite of my shaking legs, I had to try to climb up.

The first chunk of hay slipped out from the bale and I fell back on the ground. Pushing myself up, I tried again, grasping a larger handful of hay as I secured my footing between two bales. The bales were tied with twine, giving me an extra handle to hold on to, but moments later the bale I'd grabbed came tumbling down, bringing me with it.

I needed another strategy. Instead of trying to climb

straight up like Spider-Man, I needed to use the bales as a staircase. I climbed up on the bale that had hit the ground, then pulled at another one that was over my head, rocking it back and forth until it finally gave and fell down. Like children's blocks, the bales began to form giant steps.

I climbed up the second one, then the third. I stood up slowly, still wobbly from the drug as well as the tenuously stacked bales of hay that could come tumbling down at any minute.

The smoke was intense by the time I reached the top and I could see billowing gray clouds overhead. There wasn't much time before the whole maze attraction went up in flames, with me inside.

I looked out over the top of the bales, trying to orient myself, but all I could see was smoke. Where was the exit?

Suddenly, through the haze, I spotted Jake. He stood outside—thank God—along with Tiffany, and was talking on his phone. No doubt he was calling the fire department, but I was sure they wouldn't arrive in time. The hay would be a pile of ash by the time they got here. And so would I.

I was about to wave and scream at him when the bale I stood on began trembling violently. I looked down to see Crystal. She was shaking the bottom bale. There was fire in her eyes.

On the ground lay what looked like pruning shears.

I crouched down to keep my balance. I had to do something. If she knocked me off this bale tower, she was sure to kill me with those shears.

I grabbed hold of one of the bales next to me and rocked it until it gave. It rolled off and landed next to Crystal.

Missed!

She looked startled, then began violently rocking the bale that held me. I reached for another nearby bale and managed to push it down. It landed on the other side of her.

Missed again!

The smoke was beginning to burn my eyes, but Crystal didn't seem to notice as she continued to shake my foundation.

With one last violent jerk from Crystal, my footing slipped. I lost my balance and came flying down, along with the two bales that were underneath me. One of them landed on Crystal, giving me a second to scramble backward—and grab the pruning shears. The smoke enveloped us, setting us coughing.

Just in time, I saw her come at me.

I opened the shears to defend myself.

One of the blades caught her in the side. She bent over and screamed in pain.

I recoiled in horror. I had just stabbed someone! Suddenly I hoped she wasn't mortally wounded. I didn't want to be responsible for someone's death, even someone who was trying to kill me. And at the moment, I realized Crystal was my only hope of getting out of this fiery maze. If she died, I probably would too.

I dropped the shears and tried to hoist her up. As blood gushed from her wound, I wrapped her arm around my shoulder.

"Crystal, we've got to get out of here. You have to show me the way!"

Holding her side, Crystal grunted, then nodded to the left.

"This way?" I asked, hoping she wasn't planning to kill us both by leading me astray.

She grunted again. I held her close and dragged her along, following her nods and grunts. The smoke was so thick I could hardly see. My eyes burned, my throat was raw, but at least the effects of the drug had dissipated. As the cover of smoke encroached, my only thought now was praying that Crystal could find the way out.

After an eternity of turns and twists, coughing constantly, I spotted the exit sign. "We're there!" I said, adrenaline giving me the strength to make it the last few feet.

I dragged her out and we both collapsed on the ground, choking and coughing.

I thought I heard sirens. . . . Then someone was calling my name. . . . Then a familiar face appeared. . . .

"Jake," I whispered.

Chapter 25

Jake rode with me to the hospital, that much I remember. An oxygen mask was cupped over my face and two paramedics hovered over me so I couldn't see him, but I felt his hand squeezing mine—and I'd know that soft yet strong hand anywhere. They wheeled me into the Mother Lode Hospital and into Emergency, where a doctor checked me out, bandaged my twisted ankle and sore foot, and let me recover in a private room for a couple of hours before releasing me.

Jake stayed with me the whole time while I mostly slept off the drug Crystal had given me. It turned out to be Rohypnol, the date-rape drug, but luckily I didn't have much in my system, thanks to my clumsy spill.

"How're we doing?" a cheery nurse said as he entered my room. My eyes fluttered open and I glanced at Jake, who sat up in his chair next to my bed. The nurse picked up my chart from the end of the bed. His name tag read Z. Valdez.

"Much better," I said, dying to get out of the hospital and spend the rest of my recovery time under the care of Aunt Abby at the inn.

Jake gave me a relieved smile and watched as the nurse checked my blood pressure, heart rate (a gizmo attached to my index finger), IV bag, and the monitors that beeped nearby.

"Yes, you're looking remarkably good," the nurse said, cranking the bed up a few inches, so I was in a forty-five-degree angle. "The doctor will be in in a few minutes to see you."

"Will I get to go home?" I asked, sitting up even farther.

"That's up to the doctor," he replied, "but I don't see why not." He returned my chart and headed out the door.

I sat back and let out a breath of air. "Thank goodness," I said. "I hate hospitals. I just want to go home— or at least back to the inn—and check on Aunt Abby and Honey. A bowl of Aunt Abby's chicken noodle soup will do more than anything they can give me here."

Jake laughed. "I'll see what I can do about whipping up a chicken noodle cream puff for you."

I grimaced at the thought. "Don't go to trouble. Just nothing with apples, please."

He laughed again. At that moment, the doctor entered the room.

"Hi, I'm Dr. Dietz," she said. "I hear you're feeling a lot better. You had a quite a scare, didn't you."

I nodded and sat up again. "I'm hoping I can be released."

"Well, let me examine you and see about that."

After doing a rudimentary exam, Dr. Dietz listened to my breathing. I was certain she heard smoke in my lungs, the way she was frowning, but apparently that was her "doctor" expression.

"Sounds clear," she said, pulling off her stethoscope. She signed my chart, then added, "As soon as the nurse removes your IV, you're good to go."

I was dressed in my filthy clothes in less than five minutes after the nurse pulled the plug.

Jake escorted me out of the room and down the hall toward the exit. Just as I reached the double sliding glass doors, I stopped.

"Wait," I said to Jake, and turned around.

"What? Did you forget something?"

I shook my head. "Crystal's here too, isn't she?"

Jake shrugged. "I guess so. Why?"

"I need to see her."

"What for? She tried to kill you. And a minute ago you couldn't wait to get out of this hospital."

"I know, but I need to ask her something." I headed for the information desk, manned by a couple of gray-haired women wearing pink and white candy-striper outfits. Poor things, stuck in those uniforms meant for young girls who delivered magazines and snacks.

"Hi," I said to both of them. They dropped their welcoming smiles and frowned at me.

"Are you all right?" the one with bright red lipstick asked.

"Do you need a doctor?" said the other one who wore a cross around her neck.

I must have looked as if I was coming, not going, but I shook my head. "No, I'm fine. Just a little scrape. I fell. . . . Uh, do you have a patient here named Crystal Cortland?"

I sensed Jake come up behind me.

The lipsticked volunteer typed the name into the computer, then squinted at the screen. "Yes, she's in room 302."

"Are you a relative?" the cross-bearing woman asked.

"Yes," I lied. "She's my . . . aunt."

Jake cleared his throat. I tried to elbow him quiet but missed.

"Take the elevator to the third floor, then follow the yellow line to room 302."

"Thanks," I said, then headed in the direction they'd both pointed. Jake caught up with me and pulled my arm.

"What are you doing?" he said. "She could still be dangerous."

"I doubt it," I said. "I'm sure she's heavily medicated after being stitched up for that stab wound. I need to find out if she's all right."

The elevator door opened and we stepped in. I pushed the number 3 and we waited in silence as the doors shut and the car began to rise. It stopped abruptly at the third floor and we headed out through the open doors. I spotted the yellow line and followed it to Crystal's room.

I paused before entering, took a deep breath, and asked Jake to wait outside for me.

"No way," he said, frowning.

"Please? I want to ask her some questions and I'm afraid she won't open up if you're there."

Jake shook his head, but he opened the door for me and I entered—alone.

"Crystal?" I whispered as I stepped into the room. The television was on and Crystal appeared to be watching a reality show on cooking. She looked over at me and clicked off the sound.

"What are you doing here?" she said, moving her hand to her side—the spot where I had stabbed her—as if to protect it.

I winced. I could see the thick, large bandage that covered most of her right side and wondered if she was in pain.

"I . . . wanted to come by and see how you're doing," I said gently, not wanting to upset her. I was afraid she might lunge for me and hurt herself, or call the nurse to get me kicked out of her room.

"You stabbed me!" she said. "How do you think I'm doing? I'm lucky to be alive."

I stepped in closer, fairly certain that with all the wires and tubes connected to her, she wouldn't be able to really retaliate, other than throw a bedpan at me.

"Yeah, I'm sorry about that. But you did try to kill me."

"Only because you stuck your nose in where it didn't belong. What do you want?"

"I want to know why you killed Roman and Nathan. Was it all to protect your daughter, to keep Nathan out of her life?"

She looked at the TV screen for a moment, then back at me. "I'd do anything for Tiffany," she said. Tears suddenly sprang to her eyes. She sniffed. "She's everything to me. And that man doesn't deserve to be called her father."

"I understand, considering how hard it was for you to have her in the first place, but he was her father. And why kill Roman? What did he do to deserve that?"

Crystal's tears ran down her blotchy face and she grabbed a nearby tissue to wipe them. "He was blackmailing me. With all his snooping around, he found out about Tiffany's paternity and threatened to tell her and everyone else if I didn't agree to sell my place to him and get others to do the same. He was an awful, awful man, and he didn't deserve to get away with his plan."

I nodded, mostly just to keep her talking. I didn't agree with her, but I felt she needed a little understanding and sympathy.

"I still don't understand why you killed Nathan, Tiffany's biological father. Would it have been so bad if they'd had a father-daughter relationship?"

"That sleazy, womanizing alcoholic? Can you imagine having someone like him in your life and having to call him 'father'? Red is her father. He's the one who raised her from birth. He's the one who deserves the title, even if he did leave us. I couldn't stand the thought of Nathan trying to take over that role. I didn't want to take any chances. I had to stop him—permanently."

"And you didn't think telling him to stop would be enough?"

"No! Once he found out the truth—that he was Tiff's real father—he wouldn't let go of the idea of playing daddy. It made me sick. When I saw him go into the maze, I was sure he was going to meet up with Tiffany again, try to win her over. So I followed him. When I found him—alone—we argued again. He threatened me, told me he didn't care if everyone in town knew the truth. He wanted to be in Tiff's life. I had no choice. I stabbed him."

Wow, I thought, marveling at her skewed logic.

"Then you planted those seeds to make it look like Honey killed him," I added.

She shrugged. "Honey stole my husband. She was going to get what she deserved too."

I wanted to argue that Honey hadn't stolen her husband, but there was no point. I wanted to know why Crystal had done what she'd done. The district attorney could have that argument with her later.

"Did you set those fires too?" I asked.

"I only set the fires to try to make it look like those GMO people would stop at nothing to get their properties. I never meant to hurt anyone. Not then, at least."

"Well, I hope you get better soon," I said, sighing. "I better go—"

"Wait!" She tried to sit up, then held her side and lay back down. "Have you heard anything about Tiffany? Is she okay? She hasn't been by to see me."

"I'm sure she's fine. She's probably with her dad—Red. He's the only family she's got right now."

Tears flowed from Crystal's eyes again as my words hit home. I couldn't help feeling sorry for the woman, even after what she'd done. She'd been driven to the brink by pressures from the GMO company, the threat of exposing her daughter's parentage, and the loss of her husband to another woman. She just didn't realize the lies, the secrets, the tentative house of cards she'd built had to come tumbling down sometime.

"Good-bye, Crystal," I said, heading for the door.

"Please," she called out. "Tell Tiffany I love her. I did it all for her."

I nodded and left the room, eager to get back to Jake, Aunt Abby, and the comfort of some chicken noodle soup.

Chapter 26

Once again we found ourselves gathered at the inn—Aunt Abby, Detective Shelton, Jake, Dillon, and me. I'd filled in Jake on the ride back to the inn and was eager to find out if Honey had been released.

After hugs and brief explanations, I cleaned up, then joined the others at Honey's dining table. Aunt Abby had whipped up more comfort food for lunch—chicken noodle soup, fresh garden salad with ranch dressing, and slices of sourdough bread. There wasn't an apple—a real apple—in sight. Everyone had pretty much had their fill of the sinful fruit.

"This chicken noodle soup is . . ." I started to say "to die for," then changed it to: "really, really good! Thanks, Aunt Abby."

The others nodded, obviously enjoying Aunt Abby's authentic home cooking.

"I thought you might need some when you got back from the hospital," she said proudly. "I was worried about you. I'm glad you weren't the one who got stabbed."

I winced at the memory. "Any news about Honey's release?" I asked, then looked at Dillon, who sat at the table with his laptop open in front of him as he typed between bites of soup and salad.

"What are you working on?" I asked. "Now that Crystal's in custody for the murders of Roman/Reuben Gottfried and Nathan/Ethan Bramley, are there any other loose ends to tie up? Like what those e-mails between Red and Nathan meant?"

"That's obvious," Dillon said. "Red was threatening Nathan to keep away from his biological daughter, and Nathan was going to do as he pleased."

"I suppose so," I said. "Any idea what Honey and those guys were arguing about that night? I don't think you'll find that on your computer."

"Easy," he said smugly. "The GMOs. Roman was trying to get everyone to sell their farms. Honey didn't want any part of that."

"Do you really think Nathan was going to sell his farm?" Aunt Abby asked.

"If the deed was in his name, he could have. I get the feeling Nathan was all about Nathan, no matter what."

I was impressed. Dillon was proving to be quite insightful, even without his computer.

"Then what are you working on?" I asked, indicating the laptop in front of him. Before he could answer, the front door to the inn opened, and we all turned to see who it was.

"Sheriff O'Neil!" Aunt Abby said, putting down her soupspoon. "We've been waiting to hear from you." She rose from the table and rushed over to him. I hoped he had word of Honey.

He quickly stepped aside, revealing a very tired-looking but grinning innkeeper behind him.

"Honey!" Aunt Abby threw her arms around her friend, welcoming her back to her inn. "Everybody, Honey's home!" she announced unnecessarily to the rest of us.

Aunt Abby took Honey's hand and brought her over to the table, where we greeted her with hugs and smiles. No one seemed to notice a third person enter the room except me. It was Red.

Aunt Abby found seats for Honey and the sheriff, then spotted Red and added another chair. Then she rushed off to the kitchen to get the newcomers some food.

As soon as the "Welcome home!" greetings ended, I turned to Sheriff O'Neil and told him about my visit with Crystal at the hospital. "Any word on what's going to happen to her?" I still felt bad stabbing her with the pruning shears and was relieved to have found her bandaged and on the mend, but I reminded myself once again I had only done it in self-defense.

"She'll be at the hospital for a few days, under the watchful eye of my deputies, until she's released. Doc said the wound wasn't that deep and missed all the vital organs, but she'll never be able to dance the

Nutcracker again." I smiled at his attempt at humor, but mostly felt relief that I hadn't killed her. With all that blood, I had imagined the worst, and I shivered at the thought.

"Don't worry," the sheriff said. "She'll be in fine shape for the jail cell we have waiting for her, although it won't be as plush as Honey's home away from home." He winked at her. "Then it's up to the DA."

"Did she really kill Roman and Nathan?" Aunt Abby asked, returning with a tray of soup, salad, and bread. "Did she confess? Did you throw the book at her?"

The sheriff smiled indulgently at Aunt Abby's TV dialogue. "As a matter of fact, the paramedics gave her a narcotic for the pain, and she started rambling like she'd taken old-fashioned truth serum. She blabbered on and on that Roman was blackmailing her about Tiffany's paternity so she'd sell her farm—they wanted her land—and to help influence other growers to sell their farms, not to mention the fact that Nathan was going to tell Tiffany the truth, which he did. I recorded everything on my cell phone. I plan to play it back for her when she's off the meds. Her reaction should be interesting."

That was why Tiffany had looked so stunned when she came out of the hay maze, followed by Nathan, I thought. He probably told her the truth at that time. And it must have been a shock.

I nodded. "That was pretty much the same thing she'd told me, Sheriff. She must have still been on that pain medication when I talked to her. Poor Tiffany."

I noticed Honey had moved her hand over Red's at

the mention of Tiffany's name. I wondered what he thought about everything that had happened. He seemed to read my mind.

"This is all my fault," he said, glancing at Honey. "If I hadn't been so angry about all of Crystal's lies, maybe I would have seen . . ." He stopped and shook his head.

Honey squeezed his hand. "Red, you didn't do anything wrong. It was a shock for you, learning Tiffany wasn't your biological daughter, and you reacted like any human being would after realizing you'd been lied to all those years. But Tiffany *is* your daughter. You helped raise her. And there's still time. . . ."

Red nodded. "I know. I plan to make it up to her. I'll begin by telling her my side of the story. Then hopefully we can start over. Especially now that her mother will probably go to prison for murder, Tiffany's going to need me."

Everyone was quiet for a few moments, finishing up their lunches as they digested everything that had happened. I was happy to hear that Red was going to repair his relationship with his daughter—biological or not—and that Honey stood beside him. These two really did love each other.

"I have one more question," I said. "How did Roman find out all that information?"

Dillon finally broke the silence. "That's what I've been doing on the computer. I found out a little more about Roman Gold, aka Reuben Gottfried."

"Let's hear it," Jake said.

"Dude, Roman had a file called Applehead on his home computer, so I checked it out." He glanced at the detective and sheriff before continuing. The two law-men looked at each other and shook their heads. "Any-way, I recognized some of the names listed—Nathan Chapman, Adam Bramley, Crystal Cortland—even you, Honey, and Red."

Honey's eyes went wide. "What was in there?"

"Lots of stuff—birth date, address, phone number, stuff like that. There were a bunch of random details about each person, like Nathan's real name and his police record, Adam's run-in with Nathan at the bar, Red's hidden connection to his brother, Nathan. The guy also knew that Nathan was Tiffany's biological father. He probably *was* blackmailing Crystal, just like she said."

"How did he find out all this information about us?" Red asked.

Dillon shrugged. "He probably hired a hacker. There are a lot of them out there and they can find out just about anything for the right price—even if it's the wrong thing to do."

Aunt Abby smiled at Dillon. "That's a black hat, right, Dillon?" she said, then announced to the room, "Dillon is a white hat."

"Mo-om," Dillon groaned.

"So the rest of that stuff Crystal said was probably true too," Red said. "But can it be used against her?"

Jake nodded. "Spontaneous utterances are admis-sible in court," he said, going into lawyer mode. "You don't have to be Mirandized just because you're under arrest. That's only required if you're being questioned while under arrest. But if you keep talking, anything you say can then be used against you."

It was nice having "lawyer guy" around to clarify things, although I preferred "cream puff guy." Speaking of cream puffs, I was beginning to have withdrawal symptoms from Jake's creations. The apple-free ones, anyway.

Detective Shelton spoke up. "I think Dillon's right. Roman was probably blackmailing Crystal to get her to influence others to sell their farms to Eden Corporation. And he was doing the same to Nathan. Meanwhile, he had Paula go to work on Adam."

"Did she set the fires?" Honey asked.

"We don't know yet," Sheriff O'Neil answered, "but we have a unit searching her home. I'm guessing we'll find some evidence that connects her."

"Actually," I spoke up, "she pretty much admitted she did that too. She wanted it to look like the GMO company did it as a threat to the farmers so they'd sell."

"Why did she pick on Red and me?" Honey asked.

"Maybe because she knew about your affair with Red before he left Crystal to be with you," Dillon blurted. "That way she could kill two birds with one stone."

Awk-ward.

Honey glanced at Red. I saw him grip her hand tighter.

After a moment, he sighed. "Listen, it's true that we met once in a while—for coffee, or lunch, or a walk through the orchards. We were both lonely and she was a longtime friend. But it was never what you think. We only talked, nothing more. And we waited."

He looked over at Honey. She smiled at him.

"Crystal must have thought otherwise," Sheriff O'Neil said. "She was probably still in love with you, Red."

"Okay, I can understand why she set fire to my place and then Red's, but what about the fire at her festival tent?" Honey asked.

"I figure she did that to remove suspicion from herself," the sheriff explained. "I get the feeling her plans kept changing when things didn't work out the way she hoped, and she kept coming up with new ideas."

"Then after the fires at my place and Red's, she killed Roman," Honey added. It was as if a light had gone off in her head as she spoke. "So . . . she made it look like I did it by using my antique apple corer. She could easily have come into the inn and stabbed Roman with it. I should have been more careful with the keys and locking the front door, but I had no idea anyone would ever do something like that, let alone someone I knew."

"She was a very bitter, desperate woman," Red said. "All throughout our marriage she lied about things—where she'd been, what she was doing, where she was going. But I let it slide, for Tiffany's sake. When I found out the truth—that Tiffany wasn't mine and that she'd gone behind my back to get pregnant—I couldn't take it anymore."

"In her defense, Crystal didn't want you to know you might be infertile," Sheriff O'Neil added. "She did love you and she wanted to protect you—at least back then. She just didn't think it through."

The sheriff rose and patted his gut. "Thank you, Miss Abby, for the fine lunch."

Honey and Red got up. Honey hugged Sheriff O'Neil and thanked him.

"For what?" he said. "I put you in jail. These folks here were the ones who got you out."

"Well, thank you for the kind accommodations at the Apple Valley Police Inn," Honey said. "You made my stay more comfortable than I expected. I'll give you five stars on Yelp."

Everyone laughed. I admired Honey's graciousness after being in jail for nearly three days. As soon as the sheriff was gone, Aunt Abby announced it was time to get back to San Francisco and her food truck business.

"I miss my Basil," she said. "This is the longest we've ever been apart."

"The dog is probably having a ball at that overpriced doggy spa," Dillon said, closing his laptop. "I wouldn't mind staying there myself next time." He stood.

Aunt Abby turned to her longtime friend. "Thank you, Honey, for a . . . most interesting weekend."

Honey hugged my aunt tightly. She had tears in her eyes when she finally released her. "Abigail, I owe you everything," Honey said. "Your visit—and that of your family—is on the house."

Aunt Abby tried to protest, but Honey wouldn't hear of it. "If you ever get tired of cooking in that bus of yours, you can come cook for me at the Enchanted Apple Inn."

Aunt Abby smiled and took Detective Shelton's hand. "Oh, I could never leave the city and my man."

Did I see a flush of red under Detective Shelton's

mocha-colored skin? I'd swear in a court of law that the detective blushed.

"Jake and I have to go too," I said, giving Honey a hug. "Thank you so much for everything. You have a lovely inn."

"Thank you," Honey said, "for helping to find the real killer and ridding our valley of that apple pest. And I'm so sorry about everything that happened. I heard you almost died in that burning hay maze. How awful. I would never have forgiven myself if anything had happened to any of you."

"Well, I won't be going into any more mazes for a while, that's for sure," I said. "At least, not without a guide, some bread crumbs, an old-fashioned compass, a flashlight, and a pair of stilts so I can see over the tops of those hay bales. It's creepy in there."

"I don't think you'll have to worry about that particular maze," Jake said, reminding me it had burned to the ground. I shivered at the thought of how close I'd come to being turned into a crisp.

We all said our good-byes and headed for our trucks and cars. I wondered whether Willow had returned to the city or had decided to hang around J.J. awhile longer. I had a feeling Dillon had a crush on Willow too and probably didn't like the idea of his friend getting together with her, but until he stepped up and let her know how he felt, nothing was going to happen for him in the romance department.

I talked him into driving the cream puff truck home so Jake could ride with me in my car. Detective Shelton got his first taste of driving Aunt Abby's bus.

"Sorry about your birthday dinner," I said as Jake drove us past the last few apple farms along scenic Highway 49.

"No worries," Jake said, patting my leg. "I don't think I can eat for a week. And especially nothing with apples. I'm appled out."

"Well, I'll make it up to you," I said. "Are you free for dinner tonight?"

He raised an eyebrow. "What did you have in mind?"

"A home-cooked meal in my cozy Airstream bed-and-breakfast inn."

"You? Cook? Are you sure you don't want to get takeout?"

"Yes, I'm sure. We'll have a romantic birthday dinner by candlelight. I'll take care of everything."

Jake shot me a doubtful look. "All right, if you're sure."

"Yep. I've got this." I switched on a station that played music from my aunt's era and settled back in my seat for the two-hour drive. If I thawed the Costco lasagna I had tucked away in the freezer and baked it in my own oven, that counted as home-cooked, right?

"Well, then," Jake said, "I'll be dessert."

"You mean 'bring dessert,' don't you?"

He smiled. I knew exactly what he meant.

Recipes from
Death of a Bad Apple

Aunt Abby's Salted Caramel-Apple Tarts

Help yourself to a bite of Aunt Abby's Salted Caramel-Apple Tarts!

Ingredients

1½ cups plus 1 tablespoon all-purpose flour
Dash of salt
1½ sticks (6 ounces) unsalted butter, cut into ½-inch
    pieces, plus 2 tablespoons melted
⅓ cup ice water
3½ tablespoons sugar
4 large golden delicious apples—peeled, cored, and
    cut into ¼-inch-thick slices
1 cup caramel sauce
3 tablespoons sea salt

Directions

1. Combine 1½ cups of flour with salt.

2. Add butter and mix with flour in blender and whirl until contents form small balls.

3. Add ice water and blend until moistened, about five seconds.

4. Place dough on lightly floured work surface and knead two or three times.

5. Pat dough into a disk, then roll out to 16-inch round, about ¼ inch thick.

6. Line baking sheet with parchment paper.

7. Place dough on baking sheet.

8. In small bowl, combine 2 tablespoons of the sugar with remaining 1 tablespoon of flour and sprinkle over dough.

9. Place apple slices on top in overlapping concentric circles to within 3 inches of edge.

10. Fold dough over apples.

11. Brush apples with the melted butter and sprinkle with remaining 1½ tablespoons of sugar.

12. Refrigerate unbaked tart until slightly chilled, about ten minutes.

13. Preheat oven to 400°. Bake tart in center of oven for one hour or until apples are tender and golden and crust is deep golden and cooked through.

14. Brush with melted caramel sauce; lightly salt with sea salt.

15. Slide parchment onto a wire rack and let tart cool slightly before serving.

SERVES 6

Jake's Caramel-Apple Dream Puffs

Turn ordinary cream puffs into Caramel-Apple Dream Puffs!

Ingredients for Dough

1 cup water
⅓ cup butter
⅓ teaspoon salt
1 cup flour
4 eggs (beaten)

Ingredients for Apple Cream Filling

8-ounce container whipped cream (frozen)
½ cup powdered sugar
1 teaspoon vanilla extract
½ cup apple butter

Caramel Drizzle

1 cup caramel sauce

Directions for Puffs

1. Preheat oven to 375°.

2. Bring water, salt, and butter to boil in small saucepan.

3. Stir in flour until dough forms a ball in middle of saucepan.

4. Remove from heat and add eggs. Whisk until smooth.

5. Grease two mini muffin pans.

6. Scoop dough by the tablespoon into mini muffin pans.

7. Bake for twenty minutes.

8. Remove from heat and cool.

Directions for Cream Filling

1. Mix all cream ingredients together until smooth.

2. Fill piping bag with filling.

3. Poke hole in side of cooled puffs and fill with cream mixture.

Directions for Caramel

1. Heat caramel in microwave.

2. Remove and drizzle over tops of cream puffs.

MAKES 6–8

The Coffee Witch's
Caramel-Apple Cinnamon Latte

Now wash it all down with a cup of Willow's Caramel Concoction

Ingredients

½ ounce apple syrup
¼ ounce caramel syrup
¼ ounce cinnamon syrup
1–2 shots espresso
1 cup milk

Directions

1. Pour syrups into coffee mug.

2. Add espresso.

3. Fill with steamed milk.

SERVES 1

Party Planning Tip #1:

No matter how crazy the gig, the client is always right.
    And no matter how crazy the client, the event planner is liable.

Through the thick morning veil of San Francisco fog, all I could make out from the ferryboat deck was the eerie silhouette of an island. It loomed like a giant corpse floating in the bay, its form eaten away by the relentless waves.

I shivered in the penetrating cold as the wind off the Pacific whipped through my purple and gold San Francisco State University hoodie and my black jeans. Even the venti latte, my antidote for my ADHD—attention deficit/hyperactivity disorder—couldn't keep this California native warm.

Slowly, like a desert mirage, the apparition began to take shape.

Alcatraz.

I felt goose bumps break out as I thought about the former home of organized crime boss Al "Scarface" Capone, "Creepy" Karpis, "Machine Gun" Kelly, and Robert "Bird-man" Stroud. The island exuded a mystique that thrilled tourists and frightened schoolchildren. No wonder this notorious maximum-security prison was the most popular attraction in Northern California. Although no longer home to the most incorrigible criminals, it still housed plenty of legendary ghosts.

Tonight the inhospitable island would play host to the party of the century: San Francisco mayor Davin Green's "surprise" wedding to his socialite fiancée, Ikea Takeda. I held up the wedding invitation I'd created for the event and scanned it.

WANTED!

A WARRANT has been issued REQUIRING
your APPEARANCE

At the Capture and "SURPRISE" Wedlock of

MAYOR DAVIN GREEN

to

MS. IKEA TAKEDA

WITNESSES Will Be Remanded into
Custody on: OCTOBER 1

CONFINED at: Alcatraz Island

DETAINED from: 8 p.m. until Midnight

ADDITIONAL REMARKS: Come As Your
Favorite Criminal or Crime Solver

$200 Tax Deductible Donation will go to
the Alzheimer's Association

~ REWARD ~

Seafood Buffet catered by Rocco
Ghirenghelli, KBAY-TV's "Bay City Chef"

~ CAUTION! ~

Anyone caught warning the alleged Bride-
to-Be will receive a mandatory
20-years-to-life of public service.

For information concerning this docket,
contact:

PRESLEY PARKER—"KILLER PARTIES"—
415-BALLOON

It would be the biggest event since Caruso sang at
the Met.

Or the biggest disaster since the 1906 earthquake.

And I, Presley Parker, was the lucky event coordinator.

This wedding is going to be the death of me, I thought,
balancing my latte on the boat's guardrail. I shredded
the biodegradable invitation into confetti and ceremoni-
ously sprinkled it like cremated ashes into the San Francisco Bay. I only hoped it wasn't a symbolic gesture.

The sudden blast of a warning alarm startled me,
sending another chill over my already goose-pimpled
flesh. I grabbed the ferry railing, nearly spilling my

precariously balanced drink, and pulled my hood up over my bobbed auburn hair.

Prison breakout?

Nothing so exciting. Just the familiar but disquieting sound of the ubiquitous foghorn. As a seagull swooped down, I lost my grip on my latte and watched my life's blood tumble overboard. I cursed into the deafening sound.

Great. Now I'd probably be arrested for polluting the bay.

Even worse, there was no Starbucks on Alcatraz.

At least, not yet.

"Land-ho, Presley!" Delicia Jackson, my thirtysome-thing part-time assistant, called too cheerily between foghorn blasts. She appeared behind me in her quilted green parka, which made her look as if she'd been entombed in a giant bunch of grapes. Cupping her hand over her forehead like a pirate at sea, she squinted into the fog, then pointed to our destination.

"Good thing too," Delicia said, shivering in spite of the puffy jacket that nearly reached to her matching green Crocs. Her toes had to be icicles; mine were cold even in my black Uggs. "I'm getting seasick."

"How are the others doing?" I asked, referring to my minimal staff.

"They're inside. Too cold out here for those light-weights."

When she wasn't helping me host fund-raising events and kids' birthday parties for extra cash, Delicia was a part-time actress and full-time drama queen. A mixture of many cultures, she was stunningly beautiful,

with smooth mocha skin, long black hair, and discon-
certingly blue eyes. Girls loved her as characters Belle
and Ariel when she performed at my young clients' birthday events.

"Only three hours till showtime!" Delicia said, tapping her princess watch with a sparkly nail. Being an
actress, she spoke mostly in exclamation marks.

"What was I thinking?" I shouted over the rumble of
the boat engine, the squawk of the seagulls, and the relentless foghorn blasts. "This is going to be a disaster."

"It's going to be off the hook!" she shouted back.
"Perfect for your extreme career makeover!"

Extreme indeed. How did a university instructor
like me end up as an event planner? I shook my head,
recalling the day six months before—my thirtieth birthday, to be exact—when I'd received the notice in my
campus mailbox at San Francisco State University:

"Due to budget cuts . . ."

I hadn't bothered to read the rest. I knew what it
said. All of us part-timers had seen it coming. My department, psychology, had been hit especially hard.
And my specialty, ab-psych—abnormal psychology—
was one of the first to go.

That week had gone from bad to worse. Not only
had I lost my job, but my mother had been diagnosed
with early-stage Alzheimer's, and my so-called boyfriend, a professor of criminology at SFSU, had dumped
me for a grad student. I hated being a cliché.

But event planning? That was a stretch. Then again,
maybe not. Back in the days of San Francisco café soci-
ety, my mother had been famous for her Pacific Heights

parties, entertaining everyone from the mayor to the governor. I'd grown up helping her fold napkins into swans and drape fur coats in the guest room (when I was done trying them on).

She'd even written a how-to book on the subject called *How to Host a Killer Party*, a bestseller in its day. When I started doing event planning, I found her party-hosting hints handy, such as "How to Hire a Killer Caterer" and "How to Handle a Party Pooper." But instead of following in her high-heeled footsteps, I had originally gone the more academic route, like my father. Now it looked as if I had inherited her legacy after all.

"I didn't necessarily want a new career, Delicia," I said, tightening the strings on my hood. "But after being downsized thanks to the governor's slash-and-burn method of fixing the education budget, I didn't have much choice, did I? It was this or coffee barista. I should have taken the java job."

"Hey, you're a great party planner! That Harry Potter party you gave last night? It was awesome! Seriously. And that Teen *Twilight* party? Getting Duncan Grant to play the vampire was a stroke of genius. You managed to make a nerd look hot—at least temporarily."

"Event coordinator!" I reminded her. "And if I have to do one more birthday party for eight-year-old boys or twelve-year-old girls, I'm going to kill someone. Thank goodness this job came up. I still don't know exactly how I managed to get it."

Maybe I was finally receiving the recognition I'd needed. I hoped tonight's gig would get me more charitable events for important causes like Alzheimer's research, and fewer food fights between Harry Potter wannabes. I was still finding blue icing highlights in my hair from last night's frosting free-for-all.

Raising money for deserving organizations was the real reason I'd gotten into event planning. Thanks to Mom, I knew the basics of the business. When I'd been at the university, I'd help coordinate a couple of fundraisers for the library that had gone well. The mayor's surprise wedding, although under the guise of a fundraiser, would bring in a bundle for a cause dear to my heart. Since my mother had developed Alzheimer's, I'd done a lot of research on this debilitating disease, which I'd quickly learned was the sixth-leading cause of death in the US. Tears sprang to my eyes as I pushed thoughts of my mother's grim future from my mind.

"Are you all right, Pres?" Delicia asked, looking up at me.

I wiped my eyes. "Of course. It's just this fog. . . ."

"Listen, Pres," Delicia said, patting my arm. "You've hit the big time. You've snagged a superimportant shindig at a celebrated city landmark. Imagine! Presley Parker hosting Mayor Green's wedding on the Rock!"

"More like a carnival, don't you think?" I mumbled. The guests had been asked to come in costume, dressed as their favorite criminals or crime fighters. Not my idea—the mayor's. "And a decaying prison isn't exactly the most elegant setting for a wedding. It's Andi Sax who gets all the glam gigs at places like the de Young Museum and the Palace of Fine Arts."

Until the mayor's wedding, Andrea Sax, San Francisco's premiere party planner, was the go-to girl for all the best events—grand openings of prestigious restaurants, inaugurations of political figures, gala fundraisers for significant foundations. No wonder. She'd long been established in the city and owned her own party supply store. That's why I'd been so surprised when the mayor's administrative assistant called and offered me this job. The event would be impressive enough to garner a lot of publicity, thereby bringing in more gigs—and more money. But I couldn't help wondering why they hadn't used Andi again, and I was certain I'd somehow gotten the job by default.

"Well, bottom line—you need the money," Delicia said, as if reading my thoughts. "Especially now that your mom has to have full-time care."

"You're right about that." I'd had to give up my overpriced Victorian flat in the Marina District and move to cheap former naval housing on Treasure Island so I could afford her care facility in the city. Luckily TI, situated halfway between San Francisco and Oakland, was only a bridge-length away.

Delicia reached up and picked something off my bangs. "Just a little blue frosting on your hair . . . although it does bring out your green eyes."

"Great. Exactly the professional look I was going for." I pushed the hood back and gave my sticky hair a shake to fluff it up before the frosting set like concrete. I'd been too busy finishing up final touches for the wedding to wash my hair since the Potter party. Luckily a hat was part of my costume for the mayor's event.

I checked my watch: five fifteen p.m. Since Alcatraz was a national park, my crew and I couldn't set up until the place closed. Before I knew it, it would be eight p.m. and the first guests would be arriving. As the ferry docked, I hustled my coworkers down the gangplank, all arms loaded with boxes of party crap. Most of the big stuff had already been delivered and was waiting for us in the cellblock. Glancing up at the ominous cement building at the top of the hill, I shuddered, hoping the ghosts of Alcatraz would be in a partying mood tonight. Remembering a docent's spiel I'd heard on a school trip to Alcatraz, I recalled some stats about the island's fascinating and fearsome history. For nearly thirty years, the grim maximum-security federal penitentiary had housed around fifteen hundred prisoners. Thirty-six had tried to escape from the Rock. Seven were shot and killed, two drowned, five were unaccounted for, and the rest were captured. Two prisoners made it to shore but were later captured and returned, and three more escaped the island, but not the water surrounding it—presumed drowned. That was it, unless you counted the twenty-eight who escaped by dying—fifteen of natural causes, eight murdered, and five suicides.

If I didn't pull this thing off, I'd be the first to commit career suicide.

My iPhone—a luxury I refused to give up—chirped, jolting me out of my thoughts of danger, detention, and death. *Missed call*, the screen read.

"Service is really spotty here," Delicia said, checking her pink rhinestone-enhanced cell phone.

I nodded, then thumbed to the voice mail screen and found three messages waiting for me. The first was from my mother: "Pres, please call me! It's urgent!" Even though she was safely in a care facility, to my mother, every call these days was "urgent."

The second was from Chloe Webster, the mayor's admin. "Presley? We have a serious situation. Call me ASAP." And with Chloe, there was always a "serious situation." I felt for her. She was seriously overworked and no doubt underpaid, but she seemed to thrive in her status as assistant to the mayor. She'd been instrumental in getting me hired for this gig.

I saved the messages, mentally promising to return the calls—if I could find a pocket of service—as soon as I finished the more pressing matter of decorating the cellblock.

I went on to the third message.

"Presley Parker? This is Detective Luke Melvin from the San Francisco Police Department, Homicide. Would you please return my call at your earliest convenience?"

A homicide detective?

Holy shit.